Front Sales Info To Come

The Engagement

Suzanne Robinson

BANTAM BOOKS
New York   London   Toronto   Sydney   Auckland

THE ENGAGEMENT
A Bantam Book / June 1996

ISBN 0-553-56346-7

Published simultaneously in the United States and Canada

Bantam Books are published by Bantam Books, a division of Bantam
Doubleday Dell Publishing Group, Inc. Its trademark, consisting of
the words "Bantam Books" and the portrayal of a rooster, is
Registered in U.S. Patent and Trademark Office and in other
countries. Marca Registrada. Bantam Books, 1540 Broadway, New
York, New York 10036.

PRINTED IN THE UNITED STATES OF AMERICA

OPM   0 9 8 7 6 5 4 3 2 1

This book is for Janice Knobles Morrel, my cousin. Jan, I always thought of you as a hero, much like the assertive, tempestuous women about whom I write. You fight for what you want, and you look at life through a humorous, imaginative lens that makes you one of the most unique, free-spirited, and charming women I have ever had the pleasure of knowing

The Engagement

1

Texas Hill Country, 1860

Nick Ross had survived the fetid slums of White-chapel and the cutthroat labyrinths of St. Giles, but August in Texas was going to kill him. He guided his quarter horse down a path beside the Guadalupe River and wiped sweat from his face with the bandanna tied around his neck. Even under the shelter of towering cypress, oak, and hackberry the air was thick and steamy. The heat combined with the moisture to make him feel as if he were riding through boiling soup.

Overhead a red hawk circled, its wings dark against the turquoise sky. He'd been in Texas a little over a year. Arriving at the invitation of his closest friend, Jocelin Marshal, he'd learned to survive on the frontier, to ride on a Texas saddle with a high pommel and wide fenders, to use a lariat and to rope cattle without getting himself yanked off his mount or his fingers tangled and cut off by the weight of the cow.

Ranching was desperate hard work—the hours long, the work hot, dirty, and smelly. But none of it was degrading the way growing up in the festering sore of east London had been. There he'd dodged his father's fists, learned to scavenge in refuse bins for food, and later to pick pockets and rob houses to buy the moldy bread and rancid meat that kept him, his sister, and his mother alive. His mother and sister were dead, but he'd lived to escape St. Giles with Jocelin's help. Still, if he'd known about rattlesnakes and scorpions, he'd never have left England. There he had a comfortable town house near Grosvenor Square in London, country houses in several counties, and dozens of servants to kill any insects that crossed his path.

Nick removed his hat, an expensive purchase with a low crown and wide brim that had saved him from heat sickness many a time. He rubbed his shirtsleeve over his forehead and addressed his horse.

"Bloody hell, Pounder, it's not even seven o'clock. We'll be steamed to death before we reach the line camp."

As he finished speaking, a loud report bounced off the limestone hills to either side of the river. Nick hauled on Pounder's reins. The animal wheeled in a tight circle in the swift, agile manner of a horse trained to ranch work and plunged back down the path the way they'd come. Nick slapped the reins and bent over the horse's neck as they reached a full gallop. The shots had come from the direction of the ranch house he'd just left. From the pattern of gunfire he knew there was a fight.

Nick broke through the trees and galloped up a hill dotted with mesquite and cedar. Plunging down the other side, he came within sight of the house, a graceful three-story limestone building with four columns supporting a wide front porch. Between the house and the barn lay the bunkhouse. It consisted of quarters for the ranch hands and a kitchen. Between the bunkhouse and the kitchen stretched a dog trot, a cool, open hallway.

He could see several men lying behind the water trough in the corral. A fourth man staggered to the shelter of the dog trot and collapsed there, holding his arm. Two more cowboys crouched in a wagon drawn up before the barn and fired at someone high up on the windmill ladder. Pounder churned up dirt as he raced toward the ranch house.

Nick slowed the animal as they neared the porch, swung his leg over the saddle, and leaped to the ground running. Pounder swerved, skirting the corral fence, and slowed as he reached the shelter of the barn. The horse calmly walked into the dark interior while Nick jumped onto the porch. A bullet smacked into a white wooden column as he passed it. The front door opened, and Nick dived inside.

Rolling to his feet, he grabbed a rifle that was thrust at him by Liza Marshal, Jocelin's wife. Her ash-blond hair was tousled, her hazel eyes glittering with anger and fear. She rested a hand on her protruding stomach and lifted a pale oval face to him.

"It's Little Billy. He's drunk again."

"What are you doing here?" Nick shouted as he thrust her away from the windows. "You'll get yourself and the baby killed."

"Don't bellow at me, Nick Ross. Jocelin's been shot."

"Bloody hell, where is he?"

Liza lifted a shaking hand to her lips. "He's out in

the open. When Little Billy started shooting, Jocelin went out to talk to him."

Before he could stop her, she raced to the window and pulled the curtain aside. A bullet shattered the glass as Nick threw himself at Liza and pressed her against the wall. "You stay here."

He dropped to the floor and peered over the sill. From his superior position Little Billy was keeping everyone pinned down in the barn, the bunkhouse, the kitchen, the corral. And in the open yard in front of the barn, at least twenty yards from the wagon, lay the man who was more brother than friend, Jocelin Marshal, Viscount Radcliffe. He wasn't moving, and the ground was soaked with blood from a wound in his leg. His jet-black hair ruffled in the hot breeze that swirled dust across the corral.

Nick uttered a string of Cockney curses as he watched for signs of movement from his friend. It was just like Jocelin to try to talk. Jos never had entirely learned ruthlessness, not in the Crimea, not even in his crusade against debauchers of children. Little Billy was a trouble-loving young cowhand who picked fights and took offense if someone breathed in a way he didn't like. Only last week Jocelin had stopped Nick from drawing on the bastard for beating up the son of Jocelin's Mexican cook. Talk indeed.

"Dallas tried to reach Jos, but Little Billy got him in the arm," Liza said. "Oh, Nick, do something quickly."

Without a word Nick turned and ran for the stairs. Taking them three at a time, he climbed to the top floor, burst through a narrow door at the end of the landing, and raced up another flight to the sweltering attic. Once in the dark closeness of the attic,

Nick paused to catch his breath. He couldn't afford an
unsteady hand. Walking to the window on the side of
the house opposite the yard and the windmill, he un-
latched the portal and climbed onto the roof. With
the rifle in one hand he crawled up the steep slope and
poked his head cautiously over the summit.

He could see Jocelin lying on his stomach, arms
and legs spread. He hadn't moved. Dallas Meredith
was firing left-handed at Little Billy from the dog trot.
The hands behind the water trough were reloading.
Poison, the cook, was yelling insults at Little Billy
between rounds from his shotgun. A renewed burst
from the men at the water trough was his signal. Nick
slid down the roof to the limestone chimney, got to
his feet, and cocked the rifle.

Little Billy was still firing and reloading from saddlebags slung over his shoulder. Like most cowboys,
he was young, reckless, and barely literate. Also like
most, he went by his nickname and never mentioned
his real one. But unlike the rest of the hands, Little
Billy couldn't leave the whiskey bottle alone. What
was worse, Little Billy was over six feet tall and fond of
his rifle. Nick would have shot him long ago if it
hadn't been for Jocelin. He used to see the same mad-
mean look in his father's eyes just before the bastard
beat him with a coachman's whip.

Nick rested his rifle against the chimney and
sighted down the barrel. Talk. You couldn't talk to
drunks. He waited for Little Billy to turn his way. A
wide chest came into view as the drunk fired at Dallas,
then pointed his rifle down at Jocelin's prone figure.
Nick felt a stab of panic in his chest as he saw the
direction of Little Billy's aim. Then a familiar chilly

calm descended. He tilted the rifle, aiming it at Little Billy's heart, and squeezed the trigger.

The explosion of his shot hardly caused him to blink. He kept his gaze fixed on Little Billy's red long-john-covered bulk. He saw the cowboy jerk, then clutch at the windmill ladder. Little Billy dropped his rifle, then lost his grip and plummeted to the ground. His big body sent up a cloud of dust as it hit. As Nick left the roof, Dallas and the others sprang out of hiding and ran toward Jocelin. Without a twinge of conscience or a thought for the dead man, he climbed in a window and went downstairs to help carry Jocelin into the house.

Liza had sent to San Antonio for a doctor the moment her husband had been wounded, but it was sunset before the physician had finished removing the bullet from Jocelin's leg. With Dallas Meredith wounded, Nick took charge of the ranch, ordered Little Billy buried, and work resumed. The next morning he was in Dallas's room down the hall from Jocelin's when they heard a round of loud curses issuing from the master suite. There was a crash, and they bolted into the hall in time to see the boy who brought the mail in from San Antonio scamper down the stairs.

Nick was the first to enter the bedroom, where he found Jocelin sitting up in bed, emerald eyes sparkling with pent-up emotion, his leg swathed in bandages and propped up on pillows. Even in bed he wore a military bearing, his shoulders squared as though on parade with the Horse Guards. His pale face was flushed with unnatural color beneath thick, smooth waves of black hair. In his hand he held a crumpled letter, which he pounded against the mattress while

Liza stood by, arms folded, foot tapping on the floor-boards.

She glanced at Nick and said, "He got a letter from the duchess."

"Oh," Nick said. There was little else to say. Jocelin was the heir to a dukedom, but his family caused him as much misery as Nick's had.

"Hang it," Jocelin said. "Now I'll have to go home. Liza, pack for us. We're leaving tomorrow."

"Whoa, there, Marshal," Dallas said as he came in and sat on the end of the bed. "You aren't going anywhere."

"Bleeding right, toff," said Nick.

He watched Dallas's expression as he deciphered this comment. Dallas was from one of the Deep South states (he never said which) and had trouble understanding Nick's disreputable accent and language. But Nick knew an aristocrat when he saw one, and Dallas Meredith was as blue-blooded as Jocelin.

"I have to go," Jocelin said as he thrust himself upright. The movement made him grimace and curse again.

Liza unfolded her arms and pressed him back against the pillows. "You're not going anywhere."

"Begging your pardon, ma'am," Dallas said, "but neither should you."

"I know."

Jocelin waved the letter. "I have to go home." He began to move restlessly, and he seemed to pale and flush at the same time. Perspiration glistened on his forehead and upper lip.

Crossing to the bed, Nick leaned down and put a hand on Jocelin's shoulder. "Stow it, love. Let me see the bleeding letter."

The duchess was a prolific writer. Her letter was ten pages long, but most of it was repetition. Georgiana, Jocelin's younger sister, had betrothed herself to John Charles Hyde, Earl of Threshfield. Nick gave a low whistle and looked up from the letter. Liza had crossed her arms and was tapping her foot again. Her lips were compressed. She was watching Jocelin with a distracted, anxious expression while her husband moved restlessly in his bed.

"Not old Threshfield," Nick said.

Liza nodded, and Jocelin glanced at Dallas and snapped, "Yes, old Threshfield."

"Haven't I heard of Threshfield somewhere?" asked Dallas lightly.

"John Charles Hyde, the Earl of Threshfield," Nick said, "is a vicious old blister who's of an age to be Jos's grandfather."

Jocelin had been staring at Dallas, who avoided his eyes. Nick watched the silent play between the two men, growing more and more curious, but he was distracted when Jocelin sat up too quickly and gasped, clutching his leg.

"She's done it," the wounded man said. "I never thought she'd go through with it, but she has, and if I don't stop her, she'll ruin her life."

"You're not going anywhere," Liza said. She lowered herself to a rocking chair as if determined to stay there as long as it took.

"You don't understand. She told me before she came out that she was going to marry an old man so that she'd become a widow quickly."

"What kind of notion is that?" Dallas asked.

Liza smiled at him. "Georgiana has firm ideas about not marrying some young man who will tell her what to do and keep her on an allowance. She calls that slavery."

Nick's mouth fell open. He knew Lady Georgiana only slightly, and under formal circumstances. He'd always found her as quiet, nondescript, and uninteresting as most young ladies of the nobility. Sketchily educated, raised in privilege, and occupied with trivialities, she epitomized the worst faults of the English gentlewoman. While his mother had scrubbed hearths on her hands and knees to feed her children, girls like Georgiana remained abed until noon. He respected women of his own class who labored while bearing numerous children; women like Jocelin's sister were useless. And here Georgiana was embarking on this ridiculous plan to further her own selfishness.

He remembered Jocelin worrying about his sister's desire to control her own fortune and to direct the course of her life. Nick was of the opinion that she'd been disappointed in her come-out. Georgiana had Jocelin's black hair and emerald eyes, but she also had his height, which made her tower over many men. She wore gold-rimmed spectacles that gave her the look of a bluestocking. And in spite of her mother's applications of patent remedies, her nose and cheeks were sprayed with light freckles.

When she had been presented at court, she had tripped over her train as she'd backed out of the royal presence. That incident had been a harbinger of disasters to come. She had proceeded to step on the toes of every dance partner, spill tea on callers, and sneeze in the face of the prince consort, Queen Victoria's husband. Yes, Lady Georgiana ought to be able to make herself a widow no matter whom she married. The trouble was, Jocelin would make himself ill worrying about her.

"I'll wait a week," Jocelin was saying. "Then I'll go. If I wait much longer, she'll marry Threshfield before I'm halfway across the ocean."

"Your father will stop her," Nick said.

"You didn't read the rest of the letter," Liza said while she rocked. "The duke is in favor of the match."

"Strike me blind," Nick murmured.

"Indeed," Dallas said, clearing his throat and looking a bit uncomfortable. "If you will pardon me, ma'am. Allowing such an unequal alliance seems lacking in honor."

Liza put her hand on Jocelin's arm. "You know she's taken your aunt for her model. She admires Lady Lavinia, and your aunt seems quite happy as a spinster."

"Georgiana isn't Lavinia," Jocelin said as he stared at Dallas. "She'll get herself into no end of trouble. You don't know Threshfield. His chief delight in life is tormenting his family. He has a great deal of income independent of entail, and he holds it over them. Tortures them by threatening to leave his money to strangers. He's odd, too. Collects strange objects from all over the world—Africa, Australia. His house is stuffed with statues, reliefs, and columns from ancient places in Assyria, Persia, Egypt."

"Right, love," Nick said. "And he cackles when he laughs, and rolls around in a creaky wheelchair even though he's a spry old skeleton when he wants to be. Still, he's got a frittery heart. Lady Georgiana could be a widow almost as soon as she's a wife."

Jocelin groaned and sank down into his pillows.

Dallas rose from the bed along with Liza. All three of them hovered around Jocelin as he began to breathe rapidly. He covered his eyes with his forearm. Liza glanced up at Nick, her eyes filled with unshed tears.

Nick sighed and put his hand on Jocelin's shoulder. "Don't fash yerself, love. If you're that bothered, I'll go stop this mischief." Liza's hand slipped into his, and he felt her squeeze his fingers.

Jocelin lowered his arm to study him, then glanced at Dallas as if asking for his consent to the idea. "What do you think, old chap?"

Dallas's lazy blue gaze settled on Nick. "Well, sir, if anyone can disrupt a lady's marriage, it would be Nicholas."

"What does that mean, toff?" Nick straightened and glared at Dallas.

The Southerner bowed. "I was complimenting your perseverance and your intelligence, sir. And, of course, I've witnessed for myself how you charm the ladies without even trying."

"Blow that," Nick said. "You was implying I'd interfere with me best friend's sister. Well, I'll have you know Georgiana is a spoiled little miss who needs whipping, not worshiping."

"Don't go aripping and atearing at me, sir."

Nick was still scowling at Dallas. "Just you remember. I don't go fishing in blue-blooded ponds. Wouldn't have to do with any of them simpering, afraid-of-the-sun delicates. I'm only going because of me friends here."

"I never doubted it, sir."

Nick's scowl faded only to return when he found both Liza and Jocelin grinning at him. Liza stood on her toes and kissed his cheek.

"You're a dear, Nick."

"Thanks, old chap," Jocelin said.

Nick shrugged. "This heat was about to blister me insides anyway, and I was missing me studies. I got a lot of schooling to make up."

"You will stop her, won't you?" Jocelin asked, his voice strained. "I love her dearly, and I can't bear to think of her ruining her life."

"Never fear, love. Threshfield and I are friends. I put him onto a few sweet business arrangements. I'll get meself invited to his house and put him off the marriage if I have to lag him."

"Lag him?" Dallas asked.

"Send him to jail, toff."

"You'll have to be firm," Liza said. "Georgiana's as stubborn as Jocelin."

"Can't abide a stubborn woman. If she comes over me with her nonsense, I'll dodge her good."

"I hope that means you won't let her bully you," Jocelin said.

Nick stuck his thumbs into his gun belt and sauntered to the door. "Never met a woman who could."

"My, my, my," Dallas said. "I wish I was going to be there to see it—the lady against the barbarian."

"Who you calling a barbarian, toff?" Nick deliberately changed his accent to the clipped, precise one of a Cambridge graduate, straightened to an imitation of Jocelin's military bearing, and said, "Really, old chap, one adapts one's manner and speech to one's company. My compliments to you, sir. Now, if you will excuse me, I must see to my packing. A pleasant and restful day to you, my dear Jocelin, my lady."

With a last smile at Dallas, who was staring at him openmouthed, Nick strolled out of the room.

2

England, September 1860

Deep in the countryside of Sussex, nestled in the midst of vast acres of private forest and park, lay the great country seat of the earls of Threshfield. Threshfield House contained the earl, the earl's sister, his nephew, his nephew's wife, and their son, all of whom the earl could do without. The only occupant of his vast eighteenth-century home that his lordship smiled upon was, at the moment, standing in a dark hall stacked high with packing crates.

She was a tall young woman who sometimes forgot her training and attempted to hide her stature by walking bent forward at the waist. She wore gold wire-rimmed spectacles that brightened her already astonishing green eyes. Yet the studious air the glasses gave her prevented people from discerning the vulnerability that often appeared in those jewel-bright eyes. Perhaps her air of stately dignity protected her from exposure.

Dim light filtered into the corridor through gaps in the heavy velvet curtains drawn over the tall windows at either end of the hall. Trying to see by a beam of light filled with dust motes, Lady Georgiana Marshal sank her arms up to the elbows in a wooden crate, arranged the objects within, and replaced the lid. Wiping her hands on her full-length apron, she picked up the box and started down the hall.

She passed a stack of crates. Beside it, against the wall, loomed a frozen figure of a striding man with the head of a jackal. Past another collection of boxes, beside an open doorway, rested the upright mummy case of a Theban priestess. Even in the near darkness Georgiana could see the outline of the gilded human-shaped container, its black wig and lifelike painted eyes.

Georgiana entered the gallery with its statues of pharaohs; part-human, part-animal gods; sphinxes; altars; and display cases. Crossing the long chamber, she shoved open a door with her boot and entered the workroom, her footsteps echoing on the marble floor. She went to a long table piled with more boxes, books, pottery, and various other objects and set down her burden.

"Did you find it, Ludwig?" she asked.

A domed, slightly bald head shaped like a cabbage popped up from behind a stack of books topped with a bronze scimitar. "Not yet. Oh, my heart, if I've lost it, Great-uncle will never forgive me."

"You haven't lost it," Georgiana said. "I saw it not half an hour ago."

Ludwig looked helplessly at the scimitar and made swimming gestures with his hands. His egg-shaped body wavered and almost toppled from the stool upon which he was sitting. He regained his balance and tugged on his wispy mustache. Ludwig had adopted it after the style of the dashing royal dragoons and hussars in Her Majesty's cavalry.

Taking pity on him, Georgiana said, "Let me look."

She began searching between books and boxes, then sank to her knees to fumble among the items that had accumulated in piles around Ludwig's stool. She vanished under the worktable and reappeared with a slim bundle of wrapped linen. The cloth was an aged yellowish brown, the bundle almost tubular and tapering at one end. Embedded in the cloth were the skeletons of insects and several thousand years' worth of dust.

Georgiana held it out and sneezed. "Here it is."

"Oh, my heart, you've found it! How did it get down there? It's the only baby crocodile mummy we have, you know. Great-uncle bought it himself in, let me see, in twenty-four in Cairo." Ludwig took the crocodile mummy from Georgiana, laid it on the table, and picked up a pen. He scratched an entry in a heavy leather-bound volume while Georgiana returned to her carton.

"This box contains kohl tubes, unguent bottles, a chariot whip, and canopic jars holding the entrails of the high priest of Montu, eighteenth dynasty." She picked up a cosmetic bottle of Egyptian blue faience. "Amazing. This eye paint is thousands of years old."

A musical tinkling caused Ludwig to gasp. He dropped his pen, fished in a pocket of his waistcoat, and withdrew a watch. "Bless my life! It's two o'clock already and I'm not nearly finished cataloging." Ludwig fluttered his pale hands around his ostrich-egg-shaped body, found a kerchief, and wiped his forehead. "Dear Georgiana, would you be so kind as to meet the shipment from town? You're so good with workmen, and you know they'll treat that royal sarcophagus like a box of tinned meat."

"Of course, Ludwig. Don't alarm yourself. I'll attend to it at once."

"Oh, thank you. I told them to stop at the front so I could meet them. You can ride with them around to this wing."

Georgiana removed her apron, wiped her grimy hands on it, and set out on the time-consuming journey from the Egyptian Wing to the entrance to Threshfield House. She had lived all her life in grand houses, but Threshfield was unique. It consisted of a central building flanked at its four corners by pavilions linked to the main block by curved corridors. Its ground plan resembled a crab's body.

Georgiana left the southwest pavilion, called the Egyptian Wing, went down the corridor, and entered the library. Then she crossed the huge saloon with its domed glass roof. Beyond lay the vast entry hall built to resemble a Roman atrium with its twenty fluted alabaster columns, alcoves filled with Greek and Roman statues, and white plaster friezes of centaurs, trophies, and arabesques.

She stepped carefully on the slippery Italian-marble floor and at last came out onto the Corinthian portico. Broad flights of white stone steps marched up to the portico on either side. Ludwig said the facade was made to resemble the buildings on the Acropolis at Athens. Statues of Venus, Ceres, and Bacchus topped the pediments overhead, and Georgiana looked out on a wide gravel drive and expanse of lawn. Down the avenue bordered with ancient oaks clattered a wagon pulled by four draft horses. Across the drive someone rode out of the trees along one of the riding paths. Georgiana waved at her aunt Lavinia, who waved back.

She waited for the freight wagon, her hands clasped in front of her, on the portico. Her journey through the vast house would have been much more laborious and slow if she'd worn a crinoline. She would have had to maneuver it through doorways and control it on staircases, but today was a workday, and she wore a work dress. She had, in fact, two types of dresses: those made long enough to wear with a crinoline, and those fashioned to wear without one. When she worked in the Egyptian Wing, formality was cast aside, a luxury Georgiana had seldom experienced at home.

For the first time since learning of Jocelin's tragedy, she was happy. She was close to achieving independence from a father for whom she felt little but contempt. Ever since she'd pried Jocelin's secret from her mother, her rage had been growing. Jocelin had been a youth when their uncle had approached him sexually. He'd begged his parents for protection, only to be blamed for lying. Brave, sad Jocelin had been sacrificed for the sake of the family reputation, cast out as an object of disgust by those who should have safeguarded him.

When she'd learned the truth years later, she'd almost taken one of Aunt Lavinia's shotguns to Uncle Yale. Aunt Livy had stopped her, saying that soon Yale would pay for his crimes in a grotesque manner—the progressive ravages of a disease visited on the promiscuous. Aunt Livy had refused to be more specific, but

Yale was disgustingly sick now, and the plague was eating his brain.

Imagining Jocelin's suffering shot a stab of pain through her chest, and tears stung her eyes. She had never been able to distance herself from the sympathetic pain. She had nightmares in which she imagined horrible things happening to Jocelin while she stood by, unable to prevent them.

Georgiana swallowed hard and forced herself to think of more pleasant thoughts. She was most pleased at the understanding she'd reached with her father. Over the last year the duke had bungled his finances a bit, thus endangering the princely mode of living to which he was accustomed and to which he knew he was entitled. In return for the duke's consent to the marriage, the earl would settle the bulk of Clairemont's debts. She was mightily fond of Threshfield.

He was her fellow conspirator, willing to help her escape from her bear trap of a family, and asking nothing in return. However, Threshfield felt that having to live for a few years with his odd, grasping family was the sacrifice of a saint. The memory of his caustic comments upon the various Hydes in residence brought a smile to her lips as the freight wagon drew slowly alongside the double staircase.

The driver set the brake and jumped down, pulling off his cap and bowing. She listened to his description of the enormous effort he and his laborers had put forth in shifting the red-granite sarcophagus from the railcar to the wagon without damage. Walking around the wagon, she tugged on ropes and inspected the wads of padding that encased the heavy wooden crate. She was tugging on a rope that had come loose in the journey from the rail station when one of the laborers exclaimed and pointed. She looked over her shoulder, blinked, then turned around to face the oak-lined avenue.

An apparition cantered toward her on an enormous roan horse. The man on this giant beast must have seen her, for he kicked his mount into a gallop, bent over his horse's neck, and aimed right at her. The horse picked up speed in seconds, racing toward her and causing the men around her to scramble out of the way. Annoyed at this unaccountable belligerence, Georgiana shoved her spectacles up on the bridge of her nose, lifted her chin, and stood her ground. She regretted her decision at once, for she could feel the vibration of the animal's hooves through her boots. This rude stranger was trying to frighten her. He'd succeeded, which made her furious.

Rider and horse thundered directly toward her down the curved gravel drive. Pebbles shot out in all directions as each hoof slammed into the ground. Suddenly, at the last moment, the horse swerved. The rider swung one leg over the saddle, clinging to the still-cantering beast, then leaped off as he approached Georgiana. He landed at a run that brought him to a standstill a yard from her. The horse continued past her at a trot. Its owner whistled. The animal stopped sharp, whirled on its hind legs, and walked slowly back toward them.

Georgiana raised her chin a bit higher and narrowed her eyes as the stranger approached. He was almost as tall as his giant of a horse, lean, as if he'd worked hard and eaten little. He swept off his wide-brimmed hat to reveal long, shaggy chestnut hair streaked with sun-bleached amber. He swept back his long coat behind a gun belt slung low on his hip.

High-heeled boots crunched gravel, and he stuck a thumb into his gun belt as he reached her. She felt a twinge of recognition, not for the man, but because of Jocelin's description of American frontier garb.

She opened her mouth to inquire if the man had come from her brother, but he was too quick for her. A dark-blue gaze inspected her as if she were a succulent desert. Then he appeared to recognize her. His eyes crinkled, not in amusement, but in irritation.

"Well, if it ain't old George. I been looking all over creation for you. Your danged pa wouldn't tell me where you'd gone. Well, come on, girl. Time to pack up and swim."

Georgiana drew her brows together, straightened her shoulders, and said, "I beg your pardon?"

"I reckon you should."

His lips curled in a grin that was at once contemptuous and appreciative. Georgiana wasn't the daughter of a duke for nothing. Giving this barbarian a chilly nod, she turned on her heel and spoke to the Threshfield butler, who had come out of the house upon the arrival of the stranger.

"Randall, send this person on his way."

"Yes, my lady."

"Hold on a minute."

Georgiana paused in her progress around the wagon. "You appear to be looking for someone named George, sir. There is no one by that name at Threshfield."

A gloved hand settled on the revolver at the stranger's hip. Georgiana kept her features fixed in an expressionless mask that hid her uneasiness. This man spoke in a slow drawl like the one Jocelin had returned with from America, only the stranger's voice was as rough as his speech—low, throaty, and tinged with a knowing familiarity that bordered on an intrusive liberty.

"Look here, George, Jocelin sent me to fetch you, and I'm going to fetch you, so pack your duds and let's ride."

She had been certain she didn't know him. He was sun-brown, sweaty, and stubbled with two days' worth of beard. His shirt was open, and she could see his chest. His chest! No gentleman revealed his chest to a lady. But he'd called her George again, and that twinge of recognition returned. Once, years ago, a man had called her George. It had been that elegantly savage protégé of her brother's, the one whose presence turned her father's complexion vermilion.

Georgiana studied the blue eyes tinged with sapphire, the wide shoulders. Through the chestnut stubble she could discern the shallow indentation in the middle of his chin. She let out her breath on a gasp. "Dear me, it's Mr. Ross!"

"Course it's me."

"Mr. Ross," Georgiana repeated witlessly. Then she regained her composure. He was forcing her to discuss her private affairs before servants, but she wasn't going to let him into the house or talk to him alone. "I knew my brother would be concerned. I've written him a letter he's no doubt received by now, so you've come all this way for nothing. I'm sorry for it, but Jocelin does tend to be high-handed. I'm not going anywhere, especially with a mere acquaintance. Good day to you, Mr. Ross."

She turned her back to him. There was an unfamiliar sound of metal against leather, then a click. Georgiana stopped. One of the laborers swore. Darting a glance over her shoulder, she looked at the barrel of a long-nosed revolver. Her gaze lifted to the man's casual one. A snake's stare had more feeling in it.

"Now, don't get your petticoats in a twist. Jos said you'd be stubborn, and that I was to be patient, but I been clear across a continent and an ocean, and I got no use for spoiled, blue-blooded misses. Jos is laid up, and it's plain infernal meanness to worry him like you done. So I reckon I'll just have to take you back to Texas and let Jos see for himself that you ain't hitched yourself to old Threshfield."

"Why, you barbaric—"

"Don't give me no mouth." Nick's gun swerved as the freight-wagon driver and Randall moved toward him. "You fellas stay put."

There was another ominous metallic click. Everyone turned to see a woman coming toward them holding a shotgun. Georgiana smiled, and Nick's jaw dropped. The woman had silver hair, a face devoid of all but the finest age lines, and she wore breeches, riding coat, and boots.

"Aunt Livy," Georgiana said.

Lavinia nodded, keeping her gaze and her gun trained on Nick. "Good afternoon, my dear."

Nick slowly holstered his gun and lifted his hands away from his body. The shotgun lowered until it pointed at the ground. Lavinia gave him a slow, appreciative examination that evoked a grin from its subject. She noticed the grin and met his gaze with intrigued curiosity.

"Who are you, young man?"

"Nicholas Ross, ma'am. I been in Texas with Jocelin for quite a spell."

"You must have been for you to have turned gun-fighter," Lavinia replied.

"Jos sent me to fetch old George here before she up and ruined her life. He would have come himself, but he's laid up with a busted leg. Got shot up by a drunk ranch hand. He's riled himself up to a fever about his sister, and I aim to quiet him down."

"How interesting," Lavinia said. She turned to Georgiana and gave her an inquiring glance.

Georgiana hadn't realized how furious she was until Nick Ross referred to her as George in front of her aunt. Irritation rapidly boiled over into wrath. "What presumption! I have no intention of listening to this drivel, much less complying with it." Through her gold-rimmed spectacles she directed her most regal stare at her tormentor. "You have no position or claim in reference to me, sir. I have no intention of being ill-used by you further. Please give my fondest regards to my brother when you return to—Texas, was it?"

"Whoa, there," Nick snapped as she walked toward the front of the wagon. He started toward her, then stopped as Lavinia lifted her shotgun.

"Mr. Ross," Georgiana said, fighting hard not to show her embarrassment or her anger before servants again. "You seem to have mistaken me for your horse."

"Well, you're a mite more stubborn, but you got a point there."

She heard a stifled snicker from the workmen. A snicker! Color drained from Georgiana's face. Her back stiffened. Whirling in a flurry of twenty yards of skirt, Georgiana offered her hand to the wagon driver and climbed onto the seat. The driver got up beside her. Looking down, she inspected this uninvited barbarian as though he were a rat she'd found in her sewing box.

"Your indelicacy puts you beyond polite society, sir. You'll leave Threshfield immediately. If not, I'll have the earl throw you out."

Nick Ross replaced his hat, shoving it back onto his head, and grinned up at her. "I heard tell you'd grown all high-and-mighty." He glanced at Lavinia's shotgun. "Looks like it'll take me a sight longer than I thought to fix this mess. So I reckon I'll just have to stay till I can get you to leave."

To her consternation, he strolled to the wagon, leaned over, and reached out. She jumped and collided with the driver, which caused Mr. Ross to grin at her in that infuriating manner that made her feel like smacking his face. He grasped a handful of her skirt and tucked it inside the wagon away from the front wheel.

At no time did he touch her. He was wearing gloves. But the feel of his hand on her skirt created hot confusion, as if a blistering current passed from his body, through her skirt, to hers. She grew even more flustered because as he came closer, she was afforded a glimpse of that bare throat and that sun-darkened chest.

"Course, you could get rid of me now," he said softly. "Just promise me you'll pack up and go back to your pa."

"Go away, sir. I shall speak to the earl."

Nick Ross backed up and rested his hands on his hips, leering up at her with intolerable insolence. "Won't do you no good. I got myself invited to stay.

Me and Threshfield are old friends. I reckon you might as well give up now."

Lips tight, cheeks crimson, Georgiana nodded at the driver, who set the wagon in motion. She tried to ignore the chuckle that sent pinpricks of irritation down her spine.

"See you later, George. Maybe by then you'll have put on some more clothes." His voice grew louder as the wagon retreated. "I think you forgot your petticoats."

Her composure broke at this last humiliation. Twisting around in the seat, she glared back at the tall, dusty savage and for the first time in her life shouted before servants. "Drat your evil soul, Nicholas Ross. You're nothing but vermin, and I'll take great satisfaction in watching you get thrown out on your—your ear!"

3

Nick watched the wagon bearing Georgiana make a
turn on the gravel drive that took it around the northwest wing of the house. Shoving his hat lower on his
forehead, he walked over to Pounder, grabbed the
animal's reins, and handed them to one of the footmen who had followed Randall outside. He'd been
certain his wild-frontiersman tactic would work. Any
nobly born young woman threatened by a gun-toting
barbarian ought to have lifted her skirts and scurried
for the protection of her papa.

Lady Georgiana had faced him down, and now he
was stuck trying to pry her out of here some other
way. He had various other clever, and some mean,
ploys ready, but the crazed gunfighter had been the
quickest. Nick glanced at the butler and the lady in
pants. They were staring at him. Still silent, he patted
Pounder on the rump, removed his saddlebags, and
threw them over his shoulder.

For the first time since he'd set out on this mission
for his friend, he was worried. Not just worried—

damned worried. She wasn't what he'd expected. He had remembered Lady Georgiana as a bespectacled, awkward adolescent but had come face-to-face with a black-haired young noblewoman with the dignity of Her Majesty, Queen Victoria, and the queenly height to match. She didn't stumble over her feet anymore.

No one would ever mistake her for a great beauty. He was familiar with the standards of Society, and Georgiana was too tall, too determined, and had that intriguing spray of freckles across her cheeks and the bridge of her nose. He couldn't help smiling at the way her spectacles kept slipping down that delightful nose. Which was all the more reason to be furious with himself—because as soon as he hopped off Pounder and confronted her, he'd experienced a deep, gut twisting burst of desire.

Previously he'd spent no more than a few minutes in her company with no such awkward results. But she'd changed in the two years since they'd last met. He wasn't sure how, but his body didn't seem to be thwarted by his ignorance. He lusted after the sister of the man he loved like a brother.

Nick Ross, you're a disgusting prig what don't deserve to live. You think Jos, sterling bloke though he is, would want a Whitechapel thief for his sister? You owe him your life, and you ain't going to repay him by interfering with the girl he sent you to protect. Bloody hell. You stow it. Just stow it. Get this business over with, and get yourself away from her quick.

He was in luck, though. Trying to ruin her betrothal was going to make Lady Georgiana hate him. He couldn't bed a woman who hated him. He was safe; Jos was safe; the lady was safe. Satisfied, Nick returned to the woman with the shotgun.

Glancing ruefully in the direction of the vanished wagon, he shook his head. "Dang and bloody hell too."

"Indeed, young man," she said. Shifting her shotgun to one arm, she offered her hand. "I am Lavinia Stokes, Lady Georgiana's aunt."

Nick took her hand and bowed over it, saddlebags and all. "Pleased, ma'am." He eyed her man's breeches surreptitiously. He'd never seen a woman in pants, not even in all his time in Texas. It was a sight. Jos had warned him that Aunt Lavinia was Georgiana's idol, and no doubt the influence in her plan to gain independence.

"I remember you now," Lavinia continued. "I remember Jocelin speaking of you. Whatever possessed you to attempt to bully my niece in such an outlandish manner?"

"Jos sent me to break up this engagement, ma'am."

"You've failed."

"Not yet, and I got me a whole lot more to say about it."

Lavinia nodded while giving him a look of severe appraisal. "Why?"

"Uh, why?"

"There's nothing wrong with your hearing, young man. Why are you pushing yourself in where you don't belong?"

"I'm doing it for Jos, ma'am."

She gave him a sharp, sidelong glance that told him she didn't believe him. He wondered if she'd somehow perceived his disreputable reaction to her niece. What was he going to do if Aunt Lavinia pointed her shotgun at him and ordered him off the

estate? Now she was giving him a long, assessing look
that almost made him blush.

"You may remain, young man, as long as we have
an understanding."

Caught off guard, Nick concealed his surprise behind a smile he'd used on ladies and factory girls alike.
"What understanding might that be, ma'am?"

"You may try to convince my niece to give up her
plans to marry his lordship by any peaceful means, but
no more of your indelicate displays. Do we have an
agreement?"

"Just as you say, ma'am," he said softly as he
pushed his hat back farther on his head. A lock of
chestnut hair dropped over his forehead.

Lady Lavinia's gaze flicked to the errant lock and
back to his eyes. "Be careful, sir. Jocelin also mentioned that you have the charm of Byron linked with
the ruthlessness of a Cossack. I even remember his
giving me quite a long list of your conquests in Society, ladies who ought to know better than to succumb
to the devil."

"Devil, ma'am? I protest."

Lavinia walked over to him, her boots crunching
on the gravel, and spoke quietly. "Georgiana is an
intelligent girl. Far more intelligent than Jocelin has
ever realized. Please remember that in your dealings
with her. I'm trusting you because my nephew trusts
you, with his life apparently, and I respect Jocelin's
judgment. Behave yourself, Mr. Ross."

"Yes, Miz Lavinia."

"And drop that absurd accent," Lavinia said as she
headed for the monumental Corinthian portico. "You
may have fooled my niece, but you haven't deceived
me."

Nick lifted his hat, swept it off and around in a half circle, and bowed. "Yes, ma'am."

He replaced his hat, shifted his saddlebags, and beckoned to Randall, who had retreated discreetly out of hearing range. Lapsing into the manner of speech his tutors had been drilling into him for the past several years, he presented the butler with an engraved calling card.

"His lordship informed you of my visit?"

Randall glanced down at the card. His eyes widened, but he quickly recovered. "Of course, sir. Your man has just arrived with your things. May I show you to your room?"

"Thank you."

Randall offered to carry his saddlebags, but Nick declined and followed the butler's dignified progress up the stairs and into the house that was more palace than home. He entered a hall as big as a goblin-king's cave. The first thing he noticed was that it was lined with alcoves peopled with statues of naked men and women. He recognized some of them from his studies with his valet/tutor. His steps slowed as he took in the graceful curves of Ariadne.

Randall had reached the opposite end of the room as Nick passed a statue of David. It sprouted a second head from its ribs, but this one wore a close-fitting, plumed bonnet and masses of false blond curls surrounding a face full of powdered wrinkles. And it hissed at him.

"Psst!"

Nick stopped as the stranger emerged from her hiding place and gestured for him to come closer. He glanced at Randall, who was looking at the ceiling in a deliberate manner, then joined the lady. She was dressed in a pink muslin gown with a high waist, puffed sleeves, and tight, long undersleeves. He'd seen ladies dressed like this in pictures of half a century ago, but this one had the eagle's-beak nose inherited by many members of the Hyde family. The prominent feature sat oddly with the lady's air of daintiness, the curls, the plumes, the pink muslin.

He eyed her flat silk pumps, the brooch bearing a portrait of the Prince Regent affixed to her high collar, and her fringed silk parasol. Red-rimmed bean-brown eyes cut from side to side as if she expected to be attacked at any moment. She grabbed his arm with a gloved hand and pulled him into the alcove so that they were wedged between a wall and the statue.

"I saw you arrive," she said in a desperate whisper. She paused to look around suspiciously at Randall. "Have you come from the Peninsula?"

"The Peninsula?"

"From Wellesley," she said. Her voice was high and had that unfortunate squeaky quality with which some young ladies were cursed. "About the French spy. I saw you confront her. You must be clever, or she would have gotten rid of you. I wrote the marquess about her, and he said he'd sent someone to help me. Shhh."

She pulled Nick closer and lowered her voice. "Napoleon has sent her here to intercept my communications with the Prince Regent. I pass them on to Wellington, as you know."

She paused and gave him a proud look as if she expected him to reply. Nick fought the urge to gawk at this wizened little Regency belle and nodded in his most solemn manner.

"Of course, my lady."

The faint sound of a door closing made his companion jump and drop her parasol. He retrieved it for her.

"I must go. We can't be seen together. I'm glad Wellington has finally responded as is due my consequence. I'll not refine too much upon his tardiness." She poked her head out of the alcove, noted Randall's turned back, and left.

Nick watched her little slippers skid across the marble floor beneath the high hem of her gown, then came out of his amazement as she left the house. He joined Randall, who resumed his stately progress up an elegantly curved staircase covered with thick, royal-blue carpet.

"Um, Randall," Nick said.

"Yes, sir."

"That lady . . ."

"The Lady Augusta Hyde, sir. The earl's unmarried sister."

"Ah. Just so."

Randall cleared his throat. "Her ladyship has a somewhat capricious memory, sir."

"Ah. Yes, that would explain it."

"Yes, sir."

"Lady Augusta seems to think Lady Georgiana is a French spy."

"Indeed, sir. A not uncommon propensity on the part of her ladyship upon the appearance of strangers in the house. The earl has given me the responsibility of warning guests about her ladyship's singular little habits. Unfortunately, I wasn't able to do so in time, sir."

"No matter, Randall."

"Thank you, sir." Randall stopped before a white-and-gold set of double doors and opened them. "Your room is the Charles the Second on the gentlemen's side of the main house. His lordship's chambers are down the hall. Lady Lavinia and Lady Georgiana are on the east side opposite, and the family are quartered in the northwest pavilion."

Nick went inside and was immediately struck by blinding white furnishings and more gilt and gold than he'd seen since he'd bought his last country house five years ago. He waited for Randall to leave. Once the door was closed, he charged across the sitting room.

"Pertwee, where are you, Pertwee!"

"I'm at the wardrobe, sir."

Pertwee, his valet, was hanging a pair of trousers in a gilded wardrobe. His orange hair was slicked down with oil, and a monocle dangled from a ribbon on his coat. As always his clothing was pristine and free of wrinkles. Nick could never understand that, since they traveled on the same trains and rode the same distances in carriages or on horses. Perhaps it was because Theophrastus Pertwee was so thin as to resemble a stick insect, or perhaps it was because his father had been a stuffy old schoolmaster.

"Pertwee, quick. I got to get dressed and see bleeding Threshfield right away."

Pertwee shut the wardrobe door with deliberation. "Sir wished me to inform him when he lapsed in his speech or manners. Sir is now speaking as if he were a costermonger."

"Oh, hang my speech." Nick began throwing off his clothes. When Pertwee didn't move from his position and began polishing his monocle, Nick threw his shirt onto the giant four-poster bed hung with white silk damask. "Bloody hell. All right, all right."

He took a few deep breaths and began again. His shoulders pulled back. His chin elevated, and he spoke in tones that recalled Mayfair, Grosvenor Square, and royal drawing rooms. "I shall require a bath, Pertwee, and clothes for tea. Please be quick, as I must obtain an interview with his lordship immediately."

"At once, sir."

Pertwee glided out of the room as if moving on oiled wheels. Nick fell to pacing around the chamber. If he tried to find his own clean clothes, Pertwee would be annoyed. Gentlemen didn't set out their own clothing or draw their own baths. Since Jocelin had rescued him from that gutter all those years ago, he'd learned that gentlemen did bloody little for themselves if they could find someone else to do it for them.

He glanced around the bedroom. Even the bell-pull was embroidered in gold. There were flimsy little Louis XV chairs and a baroque wardrobe and chest that were more curlicue than anything else. As he looked at the ornate furnishings, that feeling came over him again. He'd lived with it for a long time now. It was a strange feeling of disjointedness.

Only recently had he discovered where it came from. Here in England he lived the life of a wealthy gentleman. His country houses were even larger than Threshfield, his town house a rival to that of any duke. He had grown used to moving among gilded surroundings. But always, deep within, he carried the east-London slums with their coat of manure mixed with coal dust and rotting garbage. The contrast between his surroundings and the fetid slime that covered his heart gnawed at him constantly.

This was why he'd accepted Jos's invitation to go to Texas. In that rough country the contrast didn't seem so great. He could enjoy the hillsides covered with veils of bluebonnets; bathe in clear streams churning with white rapids; ride beneath live oaks choking with grapevines and moss; and never once hear an upper-class accent or see a carriage blazoned with a coat of arms that would remind him of what he'd sprung from.

But now he was back in a country that was a kingdom, not a nation. Back in the place where he'd been born the son of a coachman who'd drunk himself out of every position he'd ever gained and taken his failures out on his wife and children. By the time he was eight, Pa hadn't needed the excuse of a lost position to beat his wife.

Ma would shove him and his sister, Tessie, out of their one-room apartment in St. Giles whenever Pa fell into one of his rages. Nick would always sneak back and listen to the beatings and cry—until one day when he was fifteen. That day he fled with Tessie, left her with neighbors, and sneaked back as he always had. But this time he went inside instead of cowering at the door.

This time he took a cudgel, and this time when Pa came after Ma with a broken chair leg, Nick blocked his way. The sight of his son enraged Pa further. He could still see Pa's face, red and purple with drink and violence.

"Bleeding young shaver," Pa had said with spittle wetting his lips. "Teach you to defy me, I will. Bleeding prig. I won't show no mercy. Not a hap'orth of it."

Pa had been almost twice his size, but Nick had grown up on the streets, had survived among the dodgers and prigs of Whitechapel. He beat his father senseless, told him to get out of the apartment and never come back if he wanted to live. He and Ma and Tessie had done just fine after that. Pa hadn't been there to drink up the profits he brought home from his burglaries and schemes.

"No mercy," Nick said softly to himself. He sighed, went to the bootjack, and began removing his boots. "Get the job done, Nick old chap. Get it done quick and get out. You don't belong here."

He scowled at the bootjack as he remembered Lady Georgiana's emerald eyes and the way she'd looked down at him from her perch on the freight wagon as if he were a fly on the Valenciennes lace of her gown. She reminded him of one of those statues. Which one was it? Ah, yes, the one of Athena, goddess of war. He could picture Lady Georgiana, with her majestic stature, wearing a bronze helmet and carrying a sword.

"I'll wager she'd like to whack my head off with it, too," he mused. "What a duel that would be." What would she look like, coming at him in a flimsy white gown, swinging a short sword? Her legs would be bare except for the straps of leather sandals. Her arms would be bare too, and her breasts free . . .

"Holy bleeding hell, what am I doing?"

Nick snatched up the boot he'd just removed and threw it across the room. It smacked against the wall beside the door as Pertwee came through it. The valet gasped, put a hand to his throat, and closed his eyes.

Nick heard him count to ten before he opened them again to glare at his master.

"Sir's bath is ready. If I may enter without risk to my life, I will prepare one of sir's dress day coats. The sterling-silver studs, I think, along with the silver tie pin."

"Sorry, Pertwee."

"Sir is in need of a calming influence. Perhaps if sir would care to recite a little of the Plato we were reading last night."

"Nah."

Pertwee gave him that implacable glance Nick had grown to dread. "If you please, sir. 'Beloved Pan and all ye other gods . . .'"

"Oh, all right! 'Beloved Pan, and all ye other gods who haunt this place, give me beauty in the inward soul; and may the outward and inward man be at one. May I reckon the wise to be the wealthy, and may I have such a quantity of gold as none but the temperate can carry.'" Nick became silent for a moment. Then he eyed the valet. "You're a bleeding mean old sod, Pertwee."

"Yes, sir."

"Why do you put up with me?"

"I regard sir as a challenge."

"It's 'cause you promised Jos you'd look after me, isn't it?"

"The marquess did ask me to take this position, but I wouldn't remain if I didn't consider the situation respectable, sir."

"Thanks, old chap."

"You're welcome, sir."

Nick rose and grinned at the valet. "How long do

you think it takes to unload and store a red-granite sarcophagus?"

"A what, sir?"

"Never mind. Just hurry up and make me respectable. I've got work to do. And if I'm not quick, Lady Georgiana will have me out on my ear."

4

How she wished Jocelin were here, where she could tell him what she thought of his high-handedness. She had expected him to disapprove, even to try to stop her, but she'd never expected to be pounced upon by his outrageous friend. The impudence!

Georgiana ducked under twenty yards of cream barege silk and waited while her maid, Rebecca, fastened the skirt at the back. She had been simmering near a boil for the last two hours while she'd supervised the unloading and storing of the sarcophagus. Now she wanted to get ready for tea early so that she could corner Threshfield and persuade him to oust Mr. Nicholas Ross. When she thought of this man—a near stranger—poking his nose into her personal affairs, she wanted to spit.

Her mother would never have approved of such a lapse in decorum from her daughter. It was more than irksome that men like Mr. Ross could behave with unpardonable impudence and escape with little more than a scandalized glance. But not a woman, not the daughter of a duke.

But she shouldn't lie to herself. She was angry at all men like Mr. Ross. Men whose appearance and charm allowed them to weasel their way into the affections of innocents. She had to admit to herself that she wouldn't have had much patience with Mr. Ross had he been on his best behavior—not after her experience with Lord Silverstone.

She had been introduced to Lord Silverstone during her first season, along with dozens of other suitable young men anxious to marry a duke's daughter. He was the heir to a great title, and beautiful in a pale, round-chinned way so different from the rugged Mr. Ross. Nevertheless, she had been smitten with his artistic sensibilities, his refinement, his heavy-lidded and sad brown eyes.

After one dance at a ball, Lord Silverstone had asked her father for her hand, and Georgiana had been astonished. All thoughts of independence fled her mind at the idea of becoming Silverstone's wife. She had walked around in a fluffy daze while the duke had had a series of talks with Silverstone about the marriage settlement.

The daze had lasted until her first real conversation with Silverstone. After one of the settlement discussions Silverstone had met her in the drawing room at Grosvenor Square. As she came into the room, she bent forward a little to reduce her height. Silverstone was shorter than she was. Conscious of her shortcomings, aware that Silverstone could marry any of a number of heiresses, she had been tongue-tied.

She needn't have worried about being able to say anything, because Silverstone embarked upon a lecture. He was quite sure she was aware of her duty as a wife, and he was gratified that he would be marrying a girl so well trained to undertake the responsibilities of a large household. Finally she'd gathered enough courage to mention her idea of a home for children.

"Hardly a suitable occupation for a young bride," Silverstone said. "No, there will be little time for that, what with the season and all. Establishing oneself as a major force in Society takes management, Georgiana."

"But I want—"

"I can see we need to have a frank discussion," he said. "I pride myself on my honesty, Georgiana. You'll soon learn this about me. I'm not one to keep my opinions secret. Secrecy leads to misunderstandings and quarrels between a husband and wife."

Silverstone rubbed his round chin as he gave her a severe appraisal. "I think it's best if we begin honestly. I've made a sacrifice in offering for you, because, frankly, marrying you is rather like marrying the Tower or a cathedral. I'm sure you're aware of your shortcomings in your appearance, and I'm willing to overlook them. The alliance with such a noble lineage is worth the sacrifice."

He finished with a self-satisfied glow, hardly noticing Georgiana's pallor or the way she'd drawn herself up from her slightly stooped posture.

"Your sacrifice won't be necessary," she said.

He had been gazing out the window at the carriage traffic in the square. His gaze darted to her in surprise, as if he'd never thought she would do anything but waggle her head in agreement.

"What won't be necessary?" he asked.

"Your noble sacrifice. I wouldn't hear of your

subjecting yourself to a lifetime of my company. Good-bye, my lord."

"Georgiana, you're not yourself. I shall leave and speak to you tomorrow when you've calmed down."

Behind her facade of composure Georgiana felt the ache of humiliation. Why should she let this boor get away with his insults?

"I'm not going to marry you, Silverstone, and so that you're clear on the matter, I'll tell you why. You're a mean-spirited little snake who hides his appetite for cruelty behind a guise of honesty. You admire frankness? Here's frankness—you have no chin, sir, and you're short, but neither of these mattered to me. However, I do object to marrying a self-important ass."

Dukes' daughters weren't supposed to call their fiancés asses and mean-spirited little snakes, but the breach had been worth it to see the look of red-faced outrage on Silverstone's face. The duke had been furious. And since that day Georgiana had never again given up on her plans to marry an aged suitor.

"My lady?"

Georgiana started and came out of her unhappy daydream to find Rebecca holding out the bodice to her gown. Angry with herself for indulging in thoughts that could provoke self-pity, Georgiana murmured an apology to her maid. Thrusting her arms through the tight sleeves of her bodice, she tugged on the pointed bottom hem and muttered to herself while Rebecca worked on the buttons. Then she sat before a mirror and helped the maid gather the thick lengths of her hair in coils at the back of her head.

Her hands shook with the force of her anger. If she'd been a man, like Jocelin, no one would have interfered in her plans. All her work was threatened. She'd been devising her scheme for years. It was the result of a childhood spent watching her mother and father and gradually realizing how impossible it was to be a married woman in England.

There was no particular event or conversation she could point to as the deciding ingredient in her decision to eschew the legalized slavery that was marriage. She'd simply observed her parents. Mother was far more intelligent and sensitive than Father, but because he was a man, Father controlled the family fortune. Father had legal responsibility for their children.

And yet these disparities in legal rights weren't nearly as humiliating as the small customs and acts that relegated a woman to the rank of a child—Father had to approve the newspapers, books, and magazines Mother read, the clothes she wore, the friends she made. Like a child, Mother rarely saw more than a few pounds of real money at any one time. Father had accounts with merchants, and the bills were sent to him. Georgiana would never forget accompanying Mother on a shopping trip and having to lend her money for ribbons impulsively purchased from a street vendor.

Rebecca brought out several house caps, but Georgiana rejected them in favor of a swirl of silk roses and lace that could be pinned to the back of her hair. Yes, she had been a long time forming her opinions. Having Aunt Livy nearby had offered a glaring contrast. Aunt Livy had been married young to a man more interested in his horses than in her. When he died, she refused to be put on the marriage block again and had lived her life exactly as she wanted ever since.

Society be damned, Aunt Livy had taken to wearing breeches like her friend George Sand. She would have smoked cigars if she'd liked. To Georgiana such a life seemed ideal, for she could think of nothing more deadening to the soul than to spend her time in the aimless and inane pursuits of Society. Aunt Livy called it "balls, calls, and clothes."

Georgiana was going to do something useful with her life. Jocelin had helped her realize there were too many children with no home, or with homes that were nightmares and unsafe. She was going to make a place for these unwanted young ones, a safe place, a refuge. But first she had to free herself of her parents' rule. They would never agree to letting her establish and run such a place.

In their eyes her first duty was to marry well and to breed heirs for her husband. They wanted her to spend her life with an unfeeling Narcissus like Silverstone. She'd rather die. And if Mr. Nicholas Ross thought he could order her to abandon her escape plan, he was thoroughly mistaken.

"Rebecca," Georgiana said, "I don't suppose Mr. Hyde and Lady Prudence were delayed returning from their calls."

"I'm sorry, my lady, no."

Trying not to roll her eyes in disgust, Georgiana stuck out her foot so that Rebecca could lace her kid boot. The Honorable Evelyn Hyde and his wife, Lady Prudence, were the curse of Threshfield. Unfortunately, she'd neglected to account for the Hydes in her plans to gain independence. She hadn't realized how difficult the earl's family was until she came for this betrothal visit and met them. Evelyn was Threshfield's nephew and heir, Ludwig's father. Not twenty-four hours had passed since her arrival before Evelyn had attempted to seduce her in the crimson drawing room.

Georgiana hadn't been fool enough to think Evelyn swept away by her negligible beauty. He'd been out to disgrace her before the earl. Evelyn disliked threats to his inheritance. A young bride capable of bearing sons was the last thing he wanted for his aged uncle.

And Prudence? Prudence had far-reaching plans that ended in acquiring a dukedom for Evelyn. Prudence longed to be addressed as "Your Grace." She was proof that it is possible to feel hard-done-by even when one has been born to position and wealth. Georgiana usually managed to submerge herself in her studies in the Egyptian Wing, thus avoiding Evelyn and Prudence. Poor Ludwig also took refuge there from his spiteful great-uncle and parents. Together they were cataloging and preserving the earl's neglected acquisitions.

It was her love of the ancient world that had drawn her into friendship with the earl. Threshfield had a brilliant mind and amazing imagination. Georgiana regretted that he'd allowed bitterness derived from his own uncaring parents, and a love of power over people, to sour his soul. She had a feeling the earl had agreed to her odd proposal of marriage for a cantankerous reason—to torment his family. She also knew he'd grown fond of her because she was one of the few people he couldn't bully.

As Rebecca held out a cashmere shawl, Georgiana muttered, "Mr. Ross will have an amazingly short visit."

As she turned to allow Rebecca to put the shawl

on her shoulders, she caught the maid's pop-eyed expression.

"Is something wrong, Rebecca?"

"Oh, my lady!"

"Yes?"

"Oh, my lady." Rebecca bounced up and down as she arranged the shawl in folds. "Is he as handsome as they say?"

Georgiana frowned. "He?"

"Mr. Nicholas Ross. Has he really got sunset-blue eyes, and does he look like one of those wild gunfighters from America? Nellie, the upstairs maid, got a glimpse of him. They say he's got a mysterious past and that he makes ladies and duchesses quiver in their boots when he rides by in Hyde Park."

Staring at the maid's salacious expression, Georgiana said, "Heavens, Rebecca. You know who Mr. Ross is."

"But I never saw him, my lady." Rebecca pulled the shawl down over Georgiana's arm as she chattered. "I heard Nellie telling the housekeeper that two years ago Mr. Ross fought a duel on the Continent. Some lord called him out over his wife. Nellie said Mr. Ross refused to fight the man at first. Said he never touched the woman, and that if the lord had done his lovemaking right, he wouldn't be worried about his wife finding a replacement."

"You mean he fought a duel over such a distasteful matter?"

"The lord wouldn't leave Mr. Ross alone," Rebecca said. "Mr. Ross was finally forced into the duel. Mr. Ross was clever, though. He only wounded the lord."

"How merciful of him."

Rebecca nodded violently. "And brave and gallant."

Her frown deepening, Georgiana held out her hand for her gloves.

"Rebecca, Mr. Ross is a crude barbarian, not some gallant, fairy-tale knight."

"Yes, my lady."

She dismissed the titillated Rebecca. She was ready at last and set out for the library downstairs. Her skirts floated around her, swaying gently, and soothed her irritated mood. Many women had embarrassing accidents with their crinolines. Georgiana solved the problem by refusing to wear one as wide as the current fashion dictated. Thus she could pass through doorways with little more effort than a steadying hand on her skirts.

She glided down the stairs, crossed the saloon, and knocked on the library door. The earl usually spent the two hours before tea reading and gazing out the long bank of windows that afforded him a view of the park behind Threshfield. There he and his predecessors had created an almost fairy-tale vista filled with miniature lakes, a Palladian bridge, small replicas of Grecian temples, grottos, and secluded glades dotted with classical sculpture.

The earl's voice responded to her knock, and Georgiana entered the library. John Charles Hyde, Earl of Threshfield, was near a group of chairs set before the windows that opened onto the terrace. He was standing beside his wheelchair, still tall for a man of more than eighty years. He smiled at her, but his mouth was hardly noticeable below the majestic Hyde nose. With his thick white hair swept back from his forehead, he reminded Georgiana of pictures she'd seen of an American bald eagle. In his watery eyes was that ever-present glitter composed in part of devilment, curiosity, and cynical amusement.

The earl gave her one of his admiring smiles, the brightest of which was usually reserved for a newly acquired Vermeer or Reynolds. "Georgiana, my dear, you're as graceful as a Mozart sonata. Is it time for tea already?"

"Not quite. I wanted to speak to you privately."

Leaning on an ivory-handled cane, the earl lifted a silver eyebrow and gave her a quizzical look. "Privacy? Privacy? What a rare commodity in this house."

"All the more reason for me to speak at once. Threshfield, have you indeed countenanced the visit of that barbaric Mr. Ross? I know you've heard of his absurd arrival and his rudeness to me."

"Speak up, my dear. I'm afraid my old ears aren't what they used to be. I haven't seen Mr. Ross in some time. He made an unfortunate impression upon you, I collect."

Georgiana helped the earl to his wheelchair. " 'Unfortunate' hardly describes his behavior. He rode up to me on a mad horse, nearly ran me down, and then proceeded to order me home using the most backward and offensive language. He's intrusive and ignorant. I would despise him if he weren't such a pathetic creature." She laid a gloved hand on the earl's arm and bent down to him. "His manner toward me was intolerable. Please ask him to leave, Threshfield."

The earl gave her a bleary smile, patted her hand, and glanced aside at one of the wing-backed chairs that was turned toward the windows and away from her.

'What do you say, sir?'

Georgiana gasped as a young gentleman rose and approached her. He was dressed in a Bond Street coat and trousers, pristine linen, and a silk vest as understated and elegant as any in Jocelin's wardrobe. The picture of London sophistication, he was hardly recognizable as the wild-riding barbarian of earlier that afternoon. His burnished chestnut hair had been trimmed and swept back from his face, which had been shaved. She could smell sandalwood soap, and even more amazing, he moved about the room as if he owned it. Nicholas Ross had transformed himself into a polished aristocrat too much like Rebecca's fairytale knight. She despised him.

'What do I say?' Ross replied to the earl while Georgiana gaped at him and turned pink. 'I'd say that Lady Georgiana knows a great many words that begin with the letter I—intrusive, ignorant, intolerable. I myself prefer the letter S—selfish, spoiled.' He caught Georgiana's eyes in a unruffled challenge. Gone was the drawl, the ungrammatical phraseology, the slouching posture. 'Spiteful.'

'Oh, dear,' the earl said, looking from Ross to Georgiana.

Georgiana turned on him. 'Threshfield, for shame. That wasn't handsome, not handsome at all. And you.' She rounded on the intruder. 'Your conduct is consistent with your character.'

She stopped speaking because Ross suddenly left the windows and came to stand on the other side of the earl's wheelchair. Even with the earl between them, it seemed that he was too close. For some reason she needed more distance from him than from other men. Having him so near made her jittery, and she had to stop herself from backing away as if threat-ened.

She hadn't been raised in a duke's household for nothing, though. She stood her ground. From child-hood she'd been drilled on being suitably distant to her inferiors. That's what he was—an inferior. A tall, muscled, and impudent inferior. Unfortunately, he had a way of looking at her as if she were a succulent parlor maid and he the lord of the manor.

His stare seemed to peel back the layers of her composure, to shrivel the impervious and refined wrappings with which she protected her dignity. He was grinning at her now, and holding her eyes with his, trying to embarrass her even more than he already had with his forward stare. She tore her eyes from his and snapped at the earl.

'Threshfield, are you going to dismiss this per-son?' She winced at the earl's cackle.

'I'm sorry, my dear. Too late.'

'What do you mean?'

Ross walked around the wheelchair to her side and lowered his voice. 'He means you're too late, George old chap.'

'Don't call me George, sir.' Georgiana gave her betrothed a suspicious look. 'Threshfield, what are you up to?'

'Oh, my dear, I can't offer my hospitality to your brother's dearest friend and then withdraw it. It's not in keeping with honor and duty.'

She felt her cheeks grow hot as she realized she'd lost before she'd entered the room. 'And his manner toward me is?'

'Mr. Ross has promised to improve. We must

make allowances for a man when he's spent so long in savage country.'

'There is no excuse for his intrusive and insulting conduct.'

'You really must watch the I-words, George.'

'I told you not to call me that, you wretched vermin!'

The earl banged his cane on the floor, causing Georgiana to jump. 'That's enough. Mr. Ross has come to visit and will remain. He has to, because I'm thinking of buying a painting from him.'

'What painting?' Georgiana asked suspiciously.

Ross clasped his hands behind his back and fell to studying the ceiling. 'It just so happens that I have come upon an amazing portrait of one of the Thresh-field ancestors. A Gainsborough. Quite the epitome of Gainsborough, actually. It will be the showpiece of Threshfield's new collection. Won't it, sir?'

The earl shrugged and laid his cane across his lap. 'If we can agree on a reasonable price.'

'Of course,' Nick said with a sly smile in Georgiana's direction. 'And agreeing on a suitable price takes time.'

Drawing herself up as if she had a book balanced on her head, Georgiana said, 'I see. I didn't know you were so acquisitive, Threshfield.'

'Of course you did, my dear. How else could I have amassed my Egyptian collection, my classical antiquities, and all those Dutch, Italian, and English masterpieces?'

Georgiana whirled away from the two smirking men in a wave of swaying skirts and offended dignity. 'I know what you're up to, Threshfield, but I doubt Mr. Ross does.'

'What is that?' Ross asked, still smirking.

'The earl has other hobbies besides collecting art, Mr. Ross. His favorite is pricking the sensibilities of his family. Threshfield can hardly wait for tea, because then he can watch his nephew's apoplexy when he learns that the earl is playing host to a man of ill breeding, a man in trade with the manners of a dockworker.'

She waited long enough to see Ross's smirk turn to a scowl, then sank in a curtsy and marched out of the library. Feeling as if she were sizzling on a grill, Georgiana crossed the saloon and went outside. Fortunately, tea was being held on the grassy lawn beneath a canopy of sheer gauze that gently fluttered in the breeze.

The walk down the curved stairs, past the Italian fountain with its unicorn centerpiece, gave her time to master her fury. Contrariness had always been one of Threshfield's most annoying traits. Once he fastened on an idea, he rarely abandoned it. Knowing that there was nothing Ross could do to hinder his marital plans, he'd invited the man just to upset Evelyn and Prudence. It was now up to her to make Mr. Ross so uncomfortable that he would abandon his charge and quit Threshfield. Doing so would afford her great satisfaction.

Georgiana hesitated as she neared the canopy, for Evelyn and Prudence were already seated. Enduring them would test her already burdened patience. She could see Prudence's rings flash in the late-afternoon sunlight. The lady was short, like the queen, with a body that tended to run to fat. Her features all repeated the roundness of her body—circular eyes, bulbous nose, and a mouth that pinched into a tight, round little button.

Glancing over her shoulder, Georgiana saw the infamous Mr. Ross walking beside the earl's wheelchair as Threshfield's attendant pushed him across the lawn. Four hefty footmen trailed behind. They always lingered within calling distance, ready to pick up the chair and transport their master up or down stairs.

'Do hurry up, Georgiana,' Prudence called to her in her customary sniping tone. 'I've poured your tea, and it's getting cold.'

Georgiana seated herself as far away from Evelyn as she could. This put her next to the disgruntled Prudence. Perhaps her moodiness was due to the fact that she surely knew that her marriage to the heir to an ancient earldom had depended upon her immense marriage settlement

In spite of the lack of sympathy between them, Georgiana felt compassion for this dumpy little person married to the handsome Evelyn. She was sure Prudence sought consolation by drenching herself in jewelry, especially rings, and dressing herself in the height of fashion in the most luxurious of materials. Today she wore a gown of an unfortunate mustard color that sallowed her complexion and failed to complement her oak-brown hair.

The earl and Mr. Ross arrived, and there was a great fuss to get Threshfield settled comfortably next to Georgiana. She was grateful for the distraction, because Ross had regained his smirk, possibly because Evelyn and Prudence had heard of his arrival and looked as if they'd swallowed soap.

Mr. Ross sat on a wrought-iron chair between the earl and Evelyn. Evelyn, a younger, more energetic replica of the earl, perched stiffly, sipping his tea and saying as little as possible to the new guest. Prudence wasn't so reticent.

'Mr. Ross, I don't believe I know your people. Are they from Scotland?'

Georgiana darted a quick glance from Prudence to Ross. The question was deliberate. Prudence already knew Mr. Ross's background.

Ross took a cup and saucer from Lady Prudence, stirred his tea calmly, then looked directly into his hostess's bean-colored eyes. 'As Threshfield must have told you, Lady Prudence, I have no people. I was born in St. Giles in one room of a filthy tenement. Having made my fortune, I am engaged in improving myself and seeing the world.'

In disbelief Georgiana watched Ross subject Prudence to a coy, wide-eyed regard that reduced the woman to a simpering, giggling fluster. One moment Prudence was the picture of an outraged hostess, the next she was cow-eyed and red in the face.

The earl sucked tea noisily and said, 'Young Nick here used to be a thief.' He cackled at the squawk this produced from Prudence. 'What's that word you used for 'thief,' Nick?"

"Prig, sir. And as youth I practiced the kinchin lay, which is robbing children sent on errands to various merchants. I had a snug little business."

Evelyn choked. His cup and saucer rattled, and Nick caught them before they fell. He slapped Evelyn on the back while the earl chortled. Georgiana hadn't moved, for she was beginning to feel a twinge of conscience. Whatever his transgressions, Mr. Ross must have had a terrible childhood. She had never had to steal from children to survive. She vowed that in her quarrel with him she wouldn't throw that in his face.

In her forbidden forays into newspaper reading, she'd discovered the squalor in which so many lived in neighborhoods near her own luxurious home. After that she no longer ignored the women in the Strand who sold violets, the children who offered to carry her packages. Father had been livid when he'd discovered her giving away her small allowance for things like wilted bouquets. However, Mr. Ross was a grown man. There was no excuse for his continued indelicacy. Indelicacy. Did she indeed use too many *I*-words? She hadn't been paying attention to the conversation.

"Really, Uncle," Evelyn was sputtering. "To entertain someone in trade is one thing, but to countenance the presence of a criminal. And one who behaves in such—such a debasing manner to your betrothed."

The earl's watery blue eyes sparkled, and he leered at Evelyn. "Can't say I've noticed your worrying about Georgiana lately. I'd think you'd be glad to have a handsome young man around who might catch her eye and cut me out."

"What!" Georgiana exclaimed, nearly spilling tea down the front of her gown. Prudence froze with her teacup halfway to her lips. Nick threw back his head and laughed while Evelyn made fists and bit the inside of his cheek.

"Really, Uncle, you're most improper," Prudence said as she set down her cup and fussed with the teapot while ogling Mr. Ross.

Georgiana closed her opened mouth. She happened to look at Evelyn, who was staring at her with a peculiar expression. He hadn't even noticed his wife's ambivalent reaction to Nick Ross. She gave him her most stately and chilling regard. The look seemed only to intrigue Evelyn. His gaze seemed to grow unfocused for a moment, and his lips curled into a most disgusting, slack-lipped smile. She was certain he was remembering their encounter in the drawing room. His hands had wandered to the top of her corset before she could plant her fist in his stomach.

Turning her head sharply, she encountered the quizzical scrutiny of Mr. Nicholas Ross. No doubt he thought the worst if he'd been watching that exchange with Evelyn. Jutting out her chin, Georgiana took a finger sandwich from a porcelain server, bit into it, and chewed furiously. Her mood lightened when Mr. Ross uttered a wordless exclamation, dropped his spoon and stared as Ludwig trotted up to the group, out of breath and perspiring.

"I'm late, I know," said Ludwig. "Oh, my heart, yes, terribly late, but I began to translate the inscription on the new sarcophagus, and I forgot everything else."

Georgiana smiled at her friend, for he had indeed forgotten everything. At some time during his work in the Egyptian Wing he'd donned a uraeus, a gold diadem with a cobra mounted on the front. The diadem encircled his balding head, with the serpent jutting out of his forehead. He was carrying an alabaster statue of Toth, the baboon god of wisdom. The stone image was lifelike down to the depiction of the creature's private anatomy. Ross inspected the object in horrified fascination while the earl introduced him to Ludwig.

Ludwig sat down, placing the statue on the

ground beside his chair. "Do you know anything about ancient Egypt, Mr. Ross?"

Nick watched the cobra on Ludwig's forehead and shook his head wordlessly.

"I would be glad to show you the collection and tell you something about it. Always glad to share the amazing things I'm learning. And Georgiana knows a great deal as well, oh, my heart, yes."

"I'm sure Mr. Ross isn't interested," Georgiana said swiftly.

Ross gave her that infuriating smirk. "But I am interested, Lady Georgiana. Jocelin was most anxious to learn what you're up to—your occupations, that is. May I call upon you in the Egyptian Wing, Mr. Hyde?"

"A pleasure, sir," Ludwig said with a dignity spoiled by his headdress.

"Ludwig," Georgiana said through her teeth, "we will bore Mr. Ross."

Nick leaned over and patted the baboon statue on its head. "Not at all. I find such studies uncommon jolly." Turning a brilliant smile on Ludwig, he said, "I shall be the gainer in this exchange, if you will allow me the privilege of learning from you."

"There," Ludwig replied with a triumphant look at Georgiana. "You see? Mr. Ross is delighted to share our little interests."

Mr. Nicholas Ross was gloating. If she looked at him, he would smirk at her in that infuriating way that made her want to shriek at him like a harpy. For the third time that day Georgiana found herself outmaneuvered, routed. Setting down her cup and saucer, she rose, causing the gentlemen to leave their seats.

"You will please excuse me," she said quietly.

"Aunt Lavinia has missed tea, and I want to inquire if she is feeling well."

"Oh, Georgiana, if you're going to the house, would you take this inside?"

Ludwig picked up the baboon statue and shoved it into her hands before she could protest. Georgiana found herself clutching the animal so that its anatomically realistic organs faced outward. Evelyn gave her a leer. She stumbled over a chair leg in her hasty retreat from him and backed into someone. Swinging around, she came face-to-face with Mr. Ross. Steadying her with a hand to her elbow, he said nothing but glanced from the statue's attributes to her face. She yanked her elbow free and marched past him, hissing under her breath so that only he could hear.

"Leave Threshfield, Mr. Ross. Poison my sight no longer."

He whispered as well, using that disreputable drawl he knew annoyed her. "Dang, George. Looks like I better stay put and see what other scandalous things you and Ludwig got in that old Egyptian Wing. Yep, looks like it was a good thing I showed up."

5

He was a guest in bedlam. Nick struck a match and
lighted a thin cigar as the butler passed around port to
the gentlemen. The ladies –Prudence, Georgiana,
Aunt Lavinia, and the fey Lady Augusta—had retired
to the drawing room. Dinner had been amazing in
that no one had found it odd that Lady Augusta ob-
jected to several dishes on account of Georgiana's having poisoned them. Georgiana had protested her
innocence, but not vehemently. No doubt she knew
the futility.

And there was mischief afoot. Not from poor
Lady Augusta or from the vitriolic earl, but from Evelyn Hyde. When he'd thought himself unobserved,
the bastard had given Lady Georgiana looks of brazen
familiarity. Nick knew that look. He'd used it himself
when he'd thought it would work, and it had worked
with certain ladies with too much time between calls
and the dinner gong.

But Evelyn had the subtlety of a warthog. There
was an undercurrent of tension between him and

Georgiana that crackled like the noise of a telegraph wire. Nick took a sparing sip of port from a heavy crystal snifter and listened to Evelyn argue with his son about Ludwig's immersion in his Egyptian studies.

"As a Hyde you have a duty to uphold the traditions of an ancient lineage. It's shooting season. You should have invited lots of friends. Next month pheasant season will begin, and I suppose you won't even be able to find your guns."

Ludwig slouched in his chair and mumbled, "I don't like shooting. Why should I get up before dawn and slog through the mist until I'm wet and chilled near to freezing just to slaughter hundreds of harmless birds?"

Nick eyed Evelyn with a blank expression that concealed a dislike that had sprung full-blown within him the moment he'd seen the fellow. He could stomach most aristocrats, but Hyde—with his air of entitlement, his assumption that he was superior due to an accident of birth—made Nick want to puke. And if he continued to leer secretly at Georgiana, Hyde was going to find himself strung from the earl's magnificent Corinthian portico.

The earl wheeled his way over to Nick's chair. "How do you find my family, Ross?"

"Individual, sir."

"They're a pack of useless leeches. Georgiana is worth a hundred of each of them. Don't blame her brother for wanting to watch over her. But you're daft if you think you're going to push her into changing her mind."

"You'll pardon me, sir, if I say the match is inappropriate. Lady Georgiana should marry more suitably."

"Georgiana and I have remarkably similar opinions about marriage, Ross, and you don't know her. She may look all lace and trimmings, but she's got a steel spine, like her aunt." Finishing his port in one gulp, the earl handed Nick his glass. "I'm going to retire. Late hours disagree with me. Evelyn and Ludwig will show you the way to the drawing room. Good night, Ross. I'll show you my paintings tomorrow."

Nick rose as the attendant turned the earl's chair and began pushing it out of the dining room. "Thank you, sir. Good evening."

With frigid civility Evelyn led the way to the drawing room. Nick was disappointed to find that Georgiana had retired, pleading fatigue. He paid for having toyed with Prudence at tea, for the lady descended upon him, fluttering her pudgy, beringed hands and asking him dozens of questions about his friendship with Jocelin, whom she took pleasure in referring to as "the marquess." He shouldn't have provoked her, but it had been too tempting to entice the lady and thus scandalize Georgiana. Unfortunately, Prudence was the type of woman to gush over him one moment, then eschew his low company the next. Lady Lavinia rescued him, but he soon grew uneasy when she subjected him to her own barrage of incisive questions.

His endurance was tested past bearing when Lady Augusta announced she would favor the company with a selection of pieces on the pianoforte. Attired in a girlish white silk empire gown, Augusta had once again startled him with her appearance. The neckline of her frock was low, revealing a wrinkled chest, while the deep hem was ruched and decorated with tiny blue bows. He listened to three folk songs, then slipped out of the drawing room. His long voyage was catching up with him, and he needed an extended, uninterrupted sleep to recover.

But first he would finish the cigar he'd begun in the dining room. He couldn't smoke in the presence of the ladies, but he might get away with a quiet session on the balcony overlooking the terrace and the lawn where tea had been served that afternoon. He went upstairs and through another drawing room to the balcony.

September had brought the turning of the leaves in the earl's park—beeches, chestnuts, oaks. The days were still warm for England, but the nights were chilly, bringing a mist come morning. Nick breathed in the cool air scented with leaf mold and counted himself lucky to be out of the suffocating Texas heat. There were no clouds, and he could see the constellations he had recently read about in a book Pertwee had given him.

In one group of stars he could trace a line that resembled Georgiana's statuesque figure. She had been the picture of queenly grace this evening, her manners perfect. So perfect that he'd been kept at a distance. He'd found she wouldn't look at him. She fixed her gaze upon his chin, or a point just over his shoulder.

The strategy had been bloody annoying, especially when she kept herself occupied by conversing with Ludwig and Evelyn so that she didn't have to talk to him. And at one point between dishes of roast goose and woodcock, he'd witnessed an exchange of glances between Georgiana and Evelyn. Had he been in a position of authority with Georgiana, he would have called the man out for that look of blatant lust.

True to her breeding, Georgiana hadn't responded to the unspoken message. Her gaze had settled on Evelyn's raptorlike features, then drifted on as if she found nothing out of the ordinary in his manner. Was she accustomed to it? By God, she must be, to treat the incident so casually!

Nick blew smoke and fumed as he considered the implications of his discovery. Maybe Georgiana had fooled everyone. Maybe she wasn't after the earl at all. Maybe she was after his bloody heir. Swearing under his breath, Nick threw down his cigar and crushed it beneath his polished dress boot. He had his hand on a crystal doorknob, about to leave the balcony, when out of the corner of his eye he caught a flash of white on the lawn.

Releasing the knob, he went to the railing and searched the shadows by the fountain. The moon was out, its silver light revealing a woman dressed in filmy white. It couldn't be Augusta, who was still at the pianoforte. The only other woman who wore white that evening was Georgiana. As he strained to see in the dark, the woman turned to look back at the house, revealing her face. It was Georgiana.

Nick stepped back into the shadows. Even at this distance he was certain it was she. No other woman was so tall, or moved as if she were made of mist floating on a gentle breeze. As he watched, she donned a cloak, turned and resumed her progress across the lawn. He remained there until he saw which path she took—the one the earl had said led to a Grecian temple set in a glade surrounded by forest.

"She's going on a bleeding assignation," he muttered as he hurried through the balcony doorway. "I
knew it. Precious sly and deceitful, that is. And with a
rum chap like Evelyn bloody Hyde. Done me work
for me, she has. Hung on her own hat peg. Old
Threshfield will boot her out in a dustbin. Ha!"

He raced downstairs and outside without encountering anyone, but darkness slowed his progress once
he left the terrace. The path down which Georgiana
had vanished was composed of gravel. Not wishing to
announce his presence, he walked alongside it, dodging trees and brush, thus further slowing his journey.
At last he came to the glade, with its miniature temple
gleaming whitely in the moonlight.

Skirting the tree line, he slipped behind one of the
four columns that decorated the facade. The double
doors at the entrance were ajar and revealed a dim
golden glow. Slinking inside, he paused and glanced at
an archaic iron lamp of foreign design set in a tall
tripod. It was filled with fresh oil. He was in an antechamber with a white-marble floor.

He stepped farther into the room and nearly
choked as a woman's naked figure came into view.
Then he noted the deathlike stillness, the chalky
whiteness, the plinth. There was a statue in the middle
of the room, and around it in murals were scenes of
mysterious rites. Past the statue lay an archway.

There was more dim golden light in the chamber,
but it seemed to dance on the tiled walls of the chamber beyond the archway. His imagination skipped and
leaped as he walked to the arch, careful not to make
noise on the marble floor. He paused under the arch
and listened. Hollow, watery sounds issued from the

unseen chamber. Light danced on the walls. He smelled jasmine and water.

Evelyn bloody Hyde had found himself a unique trysting place, and Nick Ross was going to wrap him around one of those white columns for it. He took a step and heard a crunch. He'd stepped on a dead leaf. Georgiana's voice floated toward him, humming, and accompanied by more watery sounds. She began to sing a song about spring and pagan rites. She sounded so blissful, her voice filled with a warmth and somnolence so at odds with her usual reserved and cool tones.

Is this what being with Hyde did to her? He wouldn't just wrap the bastard around a column, he'd flay him to it.

"Bleeding sod."

Nick charged inside only to run into a wrought-iron balustrade that prevented his rushing headfirst off a landing. Disoriented at first, he clutched at the railing and looked down into a domed chamber filled with an oval tiled pool. And in the pool gazing up at him, her mouth forming an O, was Lady Georgiana. They gaped at each other. Then each sprang into action.

Nick pointed at her. "Aha!" His arm and his jaw dropped as he realized that Georgiana was naked.

At the same time Georgiana shrieked, plunged through the water to the side of the pool, pressed her body to the tiles, and reached for a pile of clothing and towels at the edge of the pool. Her hand plucked at the closest piece of clothing, a filmy dressing gown. She dragged the length of white material against her body with one hand while she shoved her free hand into a basket next to the clothes.

Pulling her hand out, she aimed a gun at Nick. "Get out."

Ignoring her, he searched the room for Hyde, but Georgiana appeared to be alone. He'd come too soon.

"Mr. Ross," Georgiana said, her voice echoing off the high stone walls, "perhaps you didn't see my gun."

He had been watching the gown she used as cover absorb water and become almost transparent. "What?"

"This is a derringer, Mr. Ross. A Remington double-barreled, over-and-under design, forty-one caliber in rimfire, with mother-of-pearl grip and floral engraving on the barrels. It was a gift from Aunt Livy, and I'm going to shoot you with it if you don't leave immediately."

Nick's attention had strayed to the wet gown again. Stinging heat surged through his body. He'd never seen anything like this. A naked woman in an eighteenth-century plunge bath holding a gun. Her hair was piled on top of her head, but wisps had escaped to form damp curls that framed her face. In the dancing gold light he could see the hazy curves of her body, watch drops of water snake down her throat to the hollow between her breasts. And she was waiting for—

His lips curled into a nasty smile. "Well, well, well. Wot's this, wot's this? Here's a devil of a sight." He trailed his hand on the banister as he descended the curved stairs that led down to the pool.

"You stay up there!" Georgiana shouted. She cocked the pistol.

Nick stopped halfway down and leaned on the

banister. Now he could see her long legs better, although they were distorted by the water. If he came any closer, his body was going to put on an embarrassing display of its own.

"I ain't leaving until Evelyn bloody Hyde shows up."

"Ev—you think I'm here to meet him?" The derringer wobbled, then pointed at him again. "Of all the disgusting, evil assumptions. You have the mind of a degenerate, Mr. Ross."

Nick braced himself on the stair rail and leaned over it. "Speaking of degenerate. I ain't the one standing naked in a pool with a flimsy bit o' cloth that a blind frog could see through."

Georgiana looked down at herself, saw the wet, transparent material, and yelped. One arm dropped to her breasts while her gun hand dropped beneath the water to cover the dark triangle between her legs. Then she gasped, yanking the gun out of the water, only to drop it and cover herself again. Nick's delighted chuckle bounced off the walls. Georgiana plunged to the edge of the pool again, grabbed a bathing towel, and clutched it to her body. The soaked gown floated away.

Facing him again, she hissed, "I should have shot you."

Nick stopped chuckling. "How many men have you killed?"

"Don't be absurd. None."

Something in his expression must have alarmed her, because she backed into the middle of the plunge bath. He descended to the foot of the stairs, then strolled to the edge of the bath.

"None," he said softly. "Be careful who you threaten to shoot. The traps would scrag me quick if they knew how many I've killed." At her confused expression he said, "The police—they'd hang me. What did you think, that I got out of St. Giles selling violets?"

He watched her throat muscles work as she swallowed. Admiration followed when she responded in a steady voice.

"My ancestors fought the Spanish Armada and stood with Wellington against Napoleon. You aren't going to intimidate me, Mr. Ross. Now, leave, before I begin shouting for help."

"Too far away to be heard." He stooped and picked up a crystal bottle. Pulling the stopper, he sniffed. It was empty but smelled of jasmine. "Say, George. Is that water cold?"

"What do you mean? Get out!"

He knelt and trailed his fingers in the water. "Must have put in steam after it was built. But it's getting cold now."

"Are you going to leave or not?"

"Well, George, that depends."

Her thin, arched brows drew together. "Upon what?"

"On whether we can reach a deal, old chap."

"Go on," she snapped, tugging the towel closer to her hips.

"I'll leave if you promise to give up this ridiculous engagement."

"I'm going to look up an ancient Egyptian curse and use it on you."

Nick stuck his hand into the water again. "Getting colder. Course, I could come in and get you. Is that what you're waiting for?"

She backpedaled so quickly, her feet slipped out from under her and she plunged into the water. Caught by surprise, Nick knelt at the edge of the pool and chortled. She shot to the surface, sputtering water and cursing. Once on her feet, she twisted the towel around her body more securely and waded toward him. Nick stopped laughing as her voiced boomed.

"By God, sir! I'm going to make you sorry you ever left St. Giles."

He didn't respond at once, because he didn't think she would have the brazen will to do it. When she mounted the steps that led out of the pool, he realized he'd misjudged her. She was coming out, and she was going to attack him. If she touched him, all wet and bare-skinned, he wouldn't be laughing for long. He couldn't fight Jocelin's naked sister, not with his body aroused and his emotions disturbed. He began backing away as she stomped toward him. "Now, George—Lady Georgiana, remember your breeding."

"Don't speak to me of breeding, you wretched vermin."

Thrusting out a hand, Nick chuckled and shook his head.

"You don't know what you're doing, love."

She was in front of him quickly, and he was still shaking his head when she drew back a fist and punched him. She was wet, so the blow glanced off his cheek. Georgiana cried out and clutched her hand. Nick swore, more in surprise than in pain, and put a hand to his cheek as he stared at her.

He began to walk toward her. "Why, you flash little piece."

Another voice called out, "I found the other bottle of bath crystals, my lady."

Nick stopped and turned. A maid in a black gown and white apron hurried down the stairs, saw them, and nearly tripped.

"Oh. Oh, sir!" The maid was short and delicately fashioned, but she flew to her mistress and set herself between them like a furious goose protecting her brood. "For shame, sir. Off with you this instant. Go on."

"Not until I get a promise from your mistress."

"None of your excuses."

The maid held the bottle of crystals like a cudgel and started swinging at him. Nick ducked as the heavy glass sailed at his head. He began to laugh again.

"Pray don't kill me, miss."

"Rebecca, be careful," Georgiana said as she looked on with a sneer. "Don't hurt yourself."

"Don't you worry, my lady. I have five brothers, and none of them worth a bucket of coal. I know what to do about worthless blokes like this." She ran three steps and swung the bottle.

Nick sprang to the side, then jumped over the banister to land halfway up the stairs. "Perhaps I've misjudged you, George."

"If you think of yourself as my judge, you're mad. When I tell Threshfield about this, you'll be lucky to escape without arrest."

Grinning down at her, Nick said, "Blow that, George. If you peach on me, I'll have to make up me own version of the tale. Want to hear it?"

She said nothing. Their eyes met, and she slowly shook her head.

" 'Sweetest love, I do not go, / For weariness of

thee.' " Nick bowed over the banister with a flourish of his hand. 'A pleasant evening to you, Lady Georgiana."

Leaving her staring up at him in regal fury, he went up the stairs and out into the darkness.

6

Georgiana lay in bed on her stomach, her head buried
beneath two pillows, and listened to Rebecca pull
back the curtains to let in sunlight turned silver by
clouds that looked as mournful as she felt. Last night's
humiliation had given her new insight—rank means
nothing when you're naked. However, it meant quite
a lot when you were clothed and ready to demand a
man's expulsion on account of ungentlemanly behavior. Georgiana stuck her head out from under the
pillows and called to the maid.

"I shall take breakfast here instead of with the
family." She wasn't going to see Mr. Ross ever again,
and especially not the morning after he'd seen her
unclothed.

Rebecca left to inform Randall of her mistress's
wishes, and Georgiana sat up. A picture of Mr. Ross
laughing at her while she splashed around in the
plunge bath made her groan and dive headfirst under
the covers toward the foot of the bed. She'd gotten
little sleep due to the agony of her embarrassment.

The humiliation had been worse than finding out Lord Silverstone thought he was making a noble sacrifice for marrying a giant.

Reliving that first moment when she realized Mr. Ross was in the bath, she growled and beat her fists on the mattress. To have a man, a man as unchivalrous and depraved as Mr. Ross, view her unclothed! She'd never even been alone with a gentleman not a member of her family, except for the Hydes, who were soon to be family.

Nakedness and men, these were subjects Mother had avoided, except to say that both were forbidden until marriage. Georgiana had therefore concluded that nudity, men, and their private dealings with women were somehow shameful. She had worried that the whole business had something to do with what had happened to Jocelin. And that had scarred him deeply. Aunt Livy said not, but still, there seemed to be so much mystery and secrecy about the whole subject. Almost everyone seemed to think it shameful. Odd. Mr. Ross hadn't seemed to think her lack of clothing shameful. But what did he know of the standards of polite society?

Bother Mr. Ross. He'd turned an adventure into a nightmare. The earl had shown her the plunge bath when she had first come, and offered its use. It had been outfitted with hot water recently, an innovation of which Threshfield was proud. She'd been visiting the bath several times a week, and everyone knew the place was reserved for her in the evenings. Obviously no one had bothered to tell Mr. Ross.

He'd followed her expecting to discover her with Evelyn, the evil-minded lout. And his threats . . . no decent man would threaten a lady in such a manner, threaten to make up some disgusting story about their encounter in the bath. But it wouldn't do him any good. Threshfield would believe her, not him. Mr. Ross would be on his way to the town of Worth-bridge before luncheon, and on a train by nightfall.

Through layers of bed linens she heard a knock. Scrambling around to the head of the bed, she stuck her head out again and answered. One of the upstairs maids came in with a silver salver on which lay a sealed envelope. She took the envelope, dismissed the maid, and opened it.

It was a gracefully phrased apology from Mr. Ross. He'd written it in a well-formed script that belied his lowly heritage. *Dear Lady Georgiana, I must offer my abject apologies for intruding upon you last night. There is no excuse for my behavior. . . .*

She read on, somewhat amazed at the reference to Oberon spying on Titania. Then he ruined the whole thing by reminding her that if he was forced to leave, Jocelin, who was ill from his wounds, would drag himself across the ocean to save her. Liza would follow, and she was nearing her time. Both would risk their lives, and it would be her fault. *Jocelin expects regular letters from me outlining my progress with you.* There was more, but she only skimmed it.

"Wretched vermin," she muttered as she tore the note into minute pieces. Outwitted again. He knew she'd go to the earl at once and had forestalled her. She couldn't jeopardize her brother's health, or that of dear Liza and the baby. She would have to keep silent. But that didn't mean she had to endure Mr. Ross. She was good at planning. She would plan her own retreat.

For the next three days Georgiana dined in her room. She sent a note saying she had a slight cold and didn't want to infect the earl. The time was well spent reviewing descriptions of neighboring properties that might serve as her children's home. Sometimes she would leave her room after Rebecca had assured her that Mr. Ross was nowhere in sight, and spent her hours skulking in the dark cellar beneath the Egyptian Wing recording and describing objects. Yet in spite of her seclusion, she sometimes felt as if someone was nearby, as if she was being watched. She spoke to herself sternly about such feelings. Was she going to allow Mr. Ross to drive her into a brain fever?

The fourth day dawned brightly, with the sun illuminating the gold, russet, and yellow leaves of fall. October would come in a few days, and she was tired of hiding, even in the beautiful rooms the earl had given her. She was in the Lady's Suite, a series of rooms consisting of a sitting room flanked by a bed-chamber on one side and a dressing room and cabinet on the other. The colors of the suite were porcelain-blue and white. The sitting room had a balcony that looked out on the eastern park, with its miniature lake and Palladian sun temple on a little island in the middle.

Somehow the sight of that brave little temple sitting in the middle of a jewel-blue lake made her quite irritated with herself. Why was she cringing and hiding? Mr. Ross was the one at fault, the one with the disgusting habit of spying and sneaking up on people. He was the one who should be ashamed. She would be no longer. The more irritated she grew, the more her cooling anger at him heated again.

With Rebecca's help she dressed in a gown the same pale blue as her bedroom and picked up an embroidered work apron and matching cap. "I'm through hiding, Rebecca. I've had my last breakfast in this room. Mr. Ross isn't going to run me out of this house."

Rebecca had a receding chin, so when she stared at her toes, half her face vanished. Georgiana was sitting at a dressing table facing a mirror. She set the cap on her head, pushed her spectacles into place, and glanced at the maid in the mirror.

"What's wrong?"

"It's Mr. Ross, my lady. I found out he's not been here this whole time. I kept looking for him, and then I happened to overhear Mr. Randall and the housekeeper talking about him. He's been away since the morning after he—he . . ."

"The whole time," Georgiana repeated, staring at her reflection without noticing it. Suddenly she banged on the dressing table. "The monster!"

"My lady?"

"Nothing, Rebecca. Thank you."

Georgiana drummed her fingers on the dressing table. The fiend knew she would dread encountering him again. He'd gone away to prolong her agony, to make her wait in embarrassed fear while he cavorted with unsavory persons in some low haunt. But she would show him that nothing he did mattered to her. She'd face him; she'd stare straight at him and through him. No doubt he thought to find her cowering in fright, wondering when and where he'd appear.

She'd face him down. But . . . perhaps not now. Perhaps she'd do it this afternoon. By then she'd be well prepared. Her righteous anger would burn brighter if she delayed. Yes, that was an excellent plan. No sense rushing things. That was the secret to good plans. Right now there were tasks that needed attend-

ing in the basement of the Egyptian Wing. But she
wasn't hiding anymore. On that point she was quite
clear.

To prove it, she marched to the Egyptian Wing
openly, head high, her heels tapping on marble floors.
Once, when she crossed the curved corridor between
the main house and the Egyptian Wing, she thought
she heard extra echoes after her footsteps. She listened
for a moment, then stopped abruptly. The tapping
continued for two steps, then ceased. Georgiana
looked behind her but saw only the high windows
that bordered either side of the corridor, and the polished floorboards. Bright sunlight heated the chill of
the morning. Turning, she began walking and heard
no more strange sounds.

Upon reaching the Egyptian Wing, she said good
morning to Ludwig, who was busy composing a de-
tailed description and drawings of the new sarcophagus. The acquisition had pride of place in the great
work chamber that had originally been intended as a
ballroom. As usual, the rooms were dark to protect the
more delicate antiquities, and Ludwig worked by
lamplight. Ludwig showed her his drawings. She noticed that his pale, ink-stained hands were shaking.

"Aren't you well, Ludwig?"

Wiping perspiration from his chin, Ludwig rolled
up a large drawing and shook his head. "Disturbing
news. Disturbing. I spoke to Great-uncle last night,
and he mentioned he was going to leave the collection
to you." Ludwig's shoulders slumped even more than
usual, and he seemed near tears.

"Oh, no. But we only discussed making it the
basis of a museum. I thought you would be the cura-
tor."

"Well, you know how Great-uncle can twist things. And my parents would be pleased. They're always after me to give up my studies. Mother says I'll have to once Great-uncle dies and I'm heir to Threshfield. And that only makes Great-uncle furious."

Georgiana took her spectacles from a pocket of her apron and put them on. Shoving them back onto her nose, she watched Ludwig droop into a chair, the rolled drawing clutched between his knees.

"I'm so sorry," she said. "I'll speak to him. This isn't what I intended at all." She swept her arm around to indicate the multitude of objects that surrounded them. "These things need more care than we can provide by ourselves. Some of the papyri are disintegrating rapidly, Ludwig. You know that."

Nodding his cabbage-shaped head, Ludwig smiled gently at her. "I'm trying to work more quickly. Oh, my heart, yes, and I really don't mind as long as it's you to whom the collection goes. You and I will still work on it, won't we?"

"Of course, but I'll speak to Threshfield. He shouldn't play games with you. You don't deserve it."

"I didn't know it was a game." Ludwig squinted in the dim light, rose, and knelt by the red-granite sarcophagus. "I didn't see this. Look, Georgiana, at how finely carved are the wings of the goddesses."

"Yes, lovely, Ludwig."

"I must insist that Great-uncle hire a good photographer to record this. My drawings will never suffice."

She left Ludwig to his discovery, vowing to take Threshfield to task for toying with Ludwig. The earl had promised to do nothing about his collection without involving Ludwig in the decision, the wretched old liar. She went downstairs.

The basement wasn't as dark as it could have been, for barred windows at ground level allowed light to filter into the vast storage rooms. Here sat countless boxes filled with more loot from the earl's raids on ancient sites and various antiquity shops in Egypt. Some had never been opened since they'd arrived in England. In his later years the earl had discovered a new lust—for the paintings and other works of the great Western artists. He had a reputation as a collector who was eager as Catherine the Great of Russia had been.

Georgiana remained in the basement for several hours. She had opened a box that contained shabti, figurines of servants and laborers who were supposed to substitute for the deceased should he or she be called upon by the gods to do work in the afterlife. However, she couldn't concentrate for worrying about Ludwig. And when she wasn't worrying about him, memories of Mr. Ross coming upon her naked kept intruding.

Why couldn't he look as barbaric in evening dress as he had in his western garb? Her embarrassment had been all the more acute because he'd been exquisitely attired in black Saxony relieved only by the finest white linen and diamond studs. But what she remembered the most was how dark his eyes grew when he looked at her. They were blue, the blue of gentians, but the outer edges were darkest indigo. It had been a trick of the light, that sudden deepening of color. He'd had to look down into shadow to see her, that was all.

Nevertheless, she was turning crimson just thinking about how he'd stared at her. She had sensed something in that stare—that he knew how to infuse it with raw need and make it burn into his victim's soul. No wonder women seemed to deteriorate into simpletons when he came into a room. But she was confused. Why would he direct such attentions to her, a lumbering giant? Out of habit, that was why.

Georgiana glanced at the painted face of the shabti in her hand and spoke to it. "He's a poor creature, do you hear? A user of women, a miscreant, a malefactor, a sly reptile. And speaking of sly reptiles, I must talk to Threshfield."

She left the shabti and the notes she was making on it in the basement. Her concern for Ludwig was interfering with her work. She would fetch him, and together they would corner Threshfield. Upstairs she passed through the hall with its shadowed mummy cases. Pressing her hands against her skirts, she kept her crinoline from brushing a dust-laden coffin in the form of an ancient Egyptian prince.

Pausing at the door to the workroom, she felt a sudden creeping tingle that started at her fingers and crawled up her arms and spine. Turning, she looked over her shoulder, but all she saw was blankly staring statues of priests, viziers, and a sphinx of Senwosret III. Her gaze caught the shadow cast by the jackal-headed god Anubis, lord of the dead. All was dust, darkness, and stillness.

"Is anyone there?"

Silence as complete as that of a house of eternity, an Egyptian tomb. She was growing feebleminded. Next she'd begin watching for Mr. Ross to jump out at her, and she wouldn't put it past him to do so. Drat him. He'd nearly ruined her plans to gain freedom and already had succeeded in destroying her peace.

Dropping her hands to her skirts again, she eased past the prince's coffin and entered the workroom. It was deserted. Ludwig's drawing lay on the table next to the sarcophagus. The oblong granite box lay in a yellow pool of light cast by a lamp Ludwig had left on one of its corners. Nearby on the floor rested the flat stone lid. She walked between the sarcophagus and the table on her way to the room that served as a library.

As she passed the sarcophagus, its red stone glittered in the lamplight—and something rose from it. Georgiana glimpsed a frozen mask of gold, a headdress, a serpent diadem, heard a long, low groan. She screamed. Scuttling backward, she bumped against a chair, sat down, and burst into tears from the sudden fright.

"Oh, Ludwig!" she cried.

The man sitting in the coffin reached up and removed the mask. Georgiana blinked through her tears.

"You?"

"Sorry, George."

Now her tears were those of anger. Georgiana removed her spectacles. She fumbled with her apron, found her kerchief, and stuck her face in it. A thump sounded as Ross climbed out of the sarcophagus and jumped to the floor. Georgiana lowered the kerchief, scowled at him, and sobbed at the same time. Her heart was still racing from the fright.

He approached her, set the mask on the table, and knelt at her feet. "I was trying the box on for size while I waited for Ludwig. I didn't mean to scare you."

"I hate you," she said as she sniffed and swallowed back more tears. "What a contemptible trick."

Her spectacles had fallen. He picked them up and held them while she buried her nose in her kerchief.

"It wasn't a trick, Lady Georgiana. I'm sorry to have frightened you."

"Again."

He smiled at her, revealing white teeth that stood out against his sun-darkened skin. "Yes, again."

"No," she said between sniffs. "I mean you're doing it again. Speaking like a Cambridge man when at any moment you're going to drop the illusion and turn into a gunfighter or an East End thief."

Responding in the same educated accent, he said, "I promise not to do either. I shall maintain this illusion for the moment, to assuage your terror with the comfort of the familiar."

Georgiana snatched her spectacles from him.

"Why are you being polite?"

He didn't answer at once. His dark lashes dropped, concealing those blue-and-indigo eyes and contrasting with the delicate skin upon which they rested. A muscle twitched in his jaw, calling attention to the hollows in his cheeks that made him seem almost vulnerable. Then his head came up, and he gave her an off-center smile that held the menace and excitement of a forbidden pagan ritual.

"Call it a penance for scaring you, my lady." The smile faded as they looked at each other. "Never made a woman cry before. Don't enjoy it."

"You've never made a woman cry? I find that hard to believe, Mr. Ross." The more they talked, the less she sniffed.

He grinned this time, in a knowing way that irritated her. "Never. Always made them smile, or laugh." He paused this time, his gaze drifting over her face. "Groan, perhaps, but never cry."

"Groan. How could you make a lady groan unless you hurt her, sir?"

He appeared fascinated with her lips, almost distracted, which made her even more uncomfortable than she already was. At her question he started and his gaze riveted on her eyes.

"Bleeding hell."

"You're profane, sir." Georgiana's back stiffened, and she poked her kerchief back into her pocket.

"I forgot you wouldn't know about—groaning."

Suddenly his voice grew low and rough on the last word. Upon hearing it Georgiana felt a jolt of alarm that sent prickles through her body. Shifting uneasily in her chair, she glanced around the workroom.

"Where is Ludwig? He should have returned. He's probably been diverted by some book. If he becomes absorbed, he's likely to forget you." She began to rise. "I'll fetch him."

His hand closed over her arm, and Georgiana found herself gently guided back to the chair. She stiffened when the hand remained on her arm, its warmth and strength penetrating her sleeve. She darted a look at it, perceiving long, slim fingers and a gold ring engraved with a pair of winged griffins. She pulled her arm. The fingers tightened, then let go.

Georgiana swallowed and stared at the spectacles in her hand. He hadn't said a word, only detained her with his hand and the force of his silence. And that feeling was growing upon her, that feeling that she needed more distance from him. He was so close, she could smell sandalwood again, and still he didn't speak. She was going to do so herself when he broke his silence at last.

"Bleeding hell. If you know what's good for you, George, you'll scarper quick. Get out of this house and away from me."

"There," she said. "You've done it again, transformed into the rude thief who wouldn't know the letter *H* if it sat on his knee. Why can you not remain the gentleman?"

" 'Cause you don't pay no attention when I'm acting like a gentleman, but you sure as hell notice when I ain't."

"As I said, sir, you're accomplished at illusion—gentleman, thief, gunfighter. Which is real?"

Dark brows grew together. That twitch in his jaw muscle was back, and Georgiana grew alarmed as his eyes narrowed. His hands fastened on her arms, and he drew closer, making her back away from him.

"That's wot's wrong with you, George. You never had to face what's real. Maybe you need a good dose of something real to make you pay attention."

7

Nick's mind was burning as hot as his body. Was he really thinking about kissing her? He was kneeling before a woman who—in the space of a brief moment in a plunge bath—had transformed from a nuisance into an obsession. After the plunge bath he'd run away from her and Threshfield, had tried to rid himself of this unlooked-for hunger. He had thought himself successful—until he knelt before her and touched her gown.

He'd never felt like this. Touching the fabric was like drawing the tips of his fingers over the surface of pristine, still water. The sensation arced through his hand to quicken his body. It erased the memory of past conquests and even a few submissions, of nights spent in raucous pleasure.

A part of him still growled protests even as he drew closer to her, close enough to see the startled emerald eyes grow as large as coat buttons. She backed away from him but was stopped by the back of the chair. Only a few inches more to go, and he would feel her lips beneath his. She said something, but he couldn't hear her for the churning of blood in his ears.

Then her lashes fluttered and her eyes narrowed to slits the way Jocelin's did when he was surprised. *Jocelin.* He was about to kiss Jos's sister. Nick froze, then thrust himself to arm's length, searching for some way to distract himself and her.

"Mr. Ross, are you ill?"

"What? No. Yes. Yes, that's it. I've got a dashed miserable headache."

"Perhaps you should take a headache powder. I have some, which I can fetch if you're through insulting me and will move out of the way."

"Did I insult you, my lady?" he asked faintly. He had to keep her talking, because it would be embarrassing to stand up until his unruly body had calmed.

"Of course you insulted me, sir. You accused me of not knowing what's real. You've disapproved of me from our first meeting. You made that clear."

That almost jolted him out of his aroused state. "You're acting like a spoiled—bloody hell. When I think of what my sister's life was like compared to yours—"

"Pray tell me how you know I'm spoiled, Mr. Ross, when we've never spent more than a few minutes in each other's company."

"Ladies are all alike."

Georgiana lifted a thin, arched brow. "Are they?"

"I've known a few," he said with a smile that didn't quite conceal how intimate that knowledge was. "Never lift a finger to do honest work. Don't even raise their own children. Spend more blunt on petticoats than my mother ever saw in her whole life.

Throw fits if they don't get to go to fifty balls in a season."

He frowned as he remembered how raw his mother's hands had grown from scrubbing floors and fireplaces in winter. Georgiana was looking at him strangely, and the fine line of her brow had settled down from its derisive curve.

"I'm sorry that your family was poor," she said gently, "but that doesn't give you the right to assume that because mine wasn't that I have no troubles." She hesitated, as though she would say more, then tried to rise from her chair again.

"All right," he said to prevent her from forcing him to move. "Prove it."

"I beg your pardon?"

"Prove you got troubles."

Her mouth fell open in astonishment. "I shall not, sir."

" 'Cause you can't."

"Because I do not conduct intimate conversations with strangers."

Shifting his weight to his other knee, Nick pretended to think hard. "Let me see. What troubles could Lady Georgiana, the duke's daughter, have? I know. Papa won't let her spend double her allowance on Paris gowns. The shade of the carpet in her bedroom doesn't go with her dressing gown." He put a hand to his cheek in mock alarm. "And, heavens, her suitors are either of high rank or handsome, but never both at the same time." He grinned at her. His body was cooling, and he'd be able to stand soon. Her next comment hit him like the blast of a shotgun. Her hands draped off the ends of the chair arms, and she looked down at him through long lashes.

"Mr. Ross, I find intimate discussions with mere acquaintances distasteful, but your prejudices seem to rule your behavior and are in need of revision. We don't know each other well, but I do understand that you're Jocelin's closest friend, and I know what he's told you. And since he's made you privy to intimate matters concerning himself, my parents, and, worst of all, my uncle, I would think you'd have more intelligence than to assume that my life has been idyllic."

Nick straightened, suddenly alert. "Has that bastard Yale done you harm?"

"Of course not. And please guard your language, sir. Uncle Yale's brain is rotting away and he can't even feed himself anymore. He'll never harm anyone again. A just fate, in my opinion."

"So you know about him?" Nick asked, a little shocked that Jocelin had spoken of such things to her.

"I know he hurt Jocelin terribly, and that Mother and Father didn't believe my brother when he came to them for protection. But I saw his pain. His soul was in hell, and they abandoned him rather than face the truth, face the scandal. Do you know what it is to feel contempt for your own father and mother?"

Nick stood up then, turned away from her, and spoke softly. "Yes, I do. For my father, that is. He was a drunken coward who used his fists on my mother and my sister and me until the day I stopped him."

They remained silent, she in her chair and he next to her, staring into darkness past dusty shelves littered with papyrus, gold pectoral necklaces, and jars filled with ancient entrails.

"You know what it's like," she said.

He glanced at her and would have looked away,

but he was caught by the bright-green jewels that were her eyes.

She continued when he didn't reply. "You know what it's like to hate the one who gave you life. There is nothing on which to depend if you know that your own parents have abandoned their child rather than face ugliness. You must have felt that you were the man and your father the child."

"A monster child." He picked up a book and read the title, *Book of the Dead*. "It does no good to talk about it. My pa never changed. Yours won't either."

"That's true, Mr. Ross." Georgiana rose and began stacking books into neat piles on the table. "But I know how to make myself feel better."

"How? By marrying an old man who can't do you any harm?"

"No," she said. "By gaining independence. Once I do that, I can use my fortune to establish homes for children who are the victims of such monsters."

"Going to build workhouses, are you?"

"Don't be insulting, Mr. Ross. I want to build refuges, places where children can be safe and can grow up surrounded by love and gentle discipline. I want to arm them with education so that they can make their own way in the world instead of being forever at the mercy of—of evil."

Nick couldn't have been more surprised if she'd said she'd wanted to become a cook on a trail drive. Her eyes were as bright as the Mediterranean on a July morning, and she spoke with such intensity that she made him want to shovel money at her to aid her cause. He hadn't been embarrassed since he was five years old, but he was ashamed now, embarrassed at his own ignorant presumptions. It had been a long time since a woman had earned his respect.

"Strike me blind, George. You got more sense than I ever thought."

Drawing herself up, she leveled a chilly stare at him. "I have asked you repeatedly not to call me that, sir."

"Damn if you don't look like the queen taking down a lazy footman when you do that."

"I beg your pardon?"

"Spine straight as a fence post, shoulders square like the cross piece of a gibbet. Nose in the air, and those amazing emerald eyes sighting down the bridge. You could command the deck of a man-o'-war."

"You're being rude, sir."

"Just admiring your pluck, my lady."

"Pluck!" Her voice echoed off the mummy cases, and she lowered it. "You called me a fence post."

"Now, don't come over all red-faced and prissy, hang it."

They exchanged scowls. Ire lit her face with color. Her eyes glittered and enticed him despite his anger. And to his dismay his anger fed his arousal. A loud slam made both of them jump. Ludwig stood in the doorway between the library and the workroom and picked up a book he'd dropped.

"I found it," he said. "An elementary volume, but one that explains the history of ancient Egypt. And I also found a wonderful study on amulets and their meaning. Did you know that I recently purchased a collection of amulets? My favorite is a tiny falcon carved of amethyst."

"You might give an Eye of Horus amulet to Mr.

Ross," Georgiana snapped. "He's going to need it to protect his health and his feeble intelligence."

Hands on hips, Nick glared at her. "Are you threatening me, Miss Plunge Bath?"

"Oh!" Georgiana muttered something under her breath, then said, "I don't threaten rude barbarians, Mr. Ross. I ignore them."

Porcelain-blue skirts swished past him. Georgiana glided out of the room, heels tapping, head high.

Ludwig came to stand beside him, clutching his books. "She doesn't like you, you know."

Ignoring Ludwig, Nick banged his fist on the worktable. Ludwig started, then approached the table and set down his books. He cast indecisive glances at Nick, who seemed to have frozen in place with his fist pressed against the tabletop. Finally Ludwig dared to speak again.

"What did you do, Mr. Ross? A few days ago she came in here furious, saying you had the manners of a Visigoth and the sensibilities of a hog."

Nick burst into a quick stride. "Bloody hell. That woman is too bleeding gen-teel for her own good."

"Don't you want your book?" Ludwig called after him.

Georgiana was nowhere in sight when he came to the curved corridor, nor did he see her in the main house. He raced to the second floor and questioned a passing maid, who offered the information that Lady Georgiana had gone out the front door. Nick was descending the stairs two at a time when he met Lady Augusta coming in the other direction. Today she was wearing a high-waisted gown of white-sprigged muslin with puffed upper sleeves and ruffles at the neck. She was carrying a reticule and a silk bag in which rested some object nearly as long as she was tall. He bowed to her.

"Lady Augusta," he said, preparing to go on his way.

"I collect you've had an argument with her."

"Her?"

Augusta clutched her silk bag to her chest, glanced around, and whispered, "The spy."

"Oh, Lady Georgiana."

Augusta nodded so vigorously that the tiny pink flowers on her bonnet bobbed furiously. "You shouldn't have revealed your antipathy, my boy. A little more decision of character is what is wanted from you. But no matter. All will be set right, so you mustn't worry."

"All right, I won't. Pray excuse me, my lady."

Augusta swung her elongated burden up into her arms and nodded to him. "Quite right. Things to do, things to do."

Nick bowed again and raced downstairs. Striding quickly across the length of the hall between the rows of fluted columns, he burst outside and was on the gravel drive in time to see Georgiana walking across the lawn toward the bright gold, orange, and umber of the woods. Springing into a slow trot, he closed the distance between them. She heard him coming and turned to face him.

"I may be a barbarian, George, but you're not much better for marrying that old skeleton."

"I have no intention of discussing my marriage or my character with *you*, sir. Now, please leave. You should know a gentleman doesn't intrude on a lady's privacy."

As she turned her back on him, Nick folded his

arms and said, "A real barbarian would have tossed you over his saddle and made off with you."

Georgiana nearly stumbled. A gratified smile spread over his face as he watched her slowly pivot on a heel and glare at him.

"You're awfully smug for a man who knows nothing about marriage in Society."

"Marriage is marriage."

"You confirm your ignorance, Mr. Ross." She walked back to him, her skirts swaying, bell-like. Clasping her hands in front of her, she said, "The daughter of a duke must marry a man of position, preferably a nobleman. Once married, she vanishes legally, like any other woman. She no longer has power over her own property, not even those—those undergarments you mentioned."

"Petticoats?" He grinned at her.

She went on as if he hadn't spoken. "Her property is her husband's property. She can't make a contract or sue on her own, or make a will without her husband's consent. She can be locked up and even beaten by her husband if he wishes. And without funds of her own, she would be unable to afford legal representation should she wish to escape such a brutish husband."

"Not all men are monsters," Nick said.

"True. But most English noblemen are something worse. A monster doesn't hide his monstrosity behind a veneer of manners. A nobleman is a monster of entitlement. He simply assumes he's there to be served. I've seen it happen to my friends, Mr. Ross. After courtship and marriage a nobleman resumes his former life. While his wife stays at home, he prances back to his clubs, his sport, his cards, his horses. And his mistress."

"Mistr—"

"Don't gawk at me, sir, and pretend you have no familiarity with the word. Aunt Livy told me all about mistresses. Just because he's married doesn't mean a nobleman has to give up his mistress. Rather, now that he has his wife's money, he's much more able to afford to support the—the woman. All this is taken as a matter of routine, unspoken but assumed."

"You mean all the ladies know?"

She gave him a look of aggravation. "Don't be absurd. As I was saying, a daughter of a duke, like any other lady, must realize that her life and the entire household revolve around her husband. He oversees the household schedule, even the purchase of furniture. The menus, the guest lists, these are composed according to his desires. And the duke's daughter, what is her function? To produce heirs, run the household according to his pleasure, and stay out of his way."

"That's not true. Jos isn't like that." He'd never considered how it must be for the ladies he'd been with.

"Jocelin is different. I assure you, Mr. Ross, that if you will think upon it, you will admit that to an English nobleman, a wife is a necessary accoutrement to his station, not unlike a well-appointed carriage."

Nick brushed back his coat and stuck his hands into his pockets while he thought about the picture she'd painted. He couldn't imagine a life like that for himself, but women were different, and somehow he couldn't sympathize when he compared Tessie's lot to Georgiana's.

Georgiana glanced at him sideways. "Of course, there are compensations."

"Ah. I thought so."

"The duke's daughter can take a lover."

"Here! There'll be none of that, because you aren't marrying Threshfield."

"There's no need to succumb to the vapors," Georgiana said with a prim smile. "It's all quite simple. One produces an heir and a second son in case of misfortune. After that the duke's daughter is free to amuse herself. And all gentlemen know better than to approach her until after she's borne the second son. After that, well, she's married, and married women bear children, so the consequences of dalliance are negligible if she's careful." She eyed him closely. "Did you know that one of the first things my mother told me when I came out was never to comment on a likeness?"

"Why?" he asked faintly.

"Because, in case you haven't noticed, Society is a place of circumspect illegitimacy. Now, if you will excuse me, Mr. Ross, I will resume my walk."

Speechless, he watched her move away from him. As he stood there in shock, he heard something buzz by his ear and smack into the turf about a yard from Georgiana's receding skirts. She heard the small sound and swung around to give him an inquiring glance. Nick spun around and looked back at Threshfield.

They couldn't have been more than sixty yards from the house, but at first he couldn't see anything. Then he noticed a figure on the roof beside a statue of Adonis. It was Lady Augusta in her sprigged muslin gown. Georgiana joined him in gazing at the old lady.

"What is she doing?" She searched the pockets of her apron for her spectacles.

Nick shook his head. "I don't know."

Augusta had something long and thin laying across one arm. With her free hand she appeared to bite something, then put her hand to the long object. Then she set it upright and fiddled with its end. Next she produced a long rod and thrust it inside the first object. Georgiana was pulling her spectacles from her pocket, but released them when he cursed.

"Bleeding hell," Nick said. "She's got a musket." He grabbed Georgiana's hand. "Come on, run!"

Not waiting for her consent, he pulled Georgiana after him as he hurtled toward the trees. There was another shot. A ball buzzed toward them and struck the ground beside Georgiana's foot. She cried out, and Nick yanked on her arm, swinging her in front of him.

"Go!" he cried. "She won't aim at me."

He shortened his stride and ran directly behind her until they reached a line of beech trees. Then he leaped ahead, snatched her arm, and dragged her behind the thickest tree he could find. Half a minute passed before another shot threw up turf many yards short of the trees. Nick kept Georgiana between the tree and his body and craned his neck to see the house. He could feel Georgiana's body against his own. She was breathing hard, and each breath pressed her against his chest and thighs.

In the distance he could just make out Lady Augusta on the roof. She set the musket aside, put a shading hand to her bonnet brim, and surveyed the tree line. Shaking her head, she put something that must have been a powder flask in the silk bag. She picked up the musket, gathered her reticule and the silk bag, and vanished. He waited, expecting her to emerge onto the portico and come after them.

"Mr. Ross?"

"Yes?"

"She's gone. You can let me go now."

As he became aware once more of the rhythmic movement of her chest, Nick felt his body react to the feel of her. She turned around, evidently expecting him to step aside. His legs wouldn't move. Nick felt a sudden bolt of heat shoot through his body at the sight of her moist skin and gently rising breasts.

How could a woman excite him when her gown covered her from neck to toe? Without warning all the arousal he had tried to quell in the Egyptian Wing returned with double force. She could have died from a musket ball without his ever having touched her. And without a doubt he would then have suffered a pain of such devastation that he could hardly bear thinking on it.

"She almost killed you," he whispered.

Georgiana was staring at him, her face flushed, her hands trembling as they came up to press against his chest in an attempt to move him. "It's over now."

"I don't think so, George my love. I think it's just started." He didn't wait for her reply. Bending down, easing his body against hers, he touched her mouth with his.

8

She had never been so near a man unrelated to her—except for Ludwig, who was almost related. The closest she'd ever come was dancing. In less than a heartbeat Georgiana discovered that the touch of gloved hands on a ball gown wasn't remotely akin to the feel of a man's lips on hers. His mouth was soft and yet strong enough to part her lips. A tiny, muted cry escaped her as she felt his tongue slowly enter her.

It was like being consumed. His body surged against hers, which pressed against the tree. The contact drove from her mind every civilized lesson she'd ever learned. She opened her mouth wider so that his mouth was drawn more tightly against hers. Her hands ceased to press against his shoulders and dropped to his waist, where they gripped his coat.

He'd crushed her skirts between them. For the first time she felt a man's legs and hips against hers. The sensation burned itself into her consciousness, and she knew with a bright, startling insight that she would never be able to forget the feel of him.

Primitive excitement seared through her body when his lips began to suck at her mouth. Need made her brave. She wrapped her arms around him and squeezed, trying to satisfy some unfamiliar but undeniable craving. Then she slipped her hands inside his coat, beneath his waistcoat, and ran her hands over his ribs.

Suddenly his mouth lifted until their lips were barely touching. "Oh, God, no."

The words confused her, but she heard the tortured pain in his voice. Remembering Lord Silverstone, she grew afraid.

"What's wrong?"

Closing his eyes, he leaned on the tree. Mystified, Georgiana noted his labored breathing and the tautness of his face. She withdrew her hands to place them flat on his chest again. An irrelevant thought flitted through her mind; her hands seemed small against his body.

"What's wrong?" she repeated, fearing that he had found her unappealing.

He winced, as if her voice hurt him. Without answering he thrust himself away from her, walked a few steps, and stood with his back to her.

"I must go after Lady Augusta," he said roughly.

Confused, afraid to ask him why he'd kissed her, more afraid to ask him why he'd stopped, Georgiana took refuge in the topic.

"Oh, there's no need. Lady Augusta never succeeds."

Nick whirled around. "Never succeeds. You mean she's done this before?"

"Of course. Not often, but occasionally. Don't be alarmed. Her aim is terrible."

"Bleeding hell! Do you mean to tell me that Threshfield allows her to run about with a musket shooting at people?"

"Only at those she thinks are spies." *He's forgotten all about the kiss. I'll never forget.*

Nick strode toward the house. "I'm going to get that musket."

"You mustn't."

"Watch me."

Georgiana grabbed his arm, then snatched her hand back when he stopped and stared at her.

"You mustn't," she said again. "She has terrible fits if her musket is taken from her. She screams and throws herself to the floor and does harm to herself."

"And you think this is a good reason to leave her armed with a gun? Women. They got no more sense than rabbits."

"Don't interfere," she snapped. The villain had indeed forgotten their kiss. "It's not your concern."

He came closer, causing her to back into the tree.

"You're my concern," he said softly, "whether you like it or not."

"Why?" She was too confused and upset to keep the tension from her voice.

She must have startled him, because he didn't answer at once. Stuffing his hands into his pockets, he balled his fists and frowned.

"Because I owe Jos my life, and this is the only thing he's ever asked of me. We're leaving for London at once."

Somehow she'd wanted another answer from him. Taking refuge in maintaining propriety, she said, "No, and don't think of pulling any barbarian tricks on me. Aunt Livy will take her shotgun to you, and if

you succeed, Threshfield and my father will hunt you
down."

He moved even closer to her, so close she could
see the indigo in his eyes.

"Then I'll have to think of another way."

"I shall watch your efforts with interest."

The corners of his eyes crinkled in amusement.
"You're coming all over stuffy again, George."

"And you're attempting to control me."

He wasn't listening. Rubbing his chin, he said,
"First I'll have to fix the sight on that musket."

"I've already done that. I'm not a fool, you know.
Aunt Livy helped me."

"Excellent."

He appeared to lapse into thought. He had forgotten what they'd done only moments ago. How
could he remain so calm when something so unprecedented had happened? But he'd kissed women before.
Lots. Perhaps having kissed many women made him
less susceptible to this craving to have more of it. Perhaps he'd only been amusing himself with her because
there was no one more appealing to attract his attention.

His gaze was fixed on the ground while he
thought, giving her an opportunity to study him. A
soft lock of hair had fallen down over his brow. It was
a deep, warm brown, like antique wood. Sun-
lightened strands formed a spray of polished bronze
and amber through the darker hue. A fine, almost
imperceptible frown line marked a path from his nose
past his mouth. Straight, neat brows ran parallel to his
mouth, which was wide, with slender lips.

There were sculpted hollows in his cheeks below
the jawline, and a chin that would stop a ravening

mastiff with its belligerent firmness. It announced what she already knew about his character—Nicholas Ross was born to master those around him, or die trying. And nature had given him a body with which to accomplish his desires.

He was taller than Jocelin, which allowed him to look down at her. An annoying circumstance since she couldn't intimidate him with her substantial height. His shoulders and arms looked as if he'd have no difficulty lifting his own horse. Unlike poor Ludwig, he needed no tailor to pad his coat to enhance his build. Nor did he need the corset some men wore to pinch in their waists.

Georgiana found herself wishing she knew what he looked like without his clothes. Society, breeding, and convention forbade her what she wanted. Ladies didn't have such vulgar curiosity. She shouldn't even be alone with this man, but nothing seemed to matter except the fact that she wanted him to kiss her again. He had appeared to like kissing her at first. Unlike many of her other suitors, Nicholas Ross had no interest in or need of her fortune. She already knew he didn't seek connections in order to better his social position. His interest in her was for Jocelin's sake and perhaps on account of boredom, but a secret part of her didn't care.

How was she ever going to experience that amazing exhilaration again if not with him? Soon she would be married and then widowed. Widows who wished to take charge of abandoned children must have pristine reputations. But she wanted him to kiss her again. She wanted that so fiercely that the wanting trampled over the knowledge that she couldn't compare to the women he was used to. She just didn't care; she still wanted him to kiss her.

The boldness of this thought summoned a blush to her cheeks just as Nick roused from his musings and glanced at her. Recognition and surprise passed over his features. She knew he'd sensed her interest, but he made no move toward her. He thrust his hands behind his back and kept them there.

"We should go back to the house," he said.

"Mr. Ross."

"Nick."

She felt heat flow up her neck and face. "I— you . . . Would you—"

"You're babbling, George old chap."

She was so hot with embarrassment, her skin should be blistered, and she blurted out, "How do you expect a lady to ask a gentleman to kiss her? It isn't done. And don't call me George." She shut her mouth when he suddenly dropped his hands to his sides and went still.

"You want me to kiss you again?" he asked quietly.

She bit her lip and nodded. He took a step toward her, then another, until he was so close, her skirts brushed his pant legs.

Without pausing he leaned over her and murmured, "Bleeding hell, George, I wish you hadn't asked."

Once more Georgiana felt his warm, supple lips working on hers. He pressed his body against her. Tree bark jabbed her back, but she was lost in heat and a growing titillation that escalated to near pain. She had never realized it was so simple. She asked, and he came to her as if he had no will of his own.

Her arms came up around his neck and she dared to kiss him back. She opened her mouth wide and drew his lips to hers. Pressing herself against him, she was rewarded with a muffled gasp and the surge of his body in a roiling column of muscle that forced her hard against the tree. His hands began to slide up her sides. One climbed the slope of her breast while the other clasped her neck. She was going to burn alive.

Then, when she was about to try to climb his body, he suddenly tore his lips from hers and sprang backward with a curse.

"No!" he cried as she reached for him. "Don't touch me."

"But why?"

He brushed perspiration from his upper lip and swallowed. "Damn it, you've put me in hell."

"But I don't understand."

Shoving his hands into his pockets again, he clenched them into fists. "I know, and it's bleeding difficult because you don't."

"Then explain."

His eyes widened.

"Please?"

He opened his mouth, then snapped it shut. Georgiana drew near and put her fingertips on the sleeve of his coat. For some reason her voice grew low and throaty. "Please, Nick."

Drawing in his breath on a hiss, he shook his head. "I shouldn't have asked you to speak my name. God. Who would have thought your just saying my name would make it worse?" He swung away from her, out of reach, and put out a hand to ward her off when she followed. "Bloody hell, woman. Stay away from me."

"But I want—"

Without warning he was on her. He grabbed her shoulders and drew her up in a painful grip, snarling at her.

"That's the trouble. I know you want, and I know you don't understand what that means. Get out of here, love, before it's too late." He let her go so quickly, she stumbled. His voice rose until he was snarling with a violence that frightened her. "Go, my lady. If you don't, you'll be sorry. Run!"

He turned her around roughly and shoved her out of the woods. She staggered a few steps.

When she hesitated and glanced back at him, he came at her, gripped her arm so hard, she cried out, and hissed, "Stupid, foolish. Run fast and don't look back. Or you'll end up on your back underneath me, and trying to marry old Threshfield will be the least of your follies."

She understood at last. He released her and plunged back into the wood. Astonished and frightened at the same time, Georgiana lifted her skirts and sprang into a run, her legs churning. She reached the gravel avenue, raced across it, and dashed up the stairs of the portico. She kept on running until she reached her own door. Panting, she reached for the knob.

"Georgiana, where have you been!"

The earl was rolling toward her, his attendants following. His chair wheels squeaked and he stopped and poked his cane at her.

"You promised to come to luncheon this afternoon. Look at you. Your hair is falling down, and your gown has grass stains on the hem."

Catching her breath, Georgiana found her specta-

cles in her pocket and put them on. "Aunt Augusta
has been shooting at me again."

"Lavinia told me. She said she found her leaving
the roof with her musket. Are you all right, my dear?"

"Of course."

"I knew you would be. Augusta couldn't hit
Buckingham Palace from ten paces. Now, get dressed,
my dear. Everyone is to be at luncheon today. We're
having it in the fishing pavilion, and I told Ludwig not
to forget either."

"I'll be there, Threshfield."

"Good." He placed a shaking hand on her arm.
"I've missed you, my dear. I'm glad you're better."

She patted his hand. "And I you, you old mischief
maker."

"You're the only one who isn't waiting for me to
die. Did you know Evelyn and Prudence tried to get
me declared insane last year?"

"Yes, you told me."

"Might have succeeded, too, if I hadn't had the
most expensive solicitors in the kingdom." The earl
swept a finger over his eyebrow, then put both hands
on the top of his cane and leaned toward her with his
foxlike smile. "I should have told Augusta they were
both French spies."

"For shame, Threshfield." Georgiana couldn't
help responding to his wily grin.

Threshfield laid his cane across his lap and signaled
to his attendants. As he rolled away, he said, "I'll send
for Dr. Sanderson and have him prescribe something
to calm Augusta. She's been so excitable since we
announced our engagement."

Georgiana slipped inside her room and leaned
against the door. Her face burned, and she tingled

with exhilaration. Rebecca walked in from the bedroom carrying a dressing gown and saw her.

"Oh, my lady, you're a mess."

"I know, Rebecca. I know. Is my bath ready?
Good. I'm going to soak. Don't interrupt me. I don't
care if I'm late for luncheon."

She immersed herself in steaming water scented
with jasmine, growing more and more confused the
longer she remained in the bath. Until today she'd had
Nicholas Ross entered in the catalog of her mind as an
interfering bully. But then he'd spoken of his father
and become human. And once he'd kissed her, all her
neat categories exploded.

And he wanted her. She had been stunned by this
discovery. He'd been tempted too. She could still see
him, body taut with the strain of keeping himself from
touching her, his face registering a pain she now
vaguely understood.

While she'd been talking to the earl, she'd been
conscious of a driving urge to find Nick and touch
him again. Nothing seemed so important. Never had
she experienced this compulsion that obliterated all
other priorities, all other values.

He was forbidden. He wanted her to give up her
life's plan, a plan that would somehow make up for
her brother's tragedy. He thought she was a spoiled
girl with unraveled lace for brains. But he kissed her as
if his life depended upon touching her, and when he
kissed her, the various guises he adopted vanished. He
became something elemental, possessed of fire and the
power to enthrall with his very nearness.

What was she going to do? For the first time she
realized the true reason why young ladies weren't allowed to be alone with men. If she'd remained much

longer with Nick, she wouldn't have cared if they'd
ended up on the ground as he'd threatened. How
unfair of everyone to keep this secret away from
women until they married. Now she realized why
Jocelin had been so upset by her plans. This feeling
she had for Nick was what he'd wanted for her. But
Jocelin knew as well as she that her father would never
want it for her with Nicholas Ross.

And what about Nick? How did he feel? After all,
he'd sent her away. Georgiana picked up a bar of
jasmine soap. Her hands worked up a lather, then
froze. Had he sent her away because he hadn't felt as
she did? No, he'd certainly been as stirred. Ah, this
must be one of the few instances in which he had
acted the gentleman. What was she going to do? She
didn't even know if this feeling would last.

Damn her ignorance. She would talk to Aunt
Livy. Aunt Livy had been married. There were ru-
mors of her having loved a dashing young officer in
the Horse Guards long ago. She would speak to Aunt
Livy tonight when she retired.

Feeling unsettled and anxious at having to face
Nick at luncheon, Georgiana dressed and found that
she wasn't late at all. Aunt Livy stopped by to collect
her, and together they went out to the back lawn.

"You were with Mr. Ross on the lawn just now."

"Aunt Livy, is there no privacy in this house?"

"None. Be careful, Georgiana. You've little experience with men like Mr. Ross."

"You mean he's not a gentleman."

Lavinia put on her bonnet and tied its wide ribbons as they crossed the lawn. "No. I mean you've
little experience with a man who can make women's
mouths water simply by unbuttoning his coat."

"Aunt Livy!"

"That man is dangerous, child. A few years ago Lady Drille left her husband of twenty-three years to chase after him, and he hadn't even tried to seduce her. I admit Mary Drille is a selfish and soft-brained fool, but you take my point."

"Yes, Aunt Livy. I'll be careful."

Opening their parasols, they walked to the lake where the family was gathering to take boats across to the pavilion that seemed to float in the glassy water like some gleaming fairy-tale palace. Far beyond the pavilion the Palladian bridge spanned a narrower part of the lake.

Evelyn was already at the water's edge waiting for them. Georgiana allowed Aunt Livy to intercede between them with a wave of conversation. Evelyn was always polite and wary around Livy, because she'd threatened him with a load of buckshot in his posterior should he transgress against Georgiana again. Georgiana turned her back and lowered her parasol so that it screened her from him. Prudence was coming toward them from the house. As she saw Georgiana in proximity to her husband, she sped up, fairly racing down the slight slope of grass that led to the lake.

"Good afternoon, Prudence," Georgiana said.

Prudence came to a puffing halt, snapped her parasol closed, and fanned herself with it. "Augusta tried to shoot you again, didn't she? Why don't you save us all a scandal and leave before you get yourself killed?"

"A nice, warm day for luncheon outdoors, don't you think?"

"Here comes uncle," Prudence said. "I shall recommend to him that you leave for your own safety."

"You tried that before, and it didn't work."

Prudence waved a sausage-fingered hand weighted down with thick gold rings. "That was before I saw you run into the woods with Mr. Ross. I was in the drawing room of our family wing, which, I'm sure you recall, looks out on the front lawn. You were in the woods quite a long time, and then I saw you come out with him. You're ruined, Georgiana. I'm surprised at you."

"He won't believe you."

"You're going to deny it? You're going to lie?"

Georgiana tried to strangle the handle of her parasol. "No. Nothing happened."

"You know quite well that it doesn't matter. You were seen running into the woods alone with a man whose name has been linked with at least half a dozen women in Society."

"Then one more shouldn't matter much."

"There's where you're wrong, Georgiana." Prudence tapped her on the arm with the tip of her parasol. "Because those women were married. You are not."

"Don't threaten me, Pru. How many times must I tell you I have no interest in the Threshfield fortunes? You're mad at me because you secretly fancy Mr. Ross yourself. Now, if you spill that bile, I shall be forced to reveal the truth about Evelyn's disgusting conduct in the drawing room. Don't pretend you don't know about it."

Prudence's eyes bulged; her mouth worked. Georgiana smiled sweetly.

"Do mind your demeanor, Pru. You look like a dyspeptic carp."

9

The fishing pavilion, like most of Threshfield, had been built in the last century. It was partially modeled on the Roman Pantheon with a rotunda topped by a domed roof and surrounded by a colonnade. Steps led down to the water, and there was a small quay at which boats could be docked.

Beneath the shelter of the vaulted colonnade, Nick partook of luncheon with the earl and his family. He had discovered that dining outdoors with Threshfield meant that all the earl's inside luxuries came with him. The Sevres, the Spode, the silver, were ferried across the lake along with a Chippendale dining set, table linens, and an Aubusson carpet.

The butler served clear soup, roast beef, and Yorkshire pudding, venison pasties and ham with asparagus. Footmen kept glasses filled with wine and sherry. Although he'd recovered from his lapse with Georgiana in the wood, Nick was confronted with Prudence's disturbing attempts to give him flirtatious looks over serving plates.

He solved the problem by staring at his food and eating a portion from every course. By the time a plum pudding appeared, Nick was too full to eat anything else. Looking up from his plate, he found that Prudence had given up for the moment. He accepted port dispensed by the earl and watched Georgiana open her parasol and stroll over to Ludwig. Ludwig was busy on the steps assembling a model of an ancient Egyptian fishing net, which he meant to try out for the first time.

Georgiana bent down to speak to Ludwig, offering Nick an interesting view of her hips. He wished she hadn't dressed for luncheon. He preferred her habit of discarding her crinoline, but she only did that occasionally when she was going to work among her dusty and delicate artifacts. Still, he could enjoy the sight of her gleaming, Indian-black hair against the white straw bonnet she wore. She wasn't wearing her spectacles, which she used more when working. He missed them. They belonged to her, and they emphasized her bright-green eyes.

"Ross, my boy."

Nick was jolted out of his appreciation by the earl's demanding tone. "Yes, sir."

"Come over here and sit beside me." The earl indicated the chair Evelyn had vacated. Evelyn and his wife were strolling around the colonnade. Lady Lavinia was seated in the sun on the quay writing a letter, while servants prepared coffee and cleared the table. "Come on, come on. We haven't had much time to talk."

Nick picked up his port and joined the earl.

Threshfield lashed his cane at a footman who was

trying to fill his glass with more port. "Away with you. Go away, all of you."

The butler and two footmen retreated inside the rotunda, where the food had been stored. Threshfield grasped the top of his cane with both hands and leaned on it from his wheelchair. Nick found himself the subject of a calculating examination.

He raised his glass to the earl, settled back in his chair, and glanced out at the lake in a direction that allowed him to secretly keep an eye on Georgiana. He shouldn't, but he couldn't seem to stop—not since that kiss in the woods. He'd argued with himself, listed all the reasons he should never touch her again. Nothing worked. In the past he'd been able to sample a woman and leave her without further thought. His childhood had shown him how little the manipulation of body parts had to do with affection. But, still, he couldn't stop thinking about her.

"I say, Ross. When are you going to send for that Gainsborough so I can examine it?"

"What? Oh, the Gainsborough. It will take a while to pack and transport the thing. Two weeks, I should say."

Georgiana laughed at something Ludwig said, and his gaze switched from the earl to her again.

"You haven't convinced her to leave me, have you?"

This brought his eyes back to the old man. "Not yet, sir."

The earl cackled and sat back in his wheelchair, still raking Nick with his gaze. "But by now you've discovered she's not the spoiled featherwit you first assumed. Oh, don't bother to deny it, my boy. I know Georgiana quite well, you see." Threshfield paused for a moment. "I've had a letter from the duke. He thinks a May wedding would be appropriate."

Nick had been watching Georgiana again but turned to the earl. "There isn't going to be a wedding."

"Of course there is. Georgiana wants a husband who won't tell her how to breathe, what she may read, and whom she may see. Her father wants a packet of my money to help him restore a few of those rotting old houses of his. Being a duke is a trial, my boy. Too much dry rot, too many dependents to whom one owes a living." The earl fell silent again, for which Nick was grateful.

Then he felt a pain in his arm. The earl had poked him with the tip of his cane.

"Have you seduced my fiancé yet?"

"What?" Nick knocked the cane aside.

"I didn't think so."

"Sir, your accusation is offensive."

"Now, don't get your hackles raised." The earl glanced around to assure himself of his privacy. "No use pretending with me, my boy. I've known you wanted her since I saw you two together in the library."

"You bloody-minded old skeleton."

"Careful, Ross, your Cambridge accent is slipping." Lifting a white, wrinkled hand, the earl forestalled Nick's reply. "All I meant was that I would urge you to wait until after she's my wife, and preferably after I'm dead. Discretion, my boy. Society will overlook many foibles in a man as wealthy as you are, but indiscretion will get you cast out."

"I don't give a bleeding fig if I'm received or not, and you should be ashamed, you pandering old fool."

Threshfield clucked at him and shook his head. "I never expected such naïveté from you, and yet ever since we got out of the boats, you've done nothing but gawp at Georgiana. And she has done little more than sigh and blush. Ha! You didn't think you could fool a jaded old veteran of the Regent's court did you? What a disgusting display of fatuous sentiment."

"You sodding old relic."

Drawing a kerchief from his waistcoat, the earl blew his nose loudly and said, "Falling in love with one's mistress just isn't done, my boy. I'm only trying to help you, and Georgiana too. She won't thank you in the end. She has too many silly ideas about combining love and marriage. So bourgeois. I think it comes from reading too much."

"How could you ask me such a question?" Nick gripped the arms of his chair to keep from poking the old blister in the nose. "She's a virtuous lady, and you know it."

"Georgiana is sensitive and vulnerable, and she's in love with you."

Nick only stared at Threshfield, thinking him mad, while the old man grinned at him and waved his handkerchief.

"Don't say you didn't plan it. What was all that business in the plunge bath?"

"You know about that?"

"Very little that happens at Threshfield escapes me, young Ross. Now, listen to me. I'm terribly fond of Georgiana, and I saw from the first how fascinated she was with you. That's why I let you stay. Putting you two in the same room caused a veritable explosion. However, her family will never consent to a marriage between you and Georgiana, and I'm sure

you already know this. I'm also sure being around
Jocelin has taught you what's expected of a gentleman. Conduct yourself appropriately, sir. It's the
only way for you and Georgiana to be together. Let
her get married first, like all the other ladies. Heed my
advice."

"Blow your advice, you white-livered old piss
pot. Georgiana is an innocent, and you know it."

"As you say, my boy." The earl sighed and re-
arranged his lap robe. "Randall? Randall, blast you,
shove me closer to the table."

The earl grabbed a spoon and tapped it against a
crystal goblet to summon his family. "Don't go away,
young Ross. I particularly want you to hear what I'm
going to say to everyone."

"Why not? I can always throw you and your
bloody chair into the lake later."

The earl only laughed. Nick's eye caught the glint
of silver, a table knife, and he was tempted to stick it
into the earl's scrawny neck. The wrinkled old pan-
derer. Bleeding ass, telling him to wait a few months
to debauch an innocent young thing like Georgiana.
Nick thrust aside the thought that only a few moments ago he'd been contemplating that very action.

Why not? said a small, evil voice inside his head.
*She doesn't love the old skeleton. Do you want to leave her
for some flash toff what will take her sweetness and throw it
into the gutter when he's finished?*

No.

The evil voice wouldn't shut up. *She's caught—
marriage is for position and money, and love's stolen on the
sly. She knows she'll be free to pursue her own desires when
she's a widow. That's why she wants to be one.*

Her own desires be damned, Nick silently concluded.
She didn't know about real desire until I taught her.

Nick rose as the ladies approached. Prudence
passed by him and lifted her face to his, simpering and
exposing too much of her nose. It was pushed up at
the tip, resembling a pig's snout. Georgiana took her
place between Lady Lavinia and Lady Augusta, who
looked askance at her as if she expected Georgiana to
pull out a dagger and stab her.

Nick's ill humor faded as he watched Georgiana
stand in front of her chair and sit down without looking behind her. A footman was there to slide her
chair, but Nick was always amazed at how she accomplished the maneuver. Her skirts invariably floated
into place. Her back never touched the back of the
chair, and she sank into it in a smooth movement that
created the impression of royal dignity. Her perfection
of manner made him want to find a sword and kneel
with it at her feet. He'd dine on his own liver before
he'd let her marry that bloody degenerate.

The earl banged his cane on the floor. "Hurry up,
Evelyn, blast you."

Lavinia told the earl to curb his evil tongue as she
joined the group. Evelyn seated his wife and took a
chair next to Nick. He cut a glance at Georgiana that
settled on her breasts, then turned to find Nick eyeing
him with cold menace. The older man looked away
and tried to shove his chair farther away from Nick.
The earl banged his cane again for silence.

"Shut up, all of you. Your pardon, my dear Georgiana."

Georgiana shook her head, "Oh, Threshfield,
really."

The earl smiled and winked at her. Then he

stood, alerting Nick that he was up to something. The earl liked to have a clear view of his family when he provoked them.

"I've asked everyone here for two reasons. One was for the pleasure of a lovely outing for my lovely fiancée." He bowed to Georgiana, who bowed back. "The other reason was to make an announcement. For some time now each of you has had a hard time of it waiting for me to die."

"Oh, Uncle, no!" Prudence put a beringed hand to her breast.

Evelyn threw up his hands and gave a loud sigh of disgust. Ludwig's attention had already wandered back to his fishing net.

"Oh, do be quiet, Prudence," Lady Augusta said. "Such effusiveness isn't the ton."

Lady Lavinia said, "For once I agree with you, Augusta. Threshfield, your family has been waiting for you to die for a decade and you haven't cared. What has changed?"

"What's changed is Georgiana," the earl replied.

Nick sat up straight and put a forearm on the table while he fixed his gaze on the earl's watery eyes. Threshfield paused to heighten the expectancy in his audience and to survey them. He wore a look of evil anticipation and amusement.

"What has changed is that my dear fiancée has made me young again. It has come as a miracle, a sign from Providence. In short, my dear ones, Georgiana is to bear my child."

Chaos broke out. Nick jerked his head to the right to stare at Georgiana. At first she didn't move. Then her eyes blinked once before her face settled into a flat, pale mask.

Prudence fanned her face with her closed parasol. "I don't believe it, I don't believe it, I don't believe it!"

Lady Lavinia and Evelyn began to quarrel. Augusta screeched about a half-French baby spy while Ludwig tried to calm her. Threshfield stood in the middle of it all, grinning.

Without warning Nick bashed his fist against the table. The whole group shut up and stared at him.

In the silence he said, "He's lying."

"Of course," said Lady Lavinia.

"Am I?" Threshfield chortled. "What do you say, Evelyn? Soon there will be an heir between you and the title."

Evelyn was in the midst of an attempt to shred the tablecloth. "You've gone too far."

Nick paid no heed to the renewed arguments that erupted among the family. Was he the only one who had noticed that Georgiana hadn't agreed with him when he'd said the earl was lying? She was stunned, dazed. That was it. Where was she going?

Georgiana rose unnoticed by the family, turned her back on the shrill altercations that were rapidly escalating, and left the colonnade. Nick followed her out to the quay and caught her arm as she was about to step into a rowboat. She turned her blank mask on him.

"I'm sorry," he said.

"For what, Mr. Ross?"

"Nick. I'm sorry you had to be subjected to that inexcusable insult. But, after all, you put yourself in a position to be insulted by that old bag of dust and meanness."

"Pray excuse me, Mr. Ross." She moved to detach his hand from her arm, but he tightened his grip.

"You aren't furious?"

"That isn't an accurate description of my feelings."

His eyes traveled over her face again, noting her pallor and the slight trembling of her mouth. "You haven't said anything. Not a scream, not a cry, not a protest. And you're being obscure."

"As I have said many times before, Mr. Ross. I do not wish to discuss private matters with you. Please excuse me."

She pulled free and tossed her parasol into the boat. Nick caught her around the waist as she attempted to step down into the craft and turned her to face him. Now she looked angry.

"Mr. Ross, you're too familiar."

Nick took a step that brought him close to her. "I ain't the one who asked to be kissed in the woods just now. I ain't the one wot almost slipped me hands inside someone's pants." He snatched her to him and glared into her startled face. "You go back and tell them it's a lie and give that bastard his notice."

At last she was blushing. Vindicated, Nick let her go, and she straightened her bodice.

"I shall do nothing of the sort," she said.

"And just why not?"

"This conversation is distasteful to me, Mr. Ross. I have no intention of continuing it or of indulging in the rash conduct you suggest."

"Rash? Why would it be rash to call the bastard a liar . . . unless—" He shook his head and said softly, "Bloody hell."

"Your language, sir." Georgiana turned her back

to him, but he grabbed her arm and whirled her around again.

"Is this all a part of your scheme?"

"What are you talking about?"

"A surety against further interference from me or Jocelin or your parents? Strike me blind, my lady. You had me fooled right smart."

He waited for her to deny it. Instead, she let them silence between them deepen until it might as well have been a bottomless cavern. He'd faced the traps and jail and not been as afraid as he was when he finally realized she had no intention of answering him or making any denial.

"All right, Your High-and-mighty Royal Highness, if you won't give me an answer, I'll get it for myself. Tonight."

"I don't understand you, sir."

"It's real simple. I'm calling your bluff, lady. And there's only one way to do that."

He watched her brow furrow as she deciphered the meaning of his words. Then she gasped.

"You crude wretch!"

"Look, Your Highness. This morning you didn't know how to kiss. This afternoon you're increasing. Now, I know the two don't have to go together, but usually only whores do it without the kissing."

Now her face was flaming, and she hissed at him, "Stay away from me, sir. I shall lock my doors, so stay away, or I'll shoot you."

"You're not frightening me, my lady," he said in a low voice. "Shall I come wooing you with poetry like a knight to a princess? 'O! a kiss / Long as my exile, sweet as my revenge!'"

She shoved him with both hands and leaped into

the boat. Nick let her go. Steadying herself as she sat down, Georgiana grabbed the oars and shoved away from the steps that ascended from the water to the quay. Nick walked down the steps and stopped the boat with his booted foot.

"Why did you do it, love?"

"Go to hell, Mr. Ross."

10

Having escaped Nicholas Ross and gained her bedroom, Georgiana yanked the ribbons of her bonnet, tore it from her head, and threw it onto a Sheridan chair.

"Rebecca, Re—bec—ca!" She jerked each finger of her gloves. They sailed after the bonnet as she filled her lungs for another shout.

"Here, my lady." Rebecca scurried into the room. "I was looking for the mantle that goes with your gray traveling costume."

The outer door to the sitting room banged, and Aunt Livy marched into the room. "Run along, Rebecca. I'll help your mistress change."

Georgiana wrestled with the numerous buttons at the back of her bodice until the maid had gone. Then she flopped down onto the bed.

"Drat, drat, drat, drat, and drat that odious Threshfield!"

Livy lay down her parasol and folded her arms over her chest. "And just why didn't you say that when the old fool started spouting that drivel at the pavilion?"

"Oh, Aunt Livy, the disgrace." Georgiana threw her skirt over her head and began to groan.

"That's your solution? You're going to run around with your skirt over your head?"

Georgiana pulled her skirt down and peered over its folds to whisper. "When I heard him, I was too stunned to respond. If I'd been standing, my knees would have given way."

"Listen, my chick, Threshfield has gone too far this time."

"I know. He thinks he's found another goad, like threatening Ludwig with leaving the Egyptian collection to me."

"The arse delights in keeping them off balance and dancing attendance on him," Livy said. "I told him he has forty-eight hours to retract this slander or I'll take a buggy whip to him. Come here and let me help you with those buttons."

Georgiana turned her back so that Livy could unfasten the dozens of buttons. "I was too embarrassed and too furious to speak. If I had, I would either have bawled or burst into tears. It was all I could manage to stand up and walk to the boats, and then Mr. Ross followed me. He said, he said—oh—I won't repeat what he said. He's far worse than the earl."

"You should go down to dinner this evening and denounce Threshfield. Force him to retract his claim."

Stripping the bodice from her arms, Georgiana gave a sharp jerk to her head. "I have no intention of giving weight to this absurd lie by even recognizing what has taken place."

Livy pulled yards of skirt over Georgiana's head.

"There's no use taking a dignified stance. It will be lost on the family. Prudence will spread the lie across the county if we don't do something. And Evelyn is the biggest gossip in England. He'll go to his club and spew venom. Then all his cronies will flap their tongues. You'll be ruined. Raise your arms and I'll throw this skirt over your head." Livy helped her struggle through the mountain of polished gray fabric.

"Threshfield will see to it that neither of them say a word," Georgiana said as she slipped her arms through the bodice of her traveling dress. She didn't mention that her greatest humiliation had been facing Nick and having him succumb to suspicion of her virtue before her eyes. She pressed her lips together, then noticed Aunt Livy staring at her.

"What did the boy say to you?"

"Mr. Ross is a foul wretch."

"He didn't believe Threshfield. He's a right clever lad, that boy."

"I don't want to talk about it, Aunt Livy. It's too painful."

"I warn you, child. If you don't do something, Mr. Ross will. You didn't see the look he gave Threshfield after you left. Prudence and I did, and she nearly swooned."

"Are you still going house hunting with me?"

Livy gave her a skeptical look.

"I need your opinion about a house that would be suitable for about thirty children to begin with. We'll be late getting to the solicitor's." Georgiana picked up a pearl-gray bonnet with burgundy ribbons.

"You don't have to hunt for property today. Big houses like you want don't sell quickly."

"I have to get away," Georgiana said, her voice trembling. "Please hurry and change, Aunt Livy. I need your advice on choosing a home suitable for lots of children, and I want to stay away a good while, perhaps have dinner in town. I need your company."

Livy hugged her, which evoked the tears Georgiana had been withholding. She lay her head on Livy's shoulder and sobbed. It was a long time before she was able to lift her head and face leaving her room.

Late that evening she returned, having spent the afternoon touring various houses in the neighborhood. The task was a distraction from her embarrassment and from her apprehension regarding Nick. He'd threatened to invade her bedchamber, but the more she thought about it, the less likely it seemed that he would go through with the threat.

Gentlemen simply did not force their way into lady's chambers. They came stealthily by invitation. Such visits were taken for granted among house parties. That's why guests' names were often posted on bedroom doors. Georgiana remembered the year she came out at the age of eighteen. Her mother hadn't supplied the engraved name cards for the doors of the duke's guests, and an errant husband had ended up sneaking into his own wife's bed. The lady promptly kicked him out and set her shoes outside her door so that her lover wouldn't make the same mistake.

The house was quiet and dark as Rebecca helped Georgiana undress. As soon as her gown was off, Georgiana sent the maid to bed. She washed and donned a lawn-and-lace nightgown and embroidered robe. As she crossed the dressing room, Georgiana paused, then turned and went to the door. The key was in the lock. She turned it and felt much easier upon hearing the click of the lock.

Discarding her robe, she got into bed and lay staring at the light visible through the doorway between her bedroom and the sitting room. Moonbeams filtered through the long windows of the balcony. She turned onto her side and closed her eyes. Minutes passed, and she was wide-awake. She turned onto her other side. Then she lay on her back. Sighing, she punched her pillow and turned onto her stomach. She squeezed her eyes closed. She recited poetry; nothing worked. Finally she sat up, fished around in the dark for her robe, and pulled it on and her slippers as well.

In her tossing and turning her hair had come loose from its braid and tumbled over her shoulders. She thrust it away from her face and went to the glass doors that opened onto the balcony. Outside there was a chaise longue and a chair facing each other. She walked between them to stand before the wrought-iron railing and stare at the moonlight reflected in the small lake in the distance.

What had she come to that she was more insulted by the fact that Nick might believe ill of her than by Threshfield's abominable lie? She was feeling most unlike herself. She had never been kissed the way Nick had kissed her, and—now that she reflected upon it—the experience had cast her into some kind of stupor or fugue. Throughout luncheon she'd been unable to keep her eyes from him. Yet the moment he looked back at her, she turned scarlet and had to turn her gaze before she became so flustered that she giggled.

How unlike her. And how could he kiss her like that and a few hours later accuse her of—of unspeakable conduct? She hated him. The wretched vermin. Wretched, wretched vermin. The insults did little to relieve her anger, so she kicked the iron balustrade.

She forgot she wasn't wearing boots. Giving a little yelp, she hopped on one foot, then limped to the chair and rubbed her foot. She was still rubbing it when she heard a tiny sound almost beyond hearing. Her head came up, and she glanced out at the expanse of carefully kept lawn. Nothing. There it was again. She stood and leaned over the railing to look at the ground directly below. The door creaked behind her. Georgiana's back snapped straight, but before she could turn, she was surrounded by arms that pulled her backward into a hard, long body. She turned her head, and her mouth was covered even as she grabbed the arms that held her. She bit it.

"Ouch! Bleeding hell, George. You got nasty teeth, you do."

Georgiana whipped around to face her assailant. "Mr. Ross!"

"Nick."

She was speechless for a moment. He was dressed strangely, all in black, even his shirt. He wore shoes with soft soles, and he'd tied a black bandanna around his neck. Her gaze fell to the bandanna. It was silk. She wondered if the skin it concealed was as smooth as the material. What was she thinking?

"How did you get in? Release me and get out of my rooms immediately, sir." She stepped away from him, but her legs hit the balustrade as he followed her. She grasped the railing and glared at him, daring him to come closer. He did.

"You're dull as swipes if you think a lock will stop me."

"Dull as what?"

"Swipes, love. Spoiled beer."

Pointing an indignant finger at the door, Georgiana said, "Get out at once or I'll scream."

"Good, that. It'll improve your rep."

He was right. "Very well. I shall leave." She brushed past him, intent on going to Aunt Livy's room.

He caught her arm as she went by. She jerked it free but too late realized his intention. Her feet left the ground as he lifted her in his arms. Sailing in the air, she gasped when her bottom hit the chaise longue.

"What are you doing?"

His slim shadow loomed over her as he mounted the chaise longue like a quarter horse. Georgiana scooted away from him until her back hit the back of the chaise. She slipped sideways, but he planted his arms on either side of her. She was trapped.

"You still got your mouth clamped tighter than an unpaid tart's knees?"

Georgiana straightened her back, lifted her chin, and managed to look down at him even though he was taller. "You low cur. Only a contemptible villain would use such language to me. Only a base coward would force his presence on a lady who has expressed her distaste for him—keep away!"

He came at her slowly, all the while pulling her legs down so that they met his, and soon he was stretched out alongside her with one leg bent up to trap her hips. Such an action was unprecedented. Georgiana had no experience with men who refused to do as they were told in the presence of a lady. The shock rendered her speechless.

"Knew this would shut you up," he whispered.

His breath stirred the wisps of hair at her temple and made her shiver. Moonlight bathed his face in pearly light so that she could see those straight, severe brows, the shadows below his cheekbones, the curve of his lower lip.

Nick drew a finger along her throat to her chest. "You gonna tell me what I want?"

"Wh-what?"

"Say it. Say Threshfield was lying, and I'll hang him from one of his Corinthian columns."

"You're too personal, sir." She gripped one of his arms and tried to pry it from the chaise. "Allow me to rise at once!"

"Bloody hell but you're stubborn." Nick grasped one of her struggling hands and drew it down to her side, where he held it. "You're going to ruin yourself, and if you're set on it, you might as well have the fun as well as the cost."

Suddenly Georgiana heard the determination in his voice, and behind it, desperation. She remembered his struggle in the woods, how he had fought against taking further liberties, how he had warned her against himself.

She stopped fighting him and spoke in a low, wondering whisper. "Nick?"

It was a long, drawn-out breath rather than a word, more a feeling than a sound. His body went still, and his head came back so that he could look at her. She said his name again, and he sucked in his breath.

"Don't," he said. "Don't say it again."

"Nick . . ."

He sat up facing her. Crouched before her on all fours, he seemed more panther than man. He re-

mained still for a moment. Then his hand came out
slowly and picked up a fold of wispy lace and lawn.
With the fabric trailing from his fingers, he bent his
head and touched it to his face. He breathed in its
scent. His long, dark fingers drew the misty length
over his lips. Georgiana watched him, fascinated. The
sight of her lace against those strong fingers, pressing
against his lips, captured her sense and turned her
body into one mass of tingling nerves. She could have
spent eternity watching him, but he dropped the fabric and lowered his head.

"You shouldn't have said my name that way, love.
You know better."

He took her hand, turned it, and kissed the palm.
His lips slid up to her inner wrist, causing Georgiana
to gasp and sink the fingers of her free hand into the
upholstery. When he kissed the bend of her arm, she
felt her body turn to boiled pudding. It seemed natural that he came to her, fitting the whole of his body
against hers as he kissed her lips at last.

Long minutes passed in a kiss that ignited fire,
pain, and pleasure. His hand slid up her ribs and covered her breast, sending new quivers through it to a
sensitive spot between her legs. Soon her gown was
riding up her legs, and she felt his hand on her calf.
Amazing. A man was touching her leg. This man,
who drove her mad with his bullying and his kisses,
was touching her leg.

Then she felt his lips on her nipple and nearly
cried out. Her back arched and her hands groped until
they found his buttocks. She clawed at muscle through
the fabric of his pants. It wasn't enough. Driven, desperate to alleviate the compulsion he'd aroused, Georgiana followed the commands of her body, lifted her

hips, and opened her legs. He settled between them while moving his lips to her other breast.

His hand went to the waistband of his trousers and worked quickly. Georgiana was floating in a stupor of desire when she felt something hard and hot touch her. Her eyes flew open only to close again as Nick thrust himself gently against her. A low moan erupted from the depths of her body. At its sound Nick stopped all movement abruptly. He raised his head to look down at her. She could see the pain in his eyes, the grimace that distorted his features.

"Sodding bloody hell," he said. "Oh, God, I wish you weren't a f—cking virgin."

Stunned, Georgiana heard him groan, felt his flesh press against her. She cried out and shoved him. He fell to one side, nearly coming off the chaise. Scrambling from beneath him, Georgiana swept her robe around her and jumped off the chaise. Nick cursed, righted his clothing before she could straighten hers, and rounded on Georgiana.

"Where are you going?" he asked.

"L-leave me alone."

He stood before her, legs apart, hands balled into fists, breathing hard. "Now do you see? You have to leave. If you stay, it won't be long before I prove you couldn't be carrying Threshfield's get."

"I'm staying, and you're not going to prove anything, sir. If you had any honor, you wouldn't force yourself on me."

"Force isn't what happened just now, love. Take that back."

"I have no intention of retracting my words when you've invaded my chamber like some foul degenerate."

He began to walk slowly toward her, a black shadow in silver light. "Seems to me you're doing as much degenerating as me."

"Don't come any closer!"

"Too late, love. You can't have it both ways. Either you're carrying Threshfield's babe and got nothing to protect, or you're a stubborn, foolish virgin. Either way it's me you're hot to touch, and knowing that is driving me insane."

She tried to dodge to the side, but he dodged with her. She feinted the other way. Nick jumped with her. This time he grabbed the railing, and she careened into his arm. His weight shifted to rest on the balustrade, and there was a scraping sound.

Metal screamed, and Georgiana felt Nick's body hurtle past her. She cried out and grabbed him as he fell. Planting her feet, she fought their momentum as they were dragged over the edge of the balcony. His legs were hanging over the broken railing. Her foot hit the undamaged portion of the balustrade and wedged there. Pulling hard, she managed to stop Nick from plummeting over the broken railing as it lay jutting from the floor of the balcony.

"Grab my hand," she cried.

He let go of the railing, twisted, and grabbed her wrist. Her arms felt as if they would be torn from their sockets, but she held on to him as he drew himself up with the strength of his arms until his feet found purchase. His weight suddenly left her as he swung up onto the balcony again.

They fell onto the floor, gasping. After a while Nick stood up and helped her rise. They approached the gap in the balustrade and looked down. Had he fallen, Nick would have hit a pavement walk almost twenty feet below.

"Dear God," Georgiana said.

"Well, scrag me."

He knelt and touched the railing where it had separated, then whistled slowly. "Do you believe in signs from God?"

"I suppose."

"Well, I don't. Not in this case. That railing's been cut."

"Cut. What do you mean, cut?" Georgiana tried to go past him, but he stopped her.

"Stay back. It's dangerous."

They both turned as someone pounded at the sitting-room door. Evelyn's voice broke through the silence.

"Georgiana? Are you all right? I heard something."

The earl's voice was next, shouting, "What's all the noise, blast it?"

Georgiana whirled around to stare at Nick, aghast.

"Don't worry." He went into the sitting room and returned with a coiled rope. "Never look for swag without taking the proper tools." He fastened one end of the rope to the remaining balustrade, tested it, and came back to her.

"This ain't over," he said. He pulled her to him and kissed her. His mouth sucked at hers, shocking Georgiana into pounding his shoulder. He released her and grinned.

"Don't forget to untie the rope and hide it."

Georgiana gaped at him as he vanished over the balcony. She went to the edge to see him snake down the rope to the ground. He dropped on his feet, stood back, and swept his arm around in a flourish as he bowed to her.

" 'Good night, good night! Parting is such sweet sorrow / That I shall say good night till it be morrow.' "

"Shh! Stop that and get out of here," Georgiana hissed as she tugged at the knot in the rope. The pounding at the door was growing louder.

Nick put a hand on his breast. " 'A perfect Woman, nobly planned, / To warn, to comfort, and command.' "

Georgiana threw the rope at him. It hit him in the face, but he knocked it aside, pointed his toe, and swept another bow.

"You don't like Wordsworth? Pertwee is teaching me Byron. 'There be none of Beauty's daughters / With a magic like thee; / And like music on the waters / Is thy sweet voice to me.' "

"Nicholas Ross, I'm going to let them in, so you'd better get yourself inside. I wash my hands of you."

" 'She looked at me as she did love, / And made sweet moan.' "

Georgiana cupped her hands around her mouth and bent over the railing. "I'm going to put a wardrobe against my door at night!"

"If I want to get in, I will." Before she could object, he faded into the shadows. "Ta, love."

11

The next morning Nick was hunched over the writing table in his dressing room trying to finish another agitated letter to Jocelin. He'd had a damnable time communicating his concern while simultaneously concealing the fact that Georgiana was in danger. Someone had cut through that iron railing deliberately.

He didn't want Jocelin dragging himself across a continent and an ocean, and that's what he'd do if he realized someone was trying to kill his sister. And Nick didn't think it was Lady Augusta. Brain-fevered though she was, he didn't think the lady had the strength to cut through iron railings. But any other family member might except the earl.

Nick finished a paragraph laden with frank assessments of Georgiana's shortcomings—her willfulness, her defiance, her selfishness, her refusal to face things as they were. Perhaps he'd been a bit harsh, but harshness was better than risking revealing what his body became when he was with her.

Glancing up from the page, Nick beheld Pertwee brushing a morning coat. The valet's nostrils were quivering like a rabbit's. Nick blotted and folded his letter.

"What's wrong with you, my ginger-haired old cock?" he asked. "You look like you just swallowed rotten cabbage."

"Indeed, sir."

"Come on, Pertwee. I simply can't have you creeping about me like a professional mourner. Out with it."

"Sir has undertaken a nocturnal excursion."

"You been spying on me?"

"I have been mending the costume sir wears on what he calls his little jaunts."

"Relax, Pertwee. I ain't hunting degenerates at the moment, and I told you I don't do no thieving anymore. Don't have to."

"Sir has been known to grow bored and indulge himself merely for amusement."

"Not this time," Nick said as he addressed and sealed the letter. "Broke into Lady Georgiana's bedroom instead."

Pertwee dropped his clothes brush. Nick glanced up from replacing his pen in the inkstand. "Hang it, Pertwee, don't faint now. I need you to be alert. Someone's trying to harm Lady Georgiana. Last night the railing on her balcony gave way and nearly killed me."

"Sir should not be telling me this." Pertwee picked up the brush and began taking blind swipes at the morning coat. "A gentleman doesn't discuss his—his . . ."

"Strike me blind but you're weak-livered. I didn't

touch—well—the lady's virtue is intact. And don't tell me you and the rest of the household don't know about the earl's mean little story. It's a lie."

"I'm sure I don't know to what sir is referring."

Nick shot out of his chair, causing Pertwee to jump and skitter backward. "I thought toffs were hypocrites, but toffs' servants is just as bad. Lady Georgiana is irreproachable. Is that clear? I'm going to settle this mess with the earl as soon as I've spoken with her. She doesn't realize the peril she's in. Meanwhile, I want you to keep an eye out. Whoever tried to kill her last night may try again before I can get her out of here."

This time he thought he could convince her aunt to agree to a removal. That way they could all leave with propriety, as Jos would want. He could escort them back to the duke and duchess and wash his hands of Georgiana Marshal. Or could he? Knowing her as he did, he could bet she'd made a list of suitably ancient bachelors. Efficient little beast. She would find another old relic, and Nick would be right back where he started. If he left her alone, she might succeed this time.

He wasn't going to let her give herself to a decrepit. She should marry a young man, one who could make her happy, who could give her pleasure, who would make love . . .

All of a sudden this solution didn't seem as suitable as it had when he'd first arrived. He knew a great many of the eligible young aristocrats. Thinking of her with any of them made him want to puke. But what other choice was there?

Returning to the desk, Nick unsealed his letter to Jocelin and added to it. Whatever the state of his stomach, he couldn't leave her until she was settled with someone acceptable. Jos would have to provide a list of his own; Nick couldn't. Bleeding hell, he was going to have to play matchmaker for Georgiana when he would rather—no use pursuing that thought.

He finished the letter and sealed it again. Handing it to Pertwee, he donned his morning coat and set out for the dining room to corner Georgiana. After last night even she must have begun to realize the risk of remaining at Threshfield.

To his irritation Georgiana wasn't in the dining room, but Evelyn bloody Hyde was. He pointed his eagle's-beak nose in Nick's direction and muttered something that might have been good morning, then buried his face in the *Times*.

"Seen Lady Georgiana, old chap?" Nick asked as he went to the buffet and picked up a plate to help himself to eggs, bacon, kippers, and toast.

"The ladies have gone shopping in town."

"All of them? Even Lady Augusta?"

Evelyn slapped his paper down beside his plate. "Yes, and it's a good thing. I want to talk to you, Ross. I heard your voice in Lady Georgiana's room last night, and don't try to deny it. My hearing is excellent."

"You got a big mouth too."

"I was disgusted."

"You are disgusting."

"There's no use denying it, Ross. I've already spoken to the earl, though he refuses to see the truth."

Nick poured tea into a cup and placed it beside his plate on the table. "What truth is that, Hyde?"

"That this child of Georgiana's can't possibly be his. That any occasion devised to validate such a claim is merely a ruse trumped up to conceal your affair with the girl." Evelyn rose and threw his napkin onto the seat of his chair.

"I won't have it, sir. I'll not stand by and see the great name of Threshfield dragged in muck. You'll not cast dishonor on our noble heritage and compromise the family's position in Society. That trollop will never quarter the Threshfield arms or become mistress of this house."

Nick took a sip of tea. He patted his lips with his napkin and set it beside his saucer. Rising, he walked over to Evelyn, who held his ground with a sneer. Nick smiled at him and glanced aside at the buffet with its silver plate and sterling flatware. His hand shot out, plucked a carving knife from a ham, and held it in front of Evelyn's face. At the same time his other hand grabbed the man's collar, twisted it, and drew Evelyn close enough to hear his whisper.

"Now, you listen to me, Evelyn bloody Hyde. Threshfield is just trying to goad you. The story's a lie. Right?"

Evelyn's mouth worked as he tried to breathe, and his upper lip was spotted with sweat. "Erp!"

"Right. And you're not going to repeat a lie."

"Erp!"

"And you're gonna stay away from Georgiana, or you'll end up with a bloody smile in your neck. Oh, can't you breathe? Sorry, old chap."

Nick released his hold on Evelyn's collar. Choking and gulping in air, Evelyn clutched a chair. Nick stuck the knife back into the ham. Then he took his seat and dug into his breakfast.

"Aren't you going to finish your food?" Nick asked as Evelyn stumbled from the room.

The door slammed, and Nick settled back to finish his tea. He would have to follow Georgiana into town. All for the best, since he could more easily get her away from the family in some shop and make her understand her danger. Even she would have to see reason now that the threat came not from Lady Augusta, but from someone more competent.

Nick found the earl and gave him an ultimatum to retract his lies before sundown tomorrow or face retribution, then embarked on his quest of Georgiana. Worthbridge was a little less than an hour's ride on horseback from Threshfield. He arrived before noon and stabled his horse at a livery behind a bookseller.

The town was a great deal smaller than London but boasted a large and busy mercantile district, the main avenue of which was called the Quadrant. Like the Strand in the capital, the Quadrant was a long street bordered by small shops, each unique, most with a bowfront of windows divided into panes. Nick stood at one end of the Quadrant and surveyed the bustling pedestrians, the carriages, wagons, street vendors, and noisy children who skipped in and out of the traffic. The place was ablaze with color from the neatly displayed wares in the windows and from the hand-painted wooden name boards that hung over the shops.

He had emerged onto the Quadrant in front of the bookseller's. At this end of the street lay shops of interest to a gentleman—hatters, a narrow, cozy shop on the corner devoted to snuff and cigars, a boot maker, and farther down, a whip maker. Out of the door of the whip maker's establishment stepped Lady Lavinia, accompanied by an obsequious proprietor. Nick moved quickly into the doorway of the book-

seller. If possible, he wanted to catch Georgiana alone
and talk to her without anyone's knowing. Lady Lavinia seemed to be by herself. She nodded to the whip
maker and proceeded down the street, vanishing in
the crowd.

Once she'd gone, Nick stepped out of the shadows and crossed the street. His best method of locating
Georgiana was to find the Threshfield carriage and
search the shops near it. No doubt the vehicle would
progress slowly around the district with its occupants,
for he couldn't imagine either Prudence or Georgiana
loping along the dusty road like Lady Lavinia.

He found the Threshfield carriage, identifiable by
the coat of arms on the door, sitting outside a glove
shop. Strolling by, he glanced in the windows display-
ing fine French gloves, hand-sewn English gloves, and
lace mittens. He caught sight of a close-fitting bonnet
trimmed with ostrich feathers and loops of ribbon in
the Regency style. Lady Augusta, its wearer, was examining a pair of long gloves of the type she wore
with her gowns that had short puffed sleeves. A
martyred footman stood nearby holding boxes and
packages tied together with twine. Nick surveyed the
rest of the shop, but Georgiana wasn't there.

Walking down a few doors, he spied Prudence
leaving a silk mercer, accompanied by another footman. Nick saw a pair of hands reach into the shop
window and remove a bolt of sarcenet covered in a
design of giant peonies. He imagined the stunted Prudence in fifteen yards of enormous flowers and almost
winced. Nick walked behind a street vendor carrying
brushes festooned around him on frames. Prudence
marched down the street toward him without regard
to those in her path, expecting everyone to move out

of her way. Prudence charged through hapless groups of shoppers, trailed by her footman, and vanished into a jeweler's. He wouldn't expect Georgiana to be anywhere near Prudence.

His way clear, Nick left the vicinity of the brush seller. "She's got to be somewhere near."

He spotted a shawl shop and ducked inside. Not there. He tried a bonnet shop, dodging in and out of rows of lace-and muslin-caps. No luck. He tried the laceman and embroiderer, hearing talk of ruchings and rouleaux, edgings and cockades. Still no Georgiana.

Growing frustrated, he left the frills behind. Standing beside the shop window, he glanced up and down the street again. Two doors down sat an apothecary shop, its windows glittering with giant bottles of blue, green, and red waters. Delft drug jars took prominent place in the bow window. Next to it sat a china warehouse, with its plates and cups stacked outside in pyramids.

Between mountains of porcelain, a gleaming Indian-black curl caught his eye. Georgiana walked between the displays to the corner and turned down a side street. Nick strode after her. The side street was clean but devoid of the more popular shops. At the dead end, tucked away, with a small elegantly lettered sign, lay the establishment of Nan Tussett, Stay Maker. Nick slowed as he saw Georgiana's shimmering gray skirts disappear inside the shop. He came to a halt as he neared the place and caught a glimpse of twill foundations, long lengths of bone, and inside, discreetly, the lacy top edge of a corset.

Hesitating, Nick glanced around to find himself alone on the street. A pair of ladies turned the corner, saw him, and retreated. Nick grinned, pushed back his hat, and plunged into the stay maker's shop. Georgiana was talking to a woman who looked not so much dressed as upholstered in black bombazine over stays that could have squeezed the girth of a man-o'-war.

Nick removed his hat and threaded his way toward them through rows of counters and between two tables. At the tables a dozen young women bored holes in stay backs. The proprietress saw him first and stopped in midsentence to gawk at him. Georgiana turned, widened her eyes, and reddened.

"Mr. Ross, your presence in this establishment is most unseemly."

Nick bowed to them. The proprietress glanced from him to Georgiana, muttered some excuse, and scurried toward a curtained doorway. Several of the apprentices giggled and whispered behind their hands. Nick caught one of them looking at him and winked at her. This produced a cascade of twitters. He gave the lass one of his teasing smiles before turning back to Georgiana.

She wasn't there. Her crinoline swayed gently as she scudded between the tables, past the counters with their frilly corsets, and out of his sight. He replaced his hat, tipped it to the accompaniment of more giggles, and hurried out of the shop. Three long strides brought him to her side. Slipping his hand into the crook of her arm, he pulled her up short.

"Whoa, there, young George. I got to talk to you."

Georgiana twisted her elbow out of his grip and straightened her shawl on her shoulders with hands clad in kid gloves. "I'm quite busy, Mr. Ross. I should think you'd have more sense than to seek me out in so forward a manner."

"Bleeding hell, why is it you talk like some dried-up old boarding-school mistress?"

"I don't know what you mean, sir. Nor do I care to. Good day to you."

He stopped her by grabbing a hunk of the seemingly endless yards of her skirt. Twisting around, she tried to yank the fabric from him.

"Really, Mr. Ross. This is childish."

"You're not going anywhere until you listen to me. I got things to say."

Tethered, fuming, Georgiana gave a last futile jerk at her skirt, then subsided. She put her back to him, stiff with outrage. He glanced around the deserted side street. Removing a glove, he slipped his hand beneath her shawl and dragged the backs of his fingers down her back while keeping hold of her skirt with his other hand.

She jumped and whirled around to face him. "Mr. Ross!"

"Nick," he said softly.

She shook her head violently. "Oh, no. The last time I called you that, I—you—we . . ."

He sighed and let go of her gown. "You're right, love. This isn't the time. You thought about last night?"

He hadn't believed it possible for a woman to turn the color of a ruby, but Georgiana almost accomplished it.

"Sir, how odious of you to speak to me of what should remain unspoken."

"What? Oh, strike me blind, woman, I'm not talking about that. I'm talking about the railing.

Someone's trying to kill you, love. You got to scarper."

"I beg your pardon?"

"You got to leave. Now. Today, before they try again. Somebody in that family of bedlamites is trying to make sure you don't become Countess of Threshfield. It's all that old skeleton's fault for telling them you're going to have his heir."

"You're mistaken, Mr. Ross. It's only Lady Augusta up to her usual tricks."

Nick's retort died on his lips as a woman turned the corner and came toward them. Seeing him, she crossed the street and averted her face until she reached the stay maker's and went inside. Nick drew closer to Georgiana and lowered his voice.

"This ain't Lady Augusta's doing. Too subtle, too much like an accident."

Georgiana tugged on the sleeve of her glove, her brow wrinkled. "Perhaps." She appeared to think upon his point, then straightened her shawl and tugged her bonnet to the correct angle as if girding for some feminine battle. "You may be correct, and if you are, I'll not be chivied out of a hole like some fox and run away."

"Oh, I see," he said, his temper rising along with his fear for her. He should have expected her to do the opposite of what was reasonable. "You'd rather risk bashing your little skull open on the pavement below your balcony and spilling your meager brains."

"No one makes me run and hide, Mr. Ross."

In a single, smooth movement he was beside her, his lips close to her pink ear. "I can make you do both, love, and I will, if it will get you away from a murderer."

Georgiana shivered and took a quick step away from him.

"How many times must I repeat it? I'm not running away. If someone is trying to scare me, they'll do worse to Threshfield once I'm gone. Did you ever think of that, Mr.-I-Know-What's-Best-for-Everyone?"

"You ain't going to leave?"

"No."

"Sure?"

"Of course I'm sure."

Nick walked around her in a circle that put him between Georgiana and the intersection with the Quadrant. "Which do you think scares you more—what this murderer may do, or what I might do to you?"

"What an absurd question," she said as she eyed him warily.

"Is it? Let's find out."

He threw her off guard by making no abrupt movements. Instead, he merely walked toward her and kept walking. When he didn't stop, she backed from him. Moving to the side whenever she did, he easily herded her until her crinoline hit the wall beside a shuttered and abandoned shop. Georgiana turned and clamped her hand on her teetering skirt.

"Here, let me help you," Nick said, and he pressed close.

At the same time he grabbed the crinoline and flipped the back of it up so that it caught between Georgiana and the wall. She was trapped between his body and the wall. He saw her furious expression. Her lips parted. She was going to scream, so he quickly put his hands on either side of her face and whispered.

"Don't, please."

At his touch she went still and gazed at him as if transfixed. For his part, Nick hadn't counted on the feel of her skin distracting him so that he nearly forgot his name. It was like tracing liquid pearls with his fingertips. He couldn't help touching his lips to that softness.

Flattening his hands on the wall, he leaned into her and found her mouth. He sank into a hot pool of sensation, knowing and not caring that he shouldn't press his chest against her breasts or his hips against hers. He felt the mounds of softness burgeon against him, and suddenly he was fighting a ruthless, primitive impulse to drag up her skirt and abandon himself to lust. His hand left the wall and began to burrow under yards of fabric.

"Oh, my!"

A strange voice. Nick lifted his lips from Georgiana's to find that the woman who had passed them earlier had come out of the stay maker's. She was standing on the threshold of the shop, a hand over her mouth, her bonnet quivering with shock. Georgiana gave a little cry, shoved him, and began straightening her clothing. The woman scurried away.

He'd lost control of himself again and almost molested Jocelin's sister. Nick cursed himself, and Georgiana too. If she would do as she was told, he wouldn't be put in this miserable situation. He eyed her as she retied her bonnet ribbons. Damn her. She needed a good thrashing. Since he couldn't give her one, he'd do the next-best thing.

"No sense in fussing, love. I'll have you mussed in seconds."

He began his stalking again. She glanced up at him, then thrust out a hand to warn him off.

"Stay where you are."

"I was right, wasn't I? Say it." He kept coming, and she directed her steps toward the intersection rather than a wall.

"Right about what?"

"Look at you. You're shaking, love, and if I reach for you, you'll jump like a cat with a stomped tail. You're afraid of me. Told you."

Still backing way, Georgiana jutted out her chin and tried to sneer. "I'm not afraid of you, and certainly not more than some imaginary murderer."

The force of her grand claim was blunted when she caught her heel on a loose brick in the road and stumbled. Nick darted forward, caught her arms, and steadied her. He bent close enough to smell the jasmine scent of her hair.

His lips brushed her cheek as he said, "I think you're scared now, love."

Gasping, she jerked her head back, away from his lips. She froze in a startled pause. He could see the rapid beat of her pulse in a vein at her throat. He wanted to kiss it. And if he did, he might drag her into that deserted shop.

"I know what it is," he said, fighting for control through a fog of lust. "You like it dangerous."

"What?"

"That's what sets you afire, love. Danger. You might get caught making love in a street, on a balcony." He bent to mouth a hot whisper in her ear. "Maybe I should catch you in the plunge bath again."

This time she shrieked like a falcon and bashed

him aside with both arms. He got a faceful of swirling skirt as she whirled and ran from him.

"Don't go," he called after her. "Brave Lady Georgiana, who scoffs at murderers and gets all hot for danger, you're scampering like a frightened vole."

She never looked back. His lips twisted into a half smile, half grimace from touching her. Trying to ignore his too-ready body, Nick followed Georgiana into the Quadrant.

12

Georgiana rushed into the Quadrant, nearly colliding with a flower vendor, and hurried down the street. Nick Ross was a foul wretch to lure her with kisses and forbidden touches only to taunt her for the weakness he induced. Why wouldn't he leave her alone? Because he enjoyed making her foolish with desire, and he loved making her cringe with mortification.

Walking quickly, she darted a glance over her shoulder and saw him coming after her with those long strides that made him seem to wade through the heavy crowds. If he caught her, he would find more ways to make her body betray her, and then he would mock her for it. She couldn't endure such misery.

To her relief Georgiana saw the Threshfield carriage in the next block. Picking up her skirts, she began to run, dodging shoppers and street vendors. Traffic in the street had lightened and sped up, since many people had already sought home and the afternoon meal. Another glance told her that Nick was closing the distance between them.

"Hot sausages, nice and fresh. Hot sausages, inna bun!"

Georgiana skipped around the man and his cart of sausages. Only a little way to go. She could see Prudence climbing into the carriage across the street. Georgiana swerved, stepped off the curb, and heard Nick shout her name. She didn't look at him. Her gaze was fixed on the carriage. Then she heard him bellow at her. She hesitated as she crossed the street, and looked back at him.

"Look out," he shouted as he pointed behind her. "The cab!"

She turned to see a hansom careening toward her. She hurried across the street, but as she moved, the cab swerved so that she remained in its path. It barreled down on her, and she was caught in the middle of the street while an omnibus crossed her path. She turned and sprinted back the way she came. The horse drawing the cab turned and came at her, making the hansom swerve again. Georgiana made a last desperate leap to the curb.

Her gamble proved useless, for the hansom aimed at the sidewalk, scattering everyone in its path. The wheel of the cab rode over the curb, straight at Georgiana. She saw foam on the horse's mouth, the blur of the spokes on the cab wheels. Then Nick rammed into her and swept her across the walk to the shelter of a shop doorway. The cab rolled over the spot on the curb where she'd been seconds earlier.

Her heart thumped like a drum and threatened to rattle up her throat to escape her body. Nick had thrown her against the shop door and covered her with his body. He stepped back and slipped his arms around her, which was fortunate, since her legs had

turned to molasses. Her mind seemed frozen and incapable of reason. She gripped Nick's arm with both
hands; its hard strength provided a shield while she
tried to calm herself. Several passersby asked after her.
He thanked them and assured them of her welfare
while she clung to him, unable to do more than trem-
ble and blink.

When they were alone again, he grabbed both her
hands and stared into her eyes. "You all right, love?"

"I think so. Just startled." She took a deep breath
and let go of his arm. "Yes . . . yes, just startled."

"You should be more than startled," he snapped.
"You should be scared to death."

Her insides began to shake again. "It was only an
accident. A runaway."

"Bleeding hell, woman. Runaways don't aim for
anything, much less follow you onto the curb."

Gnawing at her lower lip, Georgiana glanced over
his shoulder in the direction in which the cab had
vanished. "True." She clamped her hands together.
They felt cold despite her gloves. "True."

"At last we agree. It's about time, young George.
Then we'll leave in the morning."

At his peremptory tone Georgiana frowned. "We
will not."

"And just bleeding why not?"

"I have asked you to amend your language, Mr.
Ross."

"I'm going to amend it on your backside if you
don't—"

"I'm not a fool, Nick."

She was startled when he closed his eyes and
sucked in his breath.

"Scrag me if it ain't worse when you snap at me."

"What are you talking about?"

"Say my name again, love."

Drawing her shawl about her shoulders, Georgiana scowled at him. "This is no time for familiarity, Mr. Ross. I agree that there is a possibility that this incident is no accident. However, I intend to prevent further occurrences by twisting Threshfield's ear tonight until he admits his lies. So, you see, there's no need to change my plans at all. Whoever is playing these pranks will have no need to do so after this evening."

"Pranks, my arse. Someone's trying to bloody kill you, you half-witted little beast."

Stepping out of the doorway, Georgiana said, "I shall solve this problem myself, sir. But I am indebted to you for helping me avoid the cab. You have my undying gratitude, and I can never repay you."

"Oh, I'll think of a way, love. I'll think of a way."

She recognized the rough note in his voice and didn't dare turn to face him. Instead, she crossed the street carefully, her legs still somewhat unsteady. She joined Lady Lavinia and Lady Augusta, who had just come from different directions to meet at the carriage. Lady Augusta saw Georgiana first and scrambled into the carriage before she joined them.

"Ah, Georgiana," Lavinia said, studying them curiously. "And, Mr. Ross, how pleasant to meet you here. We were just about to set off for Threshfield."

Prudence poked her head out of the carriage window, gave Nick an ingratiating smile that changed to a scowl when she saw Georgiana. "Do hurry up, Georgiana. I'm most annoyed with you for making yourself conspicuous by running in the streets."

Nick tipped his hat to Prudence. "You saw what happened?"

"Everyone in the Quadrant saw it," the lady said. She had slipped rings on over her gloves and placed one of them on her breast as she surreptitiously let her glance fall to Nick's hips.

"But you didn't warn Lady Georgiana of the cab. I would have heard you." He gazed at Prudence speculatively.

The lady plumped her skirts and huffed. "Georgiana's quite capable of taking care of herself." She gave Nick a sly, beady glance. "And, anyway, why should I deprive you of another opportunity to lay hands upon her?"

"What are you babbling about, Prudence?" Lavinia asked. "What's this about a cab, Georgiana?"

Prudence and Nick began talking at once, with Lady Augusta popping her head out the carriage window to add her own unique interpretation of the recent events. Finally an explanation was sorted out in which, due to Nick's influence, the whole affair was deemed an accident.

Satisfied that Georgiana wasn't hurt, Lavinia addressed Nick. "Will you accompany us, Mr. Ross?"

Georgiana hastened to reply before Nick could open his mouth.

"Mr. Ross has other matters to attend to, Aunt Livy."

"Oh, I'm done," he said with a smirk at her. "You ladies go on, and I'll catch up on my mount."

Georgiana fumed as he helped Lady Lavinia into the carriage. Then his hand encircled Georgiana's arm. She pulled it free and grabbed her skirts. Setting her foot on the step, she gave a small jump to lift

herself into the carriage. She misjudged the height
and landed back in the street. His hands latched on to
her waist and propelled her up again. She ducked into
the carriage only to feel his hand on her bottom,
giving her a little shove. She gasped and turned on
him as she sat down.

"Sorry, my lady," he said with an unrepentant
grin. "Didn't want you popping back out again like a
cork."

"You ill-mannered, wretched, vulgar—"

All mocking, polite solicitude left his expression.
She looked into his eyes and suddenly felt the chill of a
glacier.

"There's no more time for play," he said quietly.

He slammed the carriage door in her face. Tip-
ping his hat, he turned on his heel, leaving her pink-
faced and sputtering. The carriage set off, throwing
her back against the squabs. Aunt Livy and the others
were staring at her.

"Really, Georgiana," Prudence huffed. "One
should be conscious of one's demeanor at all times. I
would think the daughter of a duke would know
something so rudimentary and not castigate a gentleman in public like a costermonger's wife."

Georgiana settled back against the seat and let
Prudence natter. Nick was right, drat him. Someone
was trying to harm her. The thought was so strange.
She had never been important enough for anyone to
threaten. And she was beginning to feel rather foolish
at having put herself in such a dangerous position.
What hard currency Nick would make of that if he
knew. But she wasn't going to allow him the opportunity. She would forestall further disasters by making

Threshfield admit his lies tonight. She would corner him at once when they got home.

If she didn't, Nick was going to take matters into his own hands. She'd seen it in his face. He had made up his mind before her eyes. She could very well end up tossed into a trunk and hauled back to London. What would happen if he abducted her? They would be alone on the journey back to the city. The disgraceful, uncivilized part of her that responded to Nick found this prospect enticing. The duke's daughter abhorred the idea of being compromised, of losing her dignity and her reputation. By the time the carriage reached Threshfield, Georgiana had a headache.

In spite of her discomfort she went in search of Threshfield with Nick hounding her footsteps, but the earl wasn't home. He'd gone to visit his farms in a remote part of the countryside and wasn't expected back until evening. Nick said he'd simply gone to ground in order to avoid him, Georgiana, and Aunt Livy. Her headache grew worse with Nick glowering and fuming and looming over her like some protective mastiff.

She retired to her own room with his admonishments to be alert ringing in her ears. Rebecca provided a headache powder, and she lay down to rest. She hadn't thought sleep possible after such a harrowing day, but after Rebecca closed all the drapes and sat beside the bed to read to her from *A Midsummer Night's Dream*, Georgiana felt her body grow heavy, and she slept.

She woke to find her muscles stiff from her exertions. Dressing for dinner, she chose a black damask gown of intimidating severity offset by pearls and diamonds. If she was going to browbeat Threshfield, she would need to feel and look older than she was. Dinner proved to be a painfully quiet ordeal punctuated by rigid politeness on the part of the family. Ludwig forgot to show up until halfway through the fish course. Then he arrived with a copy of an ancient Egyptian medical papyrus, which he studied throughout the meal.

Augusta was upset and tapping her little slippers against the polished floorboards. "I tell you, John, Wellington will defeat the French at Salamanca and occupy Madrid." She pointed her fork at Georgiana. "You must stop her from telling Napoleon."

"Of course, my dear," said Threshfield. He was paying more attention to his favorite dish, stewed rabbit. No one else liked it, and mutton had been served as well.

Georgiana sighed and took another bite of her mutton. Her head was still foggy from her nap, and Augusta's foibles no longer amused. She glanced up to find Nick looking at her in sympathy. His fingers were entwined around a sterling fork. They were distracting, as was the rest of his hand. The nails were neat, unblemished, the joints of his fingers small, the tips square. It was a hand that could grip with the strength of a bear, yet caress with the knowing gentleness and enticement of a sorcerer.

"Georgiana, I'm speaking to you."

She blinked and turned. Everyone was staring at her.

"I beg your pardon?" she asked.

"I've been speaking to you for the past five minutes."

She looked from one face to another around the table only to end up looking at Nick. He gave her a smirk that told her he knew exactly what had captured her attention and reveled in the knowledge. She jerked her head in Prudence's direction and refused to meet his gaze for the rest of the meal. When Prudence rose as a signal for the ladies to leave the table, Georgiana stood with the rest but paused as they filed out of the dining room.

"Threshfield, I would have a word with you in the library."

The earl was watching the butler pour the port and glanced at her uneasily. "Later this evening, my dear."

"Now, Threshfield"

"It can wait, my dear."

"Threshfield, you and I are going to have a discussion full of plain talk, especially regarding your character and conduct toward me. We can have it here in the dining room in front of the staff and the gentlemen, or we can have it in the library, privately. You have one minute in which to make your decision."

Nick gave a bark of laughter and pulled out a gold watch from his waistcoat pocket. "I'll give you the time, Threshfield."

The earl rose from his wheelchair, his flaccid skin flushed. "I'll not be ordered about in my own house!"

Georgiana only folded her arms and waited.

"Forty seconds, old chap," said Nick, squinting at his timepiece.

Evelyn threw down his napkin. "Really, Georgiana, your behavior grows more bizarre by the day." He marched out of the room.

"Twenty seconds," Nick said.

"Randall, Randall, I'm retiring to my rooms at once!"

Nick snapped his watch closed and stepped between the butler and the earl and smiled. The smile
was enough to make the servant pause. Then Nick
turned to the earl.

"Do go with her to the library, sir," he said softly.
"Otherwise I'll have to push you there myself."

Threshfield banged his cane on the floor. "I'll call
my attendants and have you both thrown out of the
house."

"You will not," Georgiana said. "You're going to
do as you're told for once, or I'll break our engagement."

"What? Breach of promise, that's what it would
be."

"Whatever it is, you won't have your pending
marriage to hold over the family if I do."

Nick walked around the wheelchair and gripped
the handles. "Come on. You've danced your dance.
Time to pay the piper."

Once in the library, Georgiana thought to ask
Nick to leave. After all, the subject of her conversation
with Threshfield was delicate. Nick rolled the earl's
chair near the fireplace and stoked the coals. She
hovered in the threshold and opened her mouth as he
rose from the grate to give her a severe look.

"Forget it," he said. He leaned a shoulder against
the Italian-marble mantel.

Compressing her lips, she shut the door and
marched over to the earl. The old man rose to meet
her, bracing himself on his cane and beaming at her
with watery eyes.

"I shall be brief," she said.

"You're always admirably succinct, my dear. It's
one of your most endearing qualities."

"Don't try to butter me, Threshfield. What you've done is unforgivable. No one would blame me for rejecting you, and if you don't retract your abominable lies at once, I will reject you. Do you know what you've done? You've driven someone to try to run me out."

"Oh, yes. I did hear something about that."

Georgiana threw up her hands. "Something? You make it sound like a mere inconvenience. Someone may be trying to kill me!"

"I'm sorry you've had a few accidents, my dear, but it's only Augusta. I'll have her watched more closely."

"Your word," Georgiana said. "I'll have your word you'll tell the truth tonight."

"Now, my dear Tomorrow will do just as well."

Nick pushed away from the mantel, took the earl's arm, and guided him, protesting, back to the wheelchair. "Stow it. Your fun is over." He winked at Georgiana, who smiled back at him and preceded them to the door.

"It's a plot," the earl said, waving his cane as Nick pushed the chair past Georgiana. "What right have you to interfere, you lowborn sod? You intrude, sir. You have no call to intrude. I told you to leave her until she was a widow, now you're acting the enraged bull."

Georgiana's hand was on the knob. She let it fall and put her back to the door. "What did you say?"

"Nothing important," Nick said with a glare at the old man.

The earl cackled and banged his cane on the floor. "Think I don't know what's going on, my dear? I see the way he looks at you. A satyr amidst wood nymphs couldn't be more randy, and you flit and swish your backside at him like—"

"You quit flapping your rotten tongue," Nick snarled.

"Oh, spare me your foolish sensibilities," the earl said. "I told you I had no objections as long as you observed the proprieties."

Georgiana's hand clenched against the stiffness of her bodice. "Dear heaven, you've discussed me between you. You've decided how to hand me about, how to share me, like some prize mare."

"Now, don't come all atwitter, my dear," the earl said. He reached out and patted her hand. "You understand how these things work. Once married and a widow, a woman becomes, shall we say, available. It's all to her own good. What's the use of drying up and blowing away from being unfulfilled?"

Nick's voice was silky. "Why, you bloody-minded old carp. If you weren't ancient and frail, I'd slit your gullet and leave you to bleed your life away."

Georgiana felt sick. Her head throbbed, and she couldn't escape imagining the scene that must have taken place between the earl and Nick. Had the earl offered her, or had Nick asked to be allowed first claim? It was all rather too much like what she'd always speculated happened in brothels. Customers lined up; the first to come had the first turn with a woman. Nausea churned in her stomach. Her stays threatened to suffocate her.

"It wasn't like that, love."

She jumped at hearing Nick's voice. He was at her side, his hand sliding around her waist. She cast it off with a quiet little shriek and yanked open the door. Before he could move, she rushed out and slammed it after her. Bursting into a run, she hurtled across the saloon, up the stairs, and into her room. There she shoved a bureau in front of the door to keep Nick from stealing inside.

Out of breath, eyes blurred with tears, she heard a knock. Nick called her name gently. Backing away from the door, she covered her ears against that velvet sound. Soon the knocking turned to pounding. Tears slid down her cheeks, and she pressed her hands tighter against her ears. She could still hear him, still imagine his tall, muscled body straining against the door. Uttering a gasp and a sob, she rushed across the sitting room and down the short hall to the cabinet.

She shut herself in and turned the key in the lock. Slowly she uncovered her ears. The pounding was faint, hardly perceptible, thanks to eighteenth century workmanship. In the darkness she fumbled for the drapes and uncovered a window to let in the moonlight. Then she retreated to a corner farthest away from the sitting room, sank to the floor, and cried.

13

The cabinet had been designed as a sort of treasure room, an elegant little chamber with plastered and paneled nooks in which were set paintings by Reynolds, Titian, and Rembrandt. Delicate Louis XIV chairs were scattered about, and there was a gilt-and-red-painted marquetry chest filled with oddities collected by various Hyde ladies—a wig said to have belonged to Charles II, one of Elizabeth I's prayer books, a gilded silver ice pail born by Tritons and topped by a Venus. In the midst of these beauties and curiosities, Georgiana Marshal wept.

She cried so hard, her stays creaked. Crouched in the billowing circle of her skirts, petticoat, and crinoline, she at first failed to perceive the discomfort her position caused. Finally, however, her tears ebbed, and she grew conscious of bone pressing into her ribs, of not being able to draw a full breath, and of sweltering amid mountains of heavy cloth. She found her kerchief tucked into the sleeve of her glove and dabbed her eyes. Straightening from her hunched posture gave some relief.

She still could hardly bear thinking about Nick asking to be first in line for her favors, of his staking a claim with Threshfield. What was worse, after she'd stopped crying so hard, she had slowly realized she wouldn't be so upset if she hadn't fallen in love with Nicholas Ross.

Then she began to understand how he had brought spark and fire into her life. What had she been but a porcelain figurine, pure, gleaming Meissen on a shelf, untouched, oblivious to the bone-wrenching turmoil of desire and attraction. Her brief attraction to Silverstone had been too superficial to compare with what she felt for Nick. At heart she'd still been a majestic but merely decorative ornament to her aristocratic world. Hardly alive and in need of quickening.

Yet over the past few days Nick had burst into her life, with his scorn for falsehood and pretension, and provoked a cleansing storm. He blew gale winds of irreverence at her that tossed aside the rules and conventions behind which she sheltered for protection.

He'd refused to be intimidated by regal dignity. Nick Ross waded through proscriptions and sacrosanct tenets of civilized society as if they were stands of rotting grass. And he'd been more real, more alive, than a hundred pampered scions of the nobility.

Slowly, without thinking about it, she had succumbed to the allure of his independent, rebellious nature. Unbound by convention, he had dared her to live. True, he was interested in art, literature, civility, but for the quality these things brought to his existence, not because they would improve his social position. But these refinements masked a ruthlessness the depth of which she hadn't suspected. He had provoked her to abandon all propriety, all honor—for his own selfish purpose.

Now she understood why Nick pulled away when it seemed they would both succumb to passion. He'd taken heed of her sketch of Society and its arrangements for the sexual entertainment of married women. She had outright told him he could wait a few months and have what he wanted without the risks that came with seducing a duke's daughter. She'd been more than a fool. She'd been stupid.

And it was too late for wisdom, because, despite his ruthless manipulation, she couldn't seem to kill her desire for Nicholas Ross. Nor could she murder her love for him. She loved his bravery, his impudent humor, his championing of misused children with her brother, and most of all his emancipation from the iron rule of Society. He had done what she wished to do, what she would do.

She would continue in her plans to marry Threshfield, the old misery. There were few other options. And, after all, what was different now? Very little except that she felt as if she had a dried-up, shriveled acorn for a heart. What else could she do but marry and gain her freedom? What else was there for her to do?

First thing in the morning she would make Threshfield get a special license. They would marry, and Mr. Nicholas Ross could take himself back to Texas. There she hoped he would fall prey to Comanches or rattlesnakes, preferably both.

Meanwhile, she had cried enough for now. Dukes' daughters didn't cry the whole night over lost

loves. Dukes' daughters stiffened their spines and got
on with the business of living, even if life seemed to
offer only the prospect of unending, bleak grayness.

Using a corner table for leverage, she rose, listening for sounds outside the sitting room. All was silent.
Nick must have given up. She would remain in the
cabinet for a while longer, just in case he returned to
accost her. Hearing his voice again would bring on
more foolish tears. In the meantime she would rid
herself of this cursed crinoline.

Georgiana struggled with her gown, hiking it
over one shoulder so that she could reach behind her
back and untie her petticoat and crinoline. The hoop
and lacy covering dropped. She let go of her skirt,
lifted it, and stepped across the contraption. Picking it
up, she leaned it against the wall and draped her petticoat over a chair.

Sighing, she looked around the room for a lamp
and saw one on a small Louis XVI desk. She took a
step toward it. Her foot caught in the hem of her
gown, and she stumbled forward, nearly ending up on
the floor. She'd forgotten that the gown had been
made for use with the crinoline, and that it dragged
on the ground when unsupported.

She was gathering her skirt in both hands when
she heard a soft rush of sound behind her. Turning,
she beheld a dark shadow in an open window. It
seemed to slither into the room and loom over her in
less than a second. She was so startled, she failed to cry
out, and before she could protest, the intruder was
upon her. Georgiana gave a little cry, then filled her
lungs for a loud shout. The intruder jumped as if
surprised and clamped a hand over her mouth.

"Bleeding hell, George. That screeching would

make a ghoul piss in his shroud." Nick moved so that
he stood in a pale shaft of moonlight.

Knocking Nick's hand aside, Georgiana hissed in
a shaking voice, "Wretched vermin, you frightened
me. Must you steal about like a criminal?"

"I must if you keep barricading doors. You and I
have got to talk."

"We do not. I've no intention of speaking to you.
Ever. Get out."

"Now, George."

She couldn't endure his presence. Striding to the
door, she tried to yank it open. Her hand slipped off
the immovable knob.

"You locked it," Nick said. "That's why I came
through the window."

She turned the key in the lock and opened the
door, but it slammed back into place when Nick put
the flat of his hand on its panels.

She turned on him. "As God is in heaven, I hate
you. Get out of my sight before I scream."

"I didn't do it, love."

"What?" She was tired and confused by her pain
and fury.

Nick kept his hand against the door and leaned
down to speak softly. She could feel his breath on her
bare shoulder.

"I didn't stake a claim on you. I swear it in the
name of my dead sister. Her name was Tessie. Did you
know that? She died at the hands of a man who
bought her for an evening. She was just a little girl."

He stopped as his voice grew unsteady, then continued. "So, you see, I mean it, love. Tessie's name is
sacred to me, and I swear by it to you, because—
because you're important to me. Threshfield accused

me of wanting you and told me I should wait my turn.
I told him to stow it. He's an evil old bastard, and you
fell for one of his mischiefmaking lies."

"Oh." She was trying to make sense of her feelings—relief, uncertainty, fear.

"Oh? Is that your answer? Oh?"

"Oh, dear." She was going to cry! Dukes' daughters didn't cry in the presence of gentlemen.

He towered over her, a dark bulk that blocked out
the meager light from the moon. "What's wrong?
You sound strange. Are you all right, love?"

"I—I thought you'd taken my story about married women as advice. I thought—"

"Did you, love?"

"Please don't call me that."

"Why not?"

"It's so frivolous, and love isn't. It's most serious, I
assure you."

"What makes you think I mean it frivolously?"

She couldn't see his face well. His eyes were dark,
his expression severe, and she could barely get out her
next words.

"Am I mistaken?"

"Bloody hell, yes."

"Oh."

"Oh again. Is that all you're going to say?"

"I don't know what to do. There were no lessons
for this in boarding school." Georgiana lowered her
head and breathed Nick's name on a sigh.

At first he didn't respond. Then she felt a tug on
her hand.

"What are you doing?"

"I told you not to say my name that way." He

pulled her long glove off her hand and began to slide the other one down her arm.

"Nick," she whispered. "Nick, this isn't proper."

"Hmmm?"

His fingers touched her wrist lightly, then skimmed up the back of her arm slowly, and she shivered. His arms came around her, and she rested her head on his shoulder.

"I would never do anything to hurt you, love."

Georgiana heard the tension in his voice and lifted her head. He was staring into the darkness as if engaged in some agonizing inner argument. His body strained against hers, and his arms tightened around her. She sensed his turmoil and suspected the reason.

"Nick?"

He shut his eyes. "Bloody hell, don't say it again!"

"But I like what it does to you."

His eyes opened and he looked down at her, his lips parted in surprise. "Oh."

"Nick," she breathed. "Nick, Nick, Nicholas."

She got no further, because his lips sealed her mouth. She fell against the door, and there he shoved his body against hers. Her breasts swelled against his chest, making her respond by trying to devour his mouth. Her fingers dug through his coat to sink into his back. He groaned and thrust his hips against her.

Georgiana felt a wave of heat burst within her and rush to her head. She had never realized the power she had over him, and now she had provoked an explosion, one so full of excitement and pleasure that she was afraid it wouldn't last. To perdition with breeding and refinement. The feel of his body offered gratification incomparable to either, and she was going to have it.

His mouth was working its way from her lips to her throat, down to the tops of her breasts. She was surprised when her gown suddenly came loose and fell around her hips, and even more surprised when her corset followed the gown. Suddenly she felt cool air on her breasts. She was blushing, but it was too dark for him to see that. Not that he would have, anyway, because he was looking at her breasts.

"You are amazing, love."

He didn't give her time to answer. Bending down, he took her nipple into his mouth. Startled, Georgiana cried out. Lightning shafted through her breast and down her arms and legs. Her head fell back and bumped the door even as she thrust her breast forward and clutched his shoulders.

He nibbled at her, and she nearly went mad. Her nails clawed at his back. At the feel of them Nick cast aside his coat and shirt. When he came back to her, Georgiana stopped him and made him stay still while she stroked her palms over his shoulders in a wide sweep. His skin was smooth, and beneath it his muscles surged at the contact with her skin.

She came closer, slipped her arms around him, and raked her nails over his back. Nick arched, then rammed her against the door again. Her breasts swelled against his chest, and she felt crisp hairs prickle her skin even as his teeth skimmed across her shoulder and down to her nipples. Churning, hot tension was building between her legs, making Georgiana want to cry out.

He seemed to understand and his hands followed the ache. He caressed her hips as they smoothed her gown over them. Her undergarments vanished, but she hardly cared because she was too busy concentrating on where his fingers traveled. Without warning his mouth opened near her ear, and she felt him breathe. It was as if his sweet breath pierced her body. A jolt of delicious sensation traveled down to the triangle between her legs. She gasped, but his breath turned to reassuring whispers. Murmuring her name, he stepped back, swept his gaze over her with a look of fierce appreciation.

Only then did she realize that he was as naked as she. Taking her hands, he spread her arms wide, backed her against the door and gently crushed her between the wood and his body. She felt him press against the ache between her legs and abruptly understood that this was the way to greater pleasure. He whispered encouragement while moving against her gently.

Soon his gentleness wasn't enough. She widened her stance, allowing him to fit against her, and moved in her own rhythm. He followed her, his hips thrusting, his lips murmuring endearments against her mouth. Then, when she was gasping and clawing his back, he pulled away. She reached for him, but he was spreading her gown on the carpet.

Pulling her to him, he knelt before her and kissed the curve of her hips, her thighs, her knees. Then his tongue snaked a path up her inner thigh and touched her between her legs. His hands roamed over her to caress her breasts as his mouth began to kiss her. In moments her chest was heaving, and she couldn't stop herself from sinking her fingers into his hair. She braced her legs apart and whimpered. At the sound Nick suddenly pulled her to the floor, parted her legs, and lay between them. Georgiana was desperate now, sinking her nails into his back and moaning. He raised over her, thrust his hips against her to spread her legs farther, and stopped. She clawed at him, but he held back.

"Say it," he whispered roughly. "Say my name."

The word came out on a groan as he slipped inside her, and ended on a gasp at the pinch she felt. He eased his way into moist flesh. Georgiana felt the pressure she had been craving and forgot the pinch. When he began to move, she moved with him, feeling again the grinding, irresistible build of pleasure. He never stopped. Pushing against her relentlessly, his thrusts made the ache inside her swell and swell.

Their movements quickened, grew more violent. Georgiana grabbed his hips, lifted her own, and cried out over and over. As her cries subsided, Nick added his own as he rammed deeply inside her. She felt him swell within her body, then burst and release. She went still as she savored this strange new feeling of his erupting inside her.

Breathing hard, Nick sank on top of her to find her lips with his. He kissed her hard, then softened his touch and played with her tongue. She smiled, causing him to smile as well.

"Most improper, Mr. Ross."

"Most delicious, young George."

He nipped at the tip of her nose. She yelped and pinched his buttocks, starting a wrestling match. Georgiana twisted beneath him, dislodging him and climbing on top. She felt a rush of moisture from her body. She gasped looking down.

"Oh, dear," she said.

"It's natural." When she only stared at him, he got up, took her hand, and kissed it. "Come with me."

She followed him out of the cabinet to her bedroom, where he helped her wash in the water basin. She bathed him with a wet cloth, pausing as it smoothed over a tight hillock of muscle on his buttock. She remembered the plunge bath and wondered if it was permissible to . . .

"You're going to find out," he said.

"What?"

"You were thinking of the plunge bath, wondering if people came together in the water."

"How did you know that?"

"I know you, love. And, besides, I was thinking the same thing."

"Do you think we could go there tonight?"

"Not so soon after the first time, love. Here, you're too free with that damned cloth."

He yanked it from her hand as she slid it up his inner thigh. She slipped her arms around his bare waist. He discarded the cloth and raked his fingers through her hair until it tumbled down her shoulders and back to curl over her bottom. Then he cupped her buttocks through the sheen of curls and drew her close.

Georgiana fastened her hands in his hair and pulled his head down. She slipped her tongue inside his mouth and sucked, following his example. In an instant she felt him stir and grow against her hips.

He lifted his head. "You're tempting me, you little beast."

Her hand ran down his ribs, caressed his hip, and smoothed across his thigh. She could feel the play of sinews and the fine hairs on his leg. She explored the texture of his skin where it encased his biceps, felt with her mouth the shiver that passed over him. Fasci-

nated with the way she could make him respond, she
nibbled her way up his shoulder to gently nuzzle the
bend of his neck.

"Love," he whispered. "We shouldn't. We've already done the forbidden."

"I know. I couldn't help it." She ran her fingers
down his back to his buttocks and squeezed.

Nick gasped, then laughed. "Neither could I, and
I tried."

"You did? Yes, you did. Why?"

He didn't answer at first. Lowering his head, he
kissed her shoulder, then sighed.

"This is a grave matter. I've gone against my own
rule, and now I'm genuine damned."

"We're both sinners, but you're not making
sense," Georgiana said.

"Let's dress, and then we'll talk."

"You sound angry," she said with growing alarm.
"The more you talk, the angrier you sound."

"Don't come all atwitter at this late hour, young
George."

"It's you who seems to be coming all atwitter."

Aunt Livy's call from the sitting-room door forestalled an argument. Georgiana hurried to the blocked
door and answered.

"Come out of there. Threshfield has taken violently ill. He's so bad, the housekeeper's medicines
haven't helped, and we've sent for the doctor in town.
Georgiana, he's delirious."

Nick joined her but said nothing.

"I'll be out directly, Aunt Livy."

They turned to stare at each other.

"Awful sudden, this illness," Nick said. "Does he
take sick like this often?"

"No. He's never been delirious that I remember."

He grabbed her hand and walked quickly back to the bedroom. "Looks like we'll have to fight some other time."

"I didn't want to fight at all."

Nick threw a dressing gown at her. "That'll change quick."

"What are you talking about, Nicholas Ross?"

"Bleeding hell, woman, this is no time to go saying my name in that deep, rough voice!"

A few minutes later, after Nick had stolen back to his own rooms, Georgiana emerged from hers fully dressed in one of her work gowns. Closing the door, she pulled her spectacles from her apron pocket and put them on. Her fingers were cold, but her cheeks were still burning from her recent momentous experience. She lifted her gaze and saw Nick coming toward her. He hadn't bothered to do more than throw a coat over his open shirt. Taking her arm, he hurried her toward the earl's chambers.

"Your aunt says to come quickly, love. The old scoundrel is in a bad way."

As they entered Threshfield's sitting room, Georgiana heard the sound of breaking glass. Evelyn and Prudence burst from the bedroom, hopping over an ottoman like frightened rabbits. A china basin sailed after them and hit the suit of armor standing beside the bedroom door. A torrent of obscenities pursued the pair all the way out. Evelyn stopped long enough to give Georgiana and Nick a rancid glare before he slammed the outer door shut. Nick gripped her arm tighter when the earl's thin, hysterical voice sounded.

"Where is she, where is she, where is she, where is she?"

Aunt Lavinia appeared and beckoned to them. "Hurry, my dears. He wants to see you, Georgiana."

"Come on, love," Nick said with a reassuring squeeze of her hand.

In the bedroom, lamps cast long shadows. They danced about the dark room as people moved around the sickbed. Georgiana started as she passed a diorite statue of an Assyrian king set in a corner. Drawing courage from Nick's silent strength, she set her jaw, straightened her spine and approached the raving old man. He was propped up in the middle of a curtained bed, weaving from side to side. Dressed in a night-gown that hung limply on his thin body, the old man cursed the housekeeper and the newly arrived doctor. The physician was trying to take the earl's pulse, but the patient kept thrashing about and calling him a giant toad.

"Listen," Nick whispered to her as they neared the bed.

"He doesn't mean those things. He's delirious."

"No, *listen*."

She tried to disregard the earl's ranting, and then she heard it—a loud, steady pounding accompanied by the old man's frantic breathing.

Alarmed, Georgiana rushed to the bed. "Thresh-field!"

At the sound of her voice, the earl sprang up from the pillows and lunged at her. He grabbed her wrist and would have pulled her onto the bed if Nick hadn't thrust himself between them and broken his grip. The earl crouched before them, breathing heavily and squinting.

"I can't see. Georgiana? My dear Georgiana?"

"Threshfield, you're ill. Lay back and try to be calm while the doctor treats you." She put her hand over the earl's, but he threw her off.

"Toads!" he shrieked. "Toads hopping all over the floor. Get them off my bed. Get them off me!"

"Threshfield, listen to me, please." She reached out only to have her hand knocked away by the earl's flailing arms.

Nick put his arm around her and drew her back. The doctor tried to get the earl to drink some preparation he'd just concocted, but Threshfield knocked the cup away, lunged up, then collapsed. His body jerked and writhed as it hit the bed.

Georgiana cried out and tried to go to him, but Nick stepped in her way. Facing her, his arm came up as she tried to shove past him. He held her against his body and spoke quietly.

"No, love. He's too far gone."

She looked up into his face and saw regret, certainty, and something mysterious and foreboding. Looking from the convulsing figure on the bed and back to Nick, she asked a question with her eyes.

"I'm sorry, love."

Aunt Livy appeared again, her arms full of clean towels. She took one look at the earl's spasming body and addressed Nick.

"Get her out of here."

"But what if he calls for me again? I want to be near so that I can comfort him."

Aunt Livy exchanged glances with Nick, then left them alone. Nick took Georgiana's hands in his and

turned her so that she couldn't see the bed and what
was happening.

Drawing her close, he said, "I've seen blokes this
sick before, love." He placed his hand on her cheek.
"He isn't going to—"

"Oh, no." Tears blinded her. Quickly taking off
her spectacles, she rubbed her eyes and dropped the
glasses in her apron pocket. Then she turned back to
see the doctor and the housekeeper trying to bind the
earl's contorted body to the bed with sheets. Nick
tried to move her, but she set her feet.

"We're in the way now," he said firmly. "There's
nothing we can do for him."

She shook her head, but Nick slipped his arm
around her shoulders again, circled her wrist with his
free hand and forced her to turn away.

"I can't leave him!"

"Yes, you can, love, because you know he
wouldn't want you to see him like this. The old rascal
is bleeding proud."

Georgiana stopped resisting then and began to
sob. As Nick guided her out of the room, she cast a
last glance over her shoulder. All she saw was a
shroud-white sheet distorted by the earl's agony. Her
vision blurred, and she closed her eyes, trusting Nick
to see for them both. She knew they were in the hall
somewhere, but as they walked, she had to blink away
tears again. When her vision cleared, she found that
Nick had escorted her to a parlor near the top of the
stairs and closed the door.

He plucked her handkerchief from her sleeve and
handed it to her. "Sit down for a moment before you
join the family. They won't be any better behaved in

this situation than they have been in others less difficult."

Georgiana allowed him to take her to a settee
upholstered in gold damask. Her mind refused clarity.
Stray thoughts wandered in and out of her perception
as Nick found a liquor cabinet and poured sherry. Her
fingers traced the floral design woven into the damask.
The material was so polished she had almost slid off
the first time she'd sat on the settee.

Nick was back. He handed her a glass full of amber liquid. Georgiana took a sip, then grimaced and
handed it back to him. He took it and held it to her
lips.

"Drink it all, love. You're going to need it."

"I don't want it—oh, very well. You're such a
despot." She drank the rest of the sherry and patted
her lips with her handkerchief. She could hear hurried
footsteps in the hall outside. Her tears started falling
again. "Poor Threshfield. Poor, poor Threshfield."

Nick took the sherry glass from her and set it on
the floor. Grasping her shoulders, he turned her to
face him.

"Look at me, love. I know you're upset, but I've
got to talk to you before we go downstairs."

"How could this have happened," Georgiana
whispered. "He was fine today. His heart wasn't giving him any trouble, and he's been careful not to
overdo, used his wheelchair as the doctor ordered."

"Bloody hell, love, it ain't his heart," Nick said
harshly. At her surprised look, he swore and began
again. "Sorry love, but I seen this kind o' thing before—the loud heartbeat, the ravings, the fits. This
ain't his heart. It's something else."

Georgiana glanced at the closed door, distracted

by the voices of servants rushing between the kitchen and the earl's bedroom. "Yes?"

"I seen it in St. Giles, all over the East End. He's got hold of some drug."

Turning her gaze back to Nick, Georgiana attempted to make sense of what Nick was saying. He sat there, his dark hair falling over his forehead, his strong hands holding hers in a reassuring grip, his pliant lips taut and severe. He wasn't making some foul joke. He was serious. Her body grew suddenly cold.

"Will he die in pain," she asked.

He shook his head. "He'll fall into a stupor from which he will never recover."

"How do you know—"

"Not now, love. Just trust me."

Georgiana closed her eyes and pressed her fingertips to her temples. "I can't think. This is so bizarre." She felt his hands encircle her wrists and drag her arms down. Looking up at him, she met a gaze so intense that it banished her confusion and grief for a moment.

"You understand what I'm saying?" he asked.

Her mouth had gone dry so she nodded.

His eyes held hers without wavering. "Then you know what you have to do, love."

"Yes," she whispered.

Drawing in a long, deep breath, she rose. He dropped her wrists and stood with her.

"Evelyn and the others will be in the drawing room," Nick said. "Are you sure you're ready to face them?"

Stuffing her handkerchief into her sleeve, Georgiana gave a shuddering sigh. "Will you come with me?"

"Course. You can do it, love. It's only for a bit longer."

His hand clasped her arm again. Strangely, the feel of that warm grasp caused tears to well in her eyes again. She was losing a dear friend, and another even more dear stood at her side. She gave Nick a quick, sad smile.

"I'm ready. And don't worry. I know what I have to do."

14

Shortly after noon the next morning, Nick strode into his bedroom at Threshfield, yanked open a bureau drawer, and stuck his hands inside. He withdrew handfuls of underwear and handkerchiefs and hurled them onto the white damask bedspread. He strode over to a wardrobe, reached over his head, and pulled down a suitcase. This he threw onto the bed beside the linens.

"Pertwee, Perrrrrr —tweeeee!" Opening the suitcase, he scooped up a pile of handkerchiefs and dropped them into it. "Perrrrrrr—oh, there you are."

Pertwee marched into the bedroom holding a pair of freshly polished riding boots, nostrils quivering, bearing erect. "Sir bellowed?" The valet didn't wait for an answer. "Sir has forgotten his decorum. May I remind him of the words of Lord Chesterfield? 'Manners must adorn knowledge and smooth its way through the world.' The mark of a gentleman is that he is composed at all times."

"Sod Lord Chesterfield," Nick said as he stuck his

head inside the wardrobe to search among the coats
and waistcoats. "You can tell him that from me."

"Happily, Lord Chesterfield is no longer with us,
sir."

Hair tousled, Nick emerged from the wardrobe
with his arms full and staggered to the bed. He
dumped a load of shirts into the suitcase.

"We're going to scarper, Pertwee. Move your
arse."

"Sir can hardly remove before the funeral."

"Yes, sir can. That fool of a country doctor and
the coroner have declared Threshfield's death a natural
one. They're stupid or conniving with Evelyn bloody
Hyde. Either way, I'm not staying to find out. And
since Lady Georgiana no longer has a reason to stay
here, my work is done." Nick closed the suitcase and
picked it up.

"I overheard Rebecca, her lady's maid, say that
her mistress would remain for a few weeks."

Nick dropped the suitcase and turned on Pertwee.
"When?"

"Only a few moments ago."

Walking past the suitcase, Nick sat on the bed. "I
told her I thought he'd been poisoned."

"And Lady Georgiana said she would be leaving?"

"Hmm. She didn't actually say that."

What Georgiana had said was that she knew what
she had to do. He'd assumed she agreed with him that
they should both leave. Now he realized what he
should have known when he first revealed his suspicions. She might be grief-stricken, but Georgiana
Marshal was up to something.

He glanced at the valet. "Have you heard how the
earl died?"

"The butler said it was some kind of seizure, sir."

"Look, Pertwee, you know where I came from, and how much I've seen. That wasn't no seizure. He had a racy heart, blurred vision, galloping pulse. His skin was hot and dry and red, and you could hear his heart across the room. Later he got belligerent, then succumbed to a fever and convulsions. At the last he went into a stupor."

"How terrible."

"Right. Terrible and familiar."

Pertwee set the riding boots down and came closer, glancing around the room as if afraid of being overheard.

"Are you suggesting, er . . ."

"Right."

"Then sir must go to the authorities."

"Oh, right, Pertwee. Me, I'll just trot along to the justice of the peace, Sir Nigel bloody Mainwaring, Evelyn bloody Hyde's old school chum, and tell him I think old Threshfield was poisoned. Rum, that. Do you know the first person he'll suspect? Not his old school companion, not any of these fine, blue-blooded twits who couldn't wait to get their hands on his blunt. No. The first bloke he'll suspect is me, who ain't one of 'em, who didn't go to Oxford or Cambridge, and whose blood is plain old red."

Nick chewed on his lips, then glanced sideways at Pertwee. "You say Lady Georgiana is staying."

"Yes, sir."

Running a hand through his hair, Nick cursed silently. He hadn't wanted to admit the real reason he was in such a hurry to leave Threshfield. The cold light of this bright fall day had brought back his sanity. He had succumbed to weakness, to low, roiling lust, and betrayed his dearest friend. Jocelin had saved him from a life of squalid misery and certain hanging, and Nick had repaid him by soiling the virtue of his young sister. And he'd compounded that betrayal by falling in love with her.

Making love to Georgiana had been unlike anything he'd ever experienced. To him intercourse had always been a transaction—pleasure traded for pleasure, or money, or some other commodity. Early on, it had been something frightening, especially the night his father had traded him for settlement of a debt owed at a tavern.

After that he learned to protect himself, to hide, or to endure. As he grew older, he became master of his own body and bestowed his favors seldom. Once he'd left St. Giles and learned about Society from Jocelin, he'd kept his dalliances separate from his life among the noble and rich—at first. But he'd found that certain ladies were quite tempting, and so willing to risk their reputations for a chance to be with him. They found him enticingly dangerous and intriguing; he found them amusing, so long as they kept the affair in its proper place.

Then he'd encountered Georgiana—stately, infuriating Georgiana. Knowing her was like living with a hive of bees under his skin. He couldn't make her do what he wanted, a problem he had never had with women. Yet he couldn't dismiss her. She visited his thoughts when he least expected her, and wrought consuming, hot changes in his body without his consent. She plagued him and teased him until he'd finally lost all compunction. And being with her had been different.

Different because she hadn't wanted anything

from him except to be with him. Coming together
with her had been no transaction, no deal, no salacious game instigated by a curious and bored noblewoman. For the first time he glimpsed the feelings
heralded by the great writers he admired but never
understood and never, ever believed.

"Pertwee, where is that book by that Scottish fellow?"

"Sir Walter Scott, sir?"

"That's him."

The valet produced the book. Nick opened it and
began thumbing through the pages as he walked away
from the bed and the suitcase.

"Ah, here it is." He wandered into the sitting
room as he read.

> True love's the gift which God has given
> To man alone beneath the heaven:
> It is not fantasy's hot fire,
> Whose wishes, soon as granted, fly;
> It liveth not in fierce desire,
> With dead desire it doth not die;
> It is the secret sympathy,
> The silver link, the silken tie,
> Which heart to heart and mind to mind
> In body and in soul can bind.

He'd read that only a few weeks ago and hadn't
understood it. But last night he'd satiated himself with
Georgiana, and still he hadn't quenched this emo-
tional thirst he had for her. Always before, his interest
had faded with conquest. But last night he had looked
into Georgiana's emerald eyes and realized that he
would want to be with her next week, next year, for

as long as he could imagine. And he couldn't have her.

Once freed of the distraction Georgiana always caused in his thoughts, Nick had come to his senses. For hours he'd gone over and over the situation. He had hurt Georgiana and Jocelin, although they didn't know it yet.

Jos had endured enough pain and treachery from his own family. Jos had trusted him. Nick slumped into a chair and squeezed his eyes shut, as if to hide from the sight of his own perfidy. He had defiled Jocelin's sister. It was like defiling Jos himself. If she had been any other young woman, he could have wiped out the transgression by marrying her. But he wouldn't compound the sin by fooling himself that he could marry Georgiana.

If he did that, he would shame her and Jocelin too. No one would receive a woman who had married so far beneath her. Society would shut her out. The duke would disown Georgiana. Jocelin might put on a brave face, for he was kind and gentle, but he would be shamed nonetheless. No, he had already endangered Georgiana. He wouldn't ruin her completely.

He had decided to leave and write Georgiana a letter of apology later. That had been before he understood she was remaining at Threshfield. She couldn't stay in a household with a murderer loose.

Perhaps she hadn't believed him when he had spoken to her of poisoning. He would make her understand. And hope she understood that last night was a mistake. Surely she would. She was a duke's daughter and knew that an alliance with the likes of him would be impossible. His real worry would be that she

might want to continue to see him secretly. This he
couldn't do and keep his sanity. He would make her
understand.

With this self-sacrificing and noble aim in mind,
Nick went in search of Georgiana. He needed to meet
her secretly in order to explain himself. Yes, it was
better this way. He really couldn't scarper without
talking to her first. Stopping a maid on the landing, he
learned that Georgiana was with the family in the
drawing room where tea was being served. Callers had
begun to arrive to pay their respects and were being
received there.

He raced downstairs and went to the library. He
wanted to enter the drawing room unobtrusively
through the connecting door. He walked into the
room with its wall-to-wall bookshelves topped with
pediments. As he approached the door to the drawing
room, a click sounded in a section of bookshelves,
which began to swing back. A small, wizened face
topped with a lace cap appeared behind the shelf and
hissed at him.

"Psst!"

"Damnation, Lady Augusta, what are you doing
in there?"

"Wellington, I knew you'd come once you heard
the terrible news. In here, quickly."

She grabbed his arm, hauled him into the darkness, and pulled the shelf closed after them. He was
lost in a black void, anchored only by her thin hand.
Then he heard the click of a lock, and a narrow door
opened slightly to admit a sliver of light from the
outside.

The sky was overcast, with flat-bottomed blue-
gray clouds scudding across it. He could see Lady

Augusta now. Her childlike face was streaked with
tears, and she searched in a reticule for a lacy handkerchief, which she touched to the corners of her eyes.

"I'm sorry for your grief, Lady Augusta."

"Pray excuse me, Wellington, but this wouldn't
have happened if you'd arrested that spy as I asked.
Now you really must summon more decision of character, and speedily. Everyone thinks my brother's
death is due to some defect in his brain, but I know he
was poisoned by that French spy. You must have her
shot at once."

"My lady, I'm not Wellington—"

"Of course not. Not here among fools and spies.
No doubt you've hidden your men in the woods.
When she goes riding, set upon her. Whist! Did you
hear anything?"

Nick was still having trouble adjusting to his
change of identity. "What? No."

"You'll get rid of her, won't you? Or would you
prefer that I—"

"No, no, I'll do it." He put a hand on the lady's
arm. "Don't trouble yourself, Lady Augusta. I'll get
rid of the French spy. Don't do anything. It will take
me a few days to arrange matters so that Napoleon
doesn't suspect we're responsible. That wouldn't do,
you know. He might send more agents, and then you
might be in danger."

"Don't refine too much upon that," Lady Au-
gusta said. "I can take care of myself. But poor John
Charles couldn't." She sniffled into her handkerchief.
"Be careful, Wellington. She's clever."

Slipping through the outer door, she left him
alone in the dark. Nick felt around the walls until he
found a latch, lifted it, and pulled. The bookshelf

swung open, and he emerged into the library. Closing the shelf, he shook his head, muttering to himself.

"She thinks I'm Wellington now. Must be the strain of the earl's death. Poor lady."

Slipping into the drawing room, he found a gloomy scene waiting for him. Windows and doors had been draped with black crepe. Prudence, Evelyn, and their guests all wore black. The earl's portrait, which hung on the wall beside the fireplace, was festooned in black cloth.

On a settee in front of the fire, Lady Lavinia was comforting Ludwig, who was dabbing his eyes with a black-bordered handkerchief while clutching a volume on ancient Egyptian magic. Prudence and Evelyn were conferring with two gentlemen. They bent over a heavy volume set on a table. It appeared to be a catalog of mourning accoutrements.

Nick sidled up behind them and glanced at descriptions of mourning wares—everything from carriages, plumes, and black-bordered stationery to widows' bands. He slipped away before the group noticed him and joined Georgiana, who was staring out a window.

As he approached, she turned and saw him. Her severe expression vanished. Like emeralds flashing in the light of a thousand candles, her eyes brightened and a smile filled with the joy of angels greeted him. She had smiled at him like that last night, and he had felt his legs turn to water. Now, in the sober reflection of daylight, its brilliance increased his dread and alarm. He'd really done it this time.

She offered her hand. He held it and bent over it, brushing his lips across her skin. She murmured a greeting in that soft voice he'd never heard her use except when they were alone.

"I must speak to you," he said before she could say something he would regret.

"Yes?"

"Not here."

She was smiling again, as if she had anticipated his request.

"I thought you understood. It's dangerous here. You should leave."

"Oh, about that. If you're certain Threshfield was poisoned, I have to stay and find his murderer."

"Damn it!"

"Shhh."

He glanced around to find Lady Lavinia scowling at them in disapproval. He lowered his voice.

"We must talk, and not just about leaving. There's something else. About last night. I got to tell you something." He caught a glimpse of Evelyn staring in their direction. "Bloody hell. He's going to come over here. Look at him, all swelled up with self-importance. Looks like he swallowed a hot-air balloon. Quick, where shall we meet?"

"The grotto, after tea."

"You keep away from Evelyn bloody Hyde," he snapped.

She concealed a smile by turning to face the window again. "You're jealous."

"Am not."

"You most certainly are." Georgiana looked at him from beneath dark lashes, her cheeks pink. "Poor Threshfield is dead, and I shouldn't feel like this."

Nick saw her flush and cursed. "Listen, love, I got to ask you a question."

"I know."

"You do?"

"I have been out since I was eighteen, Nick."

"What has that got to do with—"

Evelyn was upon them, gabbling on about funeral arrangements and letters to be written to relatives, requesting Georgiana's help. Nick fell silent. He and Georgiana were dragged to the chairs around the fireplace when Randall and two footmen arrived with tea. Nick sat holding a cup of wafer-thin china and tried to figure out what Georgiana had been talking about. Her meaning eluded him, and he fell to planning what he would say to her in the grotto.

No need to mince words. She was a sensible woman, practical. He would tell her the truth, part of it anyway. That was best. He'd been wrong to get the wind up simply because she smiled at him. All in his imagination. She would understand that St. Giles didn't marry Grosvenor Square. Perhaps she would even broach the subject first. That was it. No wonder she said she knew what he wanted to say.

A burning weight of anxiety lifted from his heart. Nick sipped his tea and leaned back in his chair, relieved. Of course. She was a duke's daughter and understood how things had to be. He'd been a fool. There was nothing to worry about. Georgiana Marshal was a sensible, practical young woman.

15

After tea Georgiana slipped away from the drawing room and changed into a black riding habit with bowler hat and filmy scarf. She took a quiet little roan mare from the stables and set out on a path that wound around the perimeter of the Threshfield park. She didn't want anyone to know her real destination, so she left word that she would be riding on the bridle path that led to the ruined dower house. As soon as she was out of sight of the house, she turned off the path and headed for the wood. The grotto lay almost at its heart.

As she rode, Georgiana allowed herself to feel the happiness she'd had to conceal while among the grieving family members. Her emotions pitched violently back and forth from sadness at losing Threshfield to jubilant exhilaration at having found Nick. Once away from Threshfield's home and family, she could forget grief and suspicion about murder for a while.

She had found what she'd never thought to

have—someone to love and who loved her. Nick, with his tawny beauty and irreverent humor, had upset all her intentions and at the same time bestowed upon her a gift of unparalleled magnificence.

He had banished her old fears. Now they seemed foolish. Being touched by a man wasn't frightening; when Nick touched her, he made her want to touch him back. And he savored her body, which was an amazing discovery. Apparently no one had told him that ladies had to be small in stature, generously endowed, and delicately made. He had whispered to her that he relished her abundance of leg and her strength. Yet he was so much stronger and taller that she never felt the ungainly, loutish giant. When she was with him, all the years of feeling like a freakish colossus melted away.

She was blessed. Blessed in finding a young man who wasn't threatened by her rank, in whose eyes she was beautiful, and whom she could admire for his character and his beauty. But all the same, she was worried. Despite his defiance of Society, he was having a difficult time making a declaration. She had seen this in the drawing room. He was brave, but anyone's composure would be disturbed by the prospect of asking a duke's daughter for her hand. Several of her former suitors had been, according to her father.

It was up to her to ease the way for him. She could begin by leading the conversation to the topic of scandals. There had always been scandals about girls running off with men who were beneath them—penniless younger sons, guardsmen, grooms, footmen. She would point out that Catherine of Valois, widow of Henry V, had married her clerk of the wardrobe,

Owen Tudor. And look what happened to the
Tudors; they became kings and queens of England.

Then she might even say how she was lucky not
to be in the position of Her Majesty, Queen Victoria.
The queen had been obliged to propose to Prince
Albert because of the difference in their ranks, her
being a queen regnant. Nick knew Georgiana wasn't
so exalted. Such comments would put him at ease and
smooth his way. That was all he needed. And if all else
failed, she would make her own declaration. She
could always jolt him out of his uncharacteristic diffi-
dence by going down on one knee and asking for his
hand. They would laugh at her reversal of their parts,
and all would be settled.

Then they could get on to the serious business of
investigating the circumstances of poor Threshfield's
death. The earl had been a friend to her, a peevish and
irritating friend, but a friend. He'd been willing to
help her when she needed it most. If someone had
killed him, she wouldn't let his murderer go unpun-
ished.

She had reached the small ravine in the woods
where the earl had built the grotto. A tiny rivulet
meandered through the trees to dance over the lip of
an overhang and fall to a man-made stream below.
Thick ferns clung to the overhang and cascaded down
to partially conceal a cave in which had been placed a
white marble statue of a reclining Venus. Below the
waterfall the narrow stream had been directed to the
right and left, and Bacchus cavorted on a pedestal in
the middle of the right branch. Other statues of Greek
and Roman gods and goddesses had been placed
around the clearing bordered by the two branches. A

copy of the Apollo Belvedere stood in a nest of ferns. Cupid lurked in a nest of ivy.

Georgiana tethered her horse and descended stone stairs set in the embankment of the ravine. On her way down she passed figures of Ariadne and Mercury. Once on the floor of the ravine, she looked up at a canopy of trees bearing leaves of gold, bronze, and sunset-orange. She sat on a bench beside a fountain. In its center cavorted three satyrs. Overhead, gray-and-purple clouds streamed by while the wind whipped up leaves and made them dance. After watching them for a while Georgiana grew restless and went to examine the grotto.

She was tossing pebbles into the stream when she heard the crackle of dead leaves. Lifting her gaze, she scanned the top of the ravine but could see nothing but trees. A gust loosened a few leaves and sailed them down into the grotto. A sound made her turn in time to see Nick coming down the stairs. His boots scraped on the stones, and he gave her a tense smile as she came to meet him.

She walked into his arms, stood on her toes and kissed him before he could say anything. At first he went rigid, his lips stiff. Then, as she concentrated on his mouth, he responded, wrapping his arms around her and deepening the kiss so that she soon wanted to bite his lips. Then, abruptly, he tore his mouth free.

"Wait," he said hoarsely. "We can't."

She smiled and squeezed him so that their hips collided. Nick was already breathing hard. She heard his teeth grinding even as he drew her down onto the cushion of leaves. On their knees they faced each other. Nick pulled her to him roughly and kissed her hard. Georgiana responded by sinking her fingers into his thick hair and pressing him closer. Nick pulled his mouth away from hers again, this time to gaze at her in desperation.

"I can't do this," he said. "We got to talk first, love."

"Nick."

He jumped up and backed away from her, his hand thrust out to keep her from following. "Oh, no, you don't. You're up to your tricks again. I won't listen."

"Nicholas," she breathed.

He put his hands over his ears and started humming.

Georgiana laughed and got to her feet. "Very well. I'll refrain. For now."

Nick lowered his hands.

"What did you say?"

"I promise to behave for the moment."

"Good girl. Now I got to say something, love. You see—you're a clever girl—young lady. Practical, sensible."

"It's no good," she said.

He sighed and ran a hand through his hair. "I'm glad you realize how unsuitable the thing is."

"I'm not leaving until I'm satisfied about the circumstances surrounding Threshfield's death." Georgiana rushed on when Nick tried to interrupt. "It's no use. I'm going to look into things myself. No one else will, and I owe it to Threshfield. He may have been a mean old conniver, but he helped me when I needed it desperately, and he would have married me as I asked, if he'd lived. It's a matter of honor and friendship."

Nick had been staring at her, a series of furrows

between his brows. He looked like a brooding figure in some dark drama with the wind whipping his coat around his body, his expression as black as the clouds that skimmed by overhead.

"You ain't going to leave?"

She put a hand on his arm and looked into his eyes, which were dark indigo in the sunless ravine. "Please, Nick."

He wasn't listening and murmured to himself, "If I made you go, it would create a scandal. The whole kingdom would know I made off with you, and your reputation would be ruined. No help there."

"Don't worry about my reputation. Help me find out what really happened to Threshfield. You're right. That doctor is a fool. He's so used to treating gout and vapors, he wouldn't recognize poison even if it was fed to him."

"Look, young George. Someone fed that old skeleton belladonna."

"You're sure."

" Course I'm sure. You don't live in St. Giles and not know belladonna, opium, other drugs. The whor—never mind."

"But Threshfield didn't take belladonna. No one in the house does. I don't even think the housekeeper has any."

He rubbed his chin and studied her with a severe expression. "You're determined to do this?"

"Yes, and don't try to frighten me out of it. Now that Threshfield is gone, there's no reason for anyone to try to get rid of me. Even if someone believed I was to bear his child, it's obvious any issue would be illegitimate. I've got to do this, Nick."

"Then we got to find out where the belladonna

came from. Is there any nightshade around? That's
what it comes from."

"I suppose there's plenty in the wood." Georgiana thought for a moment. "You know, I remember
something from my childhood. The gamekeeper on
one of my father's estates once got sick from eating
rabbit. He said the creatures sometimes graze on
nightshade, and then anyone who eats them gets the
poison too."

"And old Threshfield had rabbit last night."

"We should search the game larder," Georgiana
said. "Tonight after everyone has gone to bed. Someone could have put belladonna in the rabbits just
slaughtered. There might be some tainted ones left."

"Or the dish could have been poisoned after the
rabbit was stewed."

Georgiana snapped her fingers. "You're a thief."

"Never said I wasn't," Nick snapped.

"No, I mean that you could search everyone's
rooms. To see if there's any belladonna."

"I suppose I could."

"And I'll help."

"No, you won't."

"I'll look for any leftover stew in the kitchen, but
I don't think there's any, or some of the staff would
have gotten sick from eating it."

"You get that maid of yours to ask questions in
the kitchen," Nick said. "If you set foot belowstairs,
you'll cause an uproar."

"Very well. I'll take care of the kitchen and search
the rabbit cages. They're near the stables. Then we
can meet at the game larder. I should go now and talk
to my maid."

He caught her arm. "Not yet. I still got something to say."

She waited, but he didn't go on. Covering his hand with hers, she began for him.

"You know," she said brightly, "I was thinking this morning about all the scandals I've heard about girls running off with footmen and grooms. It happens quite often. And did you know that Catherine of Valois, who was Henry V's widow, married her clerk of the—"

"Stow it!"

Her eyes grew round as he thrust her away from him and ran his hand through his hair in agitation.

"Quit gabbing and let me finish. Bloody hell, woman, can't you see this is hard for me?"

"What's wrong, Nick?"

He was standing in front of her, glowering. "Us. We're wrong. I was wrong. I never should have touched you."

He went on, but she didn't hear him. She only heard that he didn't want her. He had no intention of asking for her hand. Most likely, he never had. Her body went rigid with shock. Blood rushed to her face, then drained, leaving her feeling weak and cold. Nick was still talking. His voice seemed far away and mercifully indistinct. If she tried to concentrate on his excuses, she would burst into tears and humiliate herself even more than she had been already.

As the low rumble of his voice rolled over her, Georgiana realized that for once she was grateful for her upbringing. Dukes' daughters did not cry in front of anyone, much less the men who had seduced and jilted them. Even if the duke's daughter did wish to die rather than face a man who didn't want her. She'd

endured this before and survived; she would survive
again. Forcing back her tears, Georgiana made her
expression blank. She clasped her hands to keep them
from trembling.

Nick was pacing back and forth. "I betrayed—"

"Forgive me," she said lightly. Surely he wouldn't
notice the tiny tremor in her voice. "I'm afraid my
attention wandered, but I caught your meaning. I'm
so grateful to you for understanding my situation."

Nick stopped pacing and stared at her. "What's
wrong with you?"

"Nothing," Georgiana said, smiling with stiff lips.
"As I was trying to tell you, many upper-class girls fall
in love with men beneath them and ally themselves
with these men only to find out that the attachment
fades once disgrace ruins them. Neither of us wants
that, do we?"

Nick wet his lips and shook his head.

Georgiana went on smoothly. "Excellent. Then I
shall continue with my plans. There were several other
aged men on my list. I'll make arrangements with one
of them."

The wretch. He'd satisfied his base urges and now
was regretting it. No doubt he'd wanted to see if a
duke's daughter was as satisfying as the—the hussies he
usually bedded. Dear heaven, had he compared her to
those dashing, sophisticated women who pursued
him, and found her inadequate?

Her mind reeling with hurt and shame, Georgiana summoned her most regal bearing, nodded like
the queen reviewing the Household Cavalry, and said,
"I'm glad we understand each other." She turned on
her heel and walked toward the stairs.

"Bleeding hell, we do not!"

Nick strode after her and snatched her arm. "You didn't understand what I said."

"I did, sir, and it's of no consequence," Georgiana said as she tried to pull free.

"You listen to me, young George."

Hearing that familiar name, Georgiana almost lost her nerve. She bit the inside of her cheek to keep from bursting into tears. She stopped trying to free herself and stared coldly at the hand that gripped her arm. Nick cursed and released her. She had to make him leave her alone. She had to get out of this place before she lost all dignity and pride.

"I think it's best if you leave," she said. Her voice almost broke, but she managed to smile and shrug her shoulders. "However, you should be proud of yourself. Last night made me understand why married women take lovers. I shall be sure to avail myself of the convenience once I've taken my vows."

His eyes widened, revealing blue-gray and sapphire against tanned skin. A jolt of pain stabbed through her chest just from looking at him. Nick shook his head wordlessly, as if unable to believe what he'd heard. They stared at each other in silence. She didn't know whether to be gratified or not that she'd silenced his facile tongue. Back straight, chin elevated, Georgiana lifted her skirt and marched up the stairs. She was almost at the top when she heard him swear.

"You're a right cold-blooded bitch, Georgiana Marshal."

Whirling around, she glared at him. "Better a bitch than a lying seducer, a low, craven coward, a scheming, ignoble wretch. You're true to your breeding, Mr. Ross. St. Giles right down to your soul."

He uttered an exclamation and started up the

stairs. Georgiana saw his black expression and bolted for her horse. She was mounted by the time he reached the top of the stairs. Kicking the mare into action, she wheeled away from him as he rushed toward her. She didn't dare look back until the horse had reached a gallop. A glance over her shoulder took in Nick's tall figure leaning over the neck of a white stallion. He was gaining on her. She plunged into the wood.

Lowering her body, Georgiana slapped the mare's flanks with her reins. She darted between trees, making perilously sharp turns, and managed to stay ahead of him until they broke out of the woods. Kicking the mare, she made a run for the stables with Nick closing fast. Her horse kicked up pebbles as she slowed on the gravel path, and a stall door opened. Careening to a stop, she jumped off the mare, breathless, and threw the reins to the groom who had emerged from the stall.

To her horror Nick's stallion didn't slow as he reached the stable. As the animal plunged on, he swung a leg over the saddle and jumped to the ground. The horse kept going, and Nick hurtled toward her. She cried out, grabbed her skirts, and sprang into a run. Hands clamped down on her waist and shoulders. Her feet left the ground as he yanked her backward against his chest.

"Let go of me, you vile mongrel!"

Georgiana twisted around in his arms and tried to kick him. Nick dodged her feet, then scooped her up in his arms. She fought him, trying to land a blow to his chin with her fist. Nick stalked past an astonished stable boy to the back lawn with Georgiana ranting at him and fighting all the way. He sat down with her on

a bench beside the Italian fountain, with its unicorn
rising from sprays of silver water, and pulled her over
his lap.

"Someone ought to have whipped you a long
time ago," he said.

Red-faced and furious, Georgiana felt his hand
drawing her skirt up over her legs and hips. She let out
a screech, braced herself, and rolled sideways. She
slipped off his lap and dropped to the ground, landing
on her bottom with her skirts hiked above her knees.
She glared up at him, cursing the fact that he looked
desirable even when he'd thrown off his coat, his
damp shirt clinging to his body. Nick laughed, leaned
back on the bench, and let his gaze scour her barely
covered legs and thighs.

"Bloody hell, you were a sweet piece. And hot for
it, too."

"Ohhhhh!" She thrust her skirts down, scrambled
to her feet, and ran.

"Don't go, love," he shouted. "Come back and
lets have another roll. I'll even do you in the plunge
bath like you want!"

Vision blurred by her tears, Georgiana blundered
up to the terrace. She yanked open a door and rushed
inside, pursued by Nick's mocking laughter. As she
ran upstairs, she knew she would remember that musical, demeaning sound for the rest of her life.

16

Nick watched Georgiana disappear into the house, then went back to the stables. A groom had unsaddled Pounder and was walking him around the yard to cool him down. He took the reins from the man and dismissed him. His hands shook from raw fury born of pain. He felt dirty, as if the muck of St. Giles was oozing from his pores, leaving him soiled and disgusting in the sight of everyone, especially Georgiana.

"Precious blue-blooded bitch," he said to the horse. "Finally showed herself for what she is, old fellow. She don't mind me when I'm pleasuring her in secret, but she don't want me any other way."

Leading Pounder down a bridle path, he muttered to himself, "Ought to leave her here on her own. That's what I ought to do. Let her marry some rotting old blister. Serve her right."

She hadn't cared that he'd been in love with her, that he had set his heart at her feet, that he had been prepared to sacrifice that love for her own good. She'd hardly listened to him. Too busy stepping on his offering with both feet. In spite of all her fine talk, in her heart Georgiana Marshal's opinion of him was the same as Evelyn's and Prudence's.

The little tart didn't want him. And he would never forgive her for voicing his deepest and most painful secret—that he was forever and irrevocably polluted by St. Giles, and that he'd never be good enough for a good woman. A truly noble lady would have forgiven him his transgressions, wouldn't she? But how could a gently reared girl forgive the things he'd done —the thieving, the killing?

Even now, after years away from the slums, he could still kill without remorse, quickly, efficiently, and without hesitation. He'd done so when he'd caught Tessie's murderer and when he and Jocelin had caught one of those obscene degenerates who preyed on children. Perhaps Georgiana had sensed his lack of remorse without knowing it.

Nick walked Pounder back to the stables, tethered him, and began to wipe him with a sponge. He couldn't forget the way Georgiana had looked at him after he'd forced himself to give her up. Her nostrils had quivered as if she'd smelled the vile excrescence inside him, and she'd looked as if she were going to puke at the sight of him. Even now the memory of that look made him cringe inside, made him hate himself even more than before. She'd made him feel like a pile of steaming horse manure sitting on a silver serving platter.

Resting his cheek against Pounder's shoulder, he murmured, "To hell with her, Pounder. Let her marry whoever she wants. We'll get out of here and go back to Texas."

And face Jocelin? The little bitch was still in danger from poor Lady Augusta, and Jos would never forgive him if she got killed. So what was he going to do?

Picking up a brush, Nick stroked Pounder's back and made circles on his withers. What he wanted to do was make Georgiana as miserable as she'd made him. He couldn't do that if he left. Pain was an excellent spur to vindictiveness. He'd stay. Stay and make her pay for saying he'd taught her the pleasures of having a lover once she married. He'd hound her. No matter what poor, wrinkled sod she chose for her next betrothed, he'd find him and run him off.

He'd do the same for the next, and the one after that, until she realized her only recourse was to marry suitably. Of course, he didn't care who her suitable match was, so long as he wasn't aged or an invalid. In fact, he might be able to arrange it so that she married one of those selfish bastards she abhorred. Plenty of them around, any chap with a title ought to do. The key was to keep her from marrying some old man until Jocelin was well enough to come home and deal with her.

The groom reappeared, and Nick relinquished the brush to him. Walking back to the house, he realized he'd still have to pursue Threshfield's murderer, and he'd have to do all the work himself. He'd search the family rooms for belladonna during dinner. He wasn't hungry, anyway. Reaching his rooms, Nick had a bath brought up, and soaked in steaming water until dark.

Before he dressed in his dark thieving costume, he sent word to Prudence that he was indisposed and wouldn't be down for dinner. Then, when the whole staff was scurrying to keep up with the monumental ritual of an upper-class dinner, Nick slipped out of his room. Much of the house was dark except for dim light cast by an occasional candle in a wall sconce. The earl had yet to put in gas lighting. Nick skulked his way through the house to the wing occupied by Evelyn, Prudence, and Ludwig.

He chose to search Evelyn's room first, because in his opinion Evelyn would murder his own mother to become the noble lord of Threshfield. As he expected, the door to Evelyn's rooms was unlocked. He turned the knob and slid inside what had once been an antechamber. It had been converted into a sitting room with a heavy carved desk and uncomfortable looking armchairs.

Nick was quietly riffling a drawer when he heard a footstep in the bedroom. Closing the drawer, he floated over to the door and cracked it open. By the light of a single candle resting on the floor, he beheld Georgiana on her hands and knees, bottom in the air, peering under a bed. Nick stepped into the room and crept up behind her.

Folding his arms over his chest, he said quietly, "He wouldn't put it there."

Georgiana cried out and rose, hitting her head on a bed board. She gasped, clutched her head, and subsided onto the floor.

"Sneaking ass!" she hissed, glaring up at him.

"You keep a civil tongue about you, or I'll finish that whipping."

Scrambling to her feet, Georgiana confronted him. "You do, and I'll scream."

"Good, that. It'll bring the whole household, and then you can explain what you're doing in Hyde's bedroom, because I won't be here."

"You're a low, common—"

"Stow it, George. I heard you the first time."

He turned his back on her and scanned the room. Going to the fireplace, he began pressing various protrusions on the mantel. Georgiana followed him.

"Why are you fondling the marble?" she asked.

"These old houses got lots of hidden compartments built in. Speaking of fondling, how about another tumble now that you're broken in?"

"You are the vilest creature!"

He enjoyed the way she turned scarlet and hissed like a locomotive. He watched her hips sway as she flounced away from him and began searching a wardrobe. When he finished with the fireplace, he joined her. Shoving her aside, he ran his hand along the inner walls, searching for compartments. Georgiana made another snide comment about his vileness and opened the chest at the foot of the bed.

"At least we agree on who might have killed poor old Threshfield," he said.

"I beg your pardon?" came the chilly response.

"You tried Evelyn bloody Hyde's rooms first. You got to think he's the most likely to have done it."

"Indeed I do not," she said as she lifted a blanket out of the chest. "I simply chose a room. It's obvious that poor Augusta has gone completely mad. I'm sure she imagined Threshfield to be a spy and poisoned him. Then, when she came to her senses again, she realized what she'd done and immediately blamed me. You said she told you I murdered him."

"Why should Lady Augusta be better at killing her brother than at killing you? She hasn't even managed that."

Georgiana was bending over the chest and withdrawing pillows. "It could have been Prudence. She could have seen her plans to become a countess, and eventually a duchess, threatened."

"You just don't want to believe your precious Evelyn might have poisoned his own uncle."

Georgiana straightened and sat back on her heels to gaze at him with remote amusement. "Mr. Ross, Evelyn wouldn't dirty his hands with murder. If those two are involved, it's due to Prudence's actions and guidance."

"And of course old lost-in-the-past Ludwig couldn't have done it."

She gave him a disgusted look and resumed her examination of the chest. "Don't be absurd. The only thing Ludwig cares about is the collection."

"And you."

The reply came from the dark interior of the chest. "I would have expected that lewd suggestion from you."

"It wasn't lewd, just on the mark, Your Imperial Highness."

Nick glanced around the room, eliminating various obvious hiding places, then started to roll up the carpet. He was walking on the floorboards, testing each with his feet, when he heard a hollow creak. Georgiana looked up from the chest as he knelt and knocked on the floor.

He pulled a knife from his belt, slid the blade between two boards, and lifted. A square section of the floor came up. Georgiana closed the chest and walked over to the stand beside him. Nick stuck his hand into the compartment he'd revealed and removed a tin box. Opening it, he looked inside, but it was too dark to see the contents.

Ignoring Georgiana, he took the box to the bed-
side table where she'd moved the candle. He opened it
again and looked inside.

Nick whistled softly. "Strike me blind."

"Let me see," Georgiana said.

Nick snapped the lid closed. "Nothing here."

"Then let me see," she said, holding out her hand
in that imperious way that made him want to swat her
behind.

"You don't want to see what's in here," he said.

"I'll simply wait until you're gone if you don't
show it to me."

Bloody princess. "All right, Your Royal Highness,
have a squint." He shoved the box into her hands.

Georgiana opened the container and held it close
to the candle. Within lay a folio, which she opened to
reveal an engraving of a naked woman lying on her
back, her legs spread to reveal her most private parts.
With a squeak Georgiana slapped the cover closed on
the folio. Her hands slipped, and she nearly dropped
the box. Nick caught it and shut the lid.

"No belladonna in there," he said lightly. "Did
you get a good look?"

Georgiana whirled around so that her back was to
him. He grinned nastily and continued his search of
the room. He was almost finished when she turned to
face him.

"Men are disgusting!"

"What would you know about it, Your Majesty?"
Nick searched the spaces between the drapes and the
windows.

"I know Evelyn, and—and my uncle," she said.
Her lip curled. "And *you.*"

He let a curtain fall and stalked over to Georgiana.

"You didn't think I was so disgusting a while ago. Come to think of it, you was bloody begging for it. Panting and moaning and lifting me with your hips."

Georgiana covered her ears. "Shut up, shut up, shut up, you loathsome wretch."

"Want me to prove it?"

He took a step that brought him so close, his chest touched hers. Georgiana hopped backward with a cry.

"Don't come near me."

He took another step, and she hopped again. Amused, Nick repeated his actions, and again she leaped without looking only to back into the chest at the foot of the bed. She dropped hard into a sitting position. Nick braced his legs apart and planted his fists on his hips as he laughed down at her.

"You're all dithered 'cause you know it's the truth. You just don't want to hear it." As he gloated over Georgiana's discomfort, a sudden thought came to him. "Know what, Your Majesty?"

"Get out of my way."

She lifted her legs and tried to scoot to the side, but he moved with her, blocking her escape.

"Know what?" he repeated. "I could make you want me again. Right here, on this chest."

Her back straightened, and she lifted her nose in the air. "As I said, you are disgusting."

Nick bent over her and spoke clearly but quietly. "Tell you what. I'll leave you alone. In fact, I'll scarper. Go back to Texas. And you can marry whatever calcified old fossil you want. If . . . ."

"If what?"

"If you'll let me take another ride."

"Another ride?" Her voice was strained and disbelieving. "You want to go riding with me?"

He put his lips close to her ear. "No, love. I want to ride you. Think of the engraving."

She gave a shriek that nearly destroyed his hearing. Nick gasped and covered his ear as she shoved him aside and ran from the room. He went after her, catching her at the sitting-room door. Placing his arm against it, he held it closed with his weight while she twisted the knob. Her chest heaved, and he loved the way her eyes darted from side to side like a trapped creature. He knew she was trying to keep her composure from completely evaporating. She was nearly aflame with her outrage, his majestic Georgiana. No more reserve, just pure, distilled, enticing passion.

"There is no word for you," she ranted. "You're some kind of lewd monster."

"Then the ride's off?"

"Ohhh."

"You forgot your candle," he said with a mean grin. He watched her stomp back to the bedroom and return with the light. "Well, not much has changed, then, I guess."

Her teeth grinding, Georgiana said, "Get out of my way."

"Yes, I guess I'll just have to stay here and find the murderer and protect you from Lady Augusta, and from yourself. Want to make a bet on who finds the real murderer? I say it's Evelyn bloody Hyde, or Ludwig."

Georgiana had been glaring at him, but as he watched, her furious expression vanished, as if wiped by a cloth from her face. She was again the cool, regal duke's daughter.

"Yes, I do wish to make that wager, Mr. Ross."

"You do?"

"Indeed. Whoever has chosen the real murderer wins a forfeit from the loser. I shall choose Lady Augusta or Prudence. You're a fool if you think a woman couldn't have done it. If I win, you must take yourself back to Texas and never come near me again."

Nick chuckled, crossed his arms, and leaned against the door. "We're even more high-and-mighty than usual. We're sure of ourselves, aren't we, Your Majesty?"

"Nonsense. As you've mentioned, I'm a sensible, practical woman, Mr. Ross. Are we agreed?"

"Just a minute, Your Royal Highness. We ain't settled on your forfeit." He let his gaze wander over her figure and settle on her breasts for a long, insulting moment. "If I win, you marry someone suitable—"

"Done."

"And just to make up for all my trouble, you decorate my bed until the engagement."

"Absolutely not. The wager is off, and I have no intention of going near your bed."

"No? Suit yourself. I'll just have to content myself with making you miserable until you see reason. Come on, Your Royal Highness. Let's search Prudence's room, and I'll describe the other engravings in Evelyn's collection. There was one with a lady on her hands and knees, and this chap with a huge, huge—er—member, was behind her, and he was—"

Georgiana covered her ears again. "Be quiet, you animal."

"You see, if you're on all fours," he said as he pulled her hands down. "Listen, this is the good part. If you're on your hands and knees, a chap can come up behind you and slip it in from behind. Want me to show you?"

"All right!" Georgiana threw her hands out before her as if to ward off the assault of words.

"Bleeding hell, that's ripe, that is. I didn't think you'd want to do it. Just get on the floor and I'll lift your skirts over your head."

By this time Georgiana was sputtering and had covered her ears again. "No, no, no, no, no. I agree to the wager, you perverted beast."

"Aw, are you sure?"

"Yes, *yes*, I'm sure. Now, shut up."

"Too bad. Some ladies I've known really liked it like that. Course, while I'm doing it, I make sure I keep them hot and ready. That's the trick."

"There's no need to be vulgar anymore, Mr. Ross. I've agreed to your wager."

Nick opened the door, bowed, and said, "Sorry, Your Majesty. Must be the St. Giles in me, like you said. Kept it bottled up too long, and now it's got to escape. No telling when that's going to happen. So you'll just have to endure it, unless you want to do this search separately."

"And have you come upon the answer before I do? I'm not a fool, sir."

Strolling down the hall to Prudence's room, Nick glanced back at her. "Suit yourself, but we've got a bet, lady, and nobody goes back on a wager with me. If I win, I'm going to collect, and you're going to pay."

17

Georgiana had never been more miserable. This evening hadn't gone the way she'd planned. Nick Ross
had ruined everything by appearing in Evelyn's room
like a curse and hectoring her until she agreed to that
sinful, disgusting wager. How could she have con-
sented to it? She wouldn't have if he hadn't fogged her
brain with his lewd and lascivious suggestions and language. Dear God, she'd never imagined some of the
things he'd described!

And he knew it. He'd embarrassed her on purpose, to make her commit herself to this horrible
wager. Now she had to prove her judgment correct
about the identity of the earl's murderer or suffer even
more terrible humiliation.

They had already searched the family rooms and
found nothing. Nothing related to the murder, that is.
In Augusta's rooms they'd found dozens of high-
waisted gowns, as many different reticules, and, of
course, her musket. In Prudence's chambers Nick had
located her secret wall safe in which the lady had

secreted her jewels. Nick had hesitated over them until Georgiana had firmly closed the jewel case and the
safe as well.

A search of Ludwig's room yielded nothing more
sinister than a model of an ancient Egyptian funeral
boat. She'd been gratified when the life-size black-
granite statue of Ramses II had given Nick a start.
He'd backed into it and whirled around to face what
he thought was a real man, his body crouched to meet
an attack.

It was growing late. They were in the midst of
searching the rooms used by the servants. It was during this exploration that Georgiana realized anew that
Nick could get into any locked room he wished. So
far they'd inspected the butler's pantry, the knife,
plate, and lamp rooms, the wine cellar and stillroom.
None of these had taken much time, because neither
of them believed that a murderer would be foolish
enough to leave nightshade in them where it could be
found by servants.

Now they had reached the kitchen. Georgiana
found the bins used for rubbish and pointed to them.
Nick strolled over to glance down at them, holding
the candle she'd brought so that the muck within was
revealed.

He bowed and swept his arm. "My lady."

Scowling at him, Georgiana came forward and
looked into the smelly interior of the first bin. Wrin-
kling her nose, and using her fingertips, she picked up
a broken piece of crockery splattered with food.

"This is the right one, the food bin," she said.
"You may proceed."

"Not bloody likely. Food is women's work."

"You're a foul creature—"

"We ain't got all night, Your Graciousness."

He wasn't even going to help. He just stood there smirking. Wishing she were a man so she could bash that superior sneer from his face, Georgiana began searching through the decomposing food using the broken piece of crockery. Long minutes of nauseating work produced nothing.

Georgiana dropped the crockery into the bin and brushed her hands. "If there was any stew left, it's gone."

"Well, my, my, what's this?" Nick tipped the bin beside the one she'd searched, and Georgiana caught a whiff of old rabbit stew.

She thought her head would explode from rage. "You knew that was there all the time, and you let me root around in that muck!"

"Why, George, how suspicious you are."

"Oh, shut your mouth and help me find a bowl."

Nick produced one he'd been holding behind his back, grinning all the while. "This ought to do, Your Royal Perfection."

Snatching the vessel, Georgiana scooped up a gob of congealed stew, turned, and marched out of the kitchen through a mudroom. Nick slipped past her to unlock a door, and they stepped out into the night. It was some time in the early morning. An icy chill had set in, and Georgiana immediately regretted not having brought a mantle. She thought of going back, but she couldn't imagine Nick's waiting for her. They were supposed to search the game larder. She would just have to be cold.

Georgiana led the way across the kitchen yard, past the stables, and down a small gravel path to a copse of trees. In their midst sat the game larder, a little building faced with white stone. It was mostly windows fit with screens and framed with vents. Nick made quick work of the lock, slipping a slender, hooked tool into the hole and working it neatly until the mechanism snapped open.

Inside were two rooms floored with slate. The first was equipped with a high ceiling rack constructed like the spokes of a wagon wheel. From this hung smaller game. Shivering, Georgiana reached up and spun the rack.

"There," she said, pointing to a small carcass amid those of ducks.

Nick grunted and walked past her to the inner room. Larger carcasses were hung from rails—venison, chiefly. He searched among the marble shelves in several alcoves that provided cold storage and came back with another rabbit.

"Bloody hell," he said as he glanced around the ornate little structure with its abundance of freshly killed game. "When I think of all the tykes going hungry in London."

Georgiana stretched to reach the hanging rabbit but failed to touch it. "Precisely. That's why Aunt Livy and I are going to buy a house like this. It will come with a large park and wood, and the children can learn all sorts of skills—gamekeeping, butlering, cookery."

She tried jumping but missed. Nick snorted and plucked the carcass from its hook.

"Right. And just what would Your Almighty Majesty know about any of them things?"

"You seem to have lost every bit of your counterfeit gentleman's accent, Mr. Ross, and your gunslinger's grammar as well. I'm sorry to disappoint your preconceptions, but I know quite a bit about such things. How do you think ladies manage large households without knowing the intricacies of domestic arrangements?"

Georgiana nodded in the direction of the kitchen. "Do you know how to stock a housekeeper's storeroom? One lays in provisions several times a year to take advantage of seasonal prices. Rice can be kept more than three years if stored properly. Pickles and preserved fruit should be stored upside down. Tea, sugar, and spices must be placed in a locked cupboard with folding doors. Coffee has to be stored separately so that it doesn't contaminate the tea. Would you like to know what brushes and soaps one should provide for the laundry maids?"

Nick dangled the rabbit from his fingers. "All that proves is you're just like all the other spoiled ladies, good at getting other people to do all the work, Your Imperial Laziness." Shaking the carcass at her, he said, "I got to pack up this lot and send it to my doctor friend in Harley Street. Get the bowl of stew, Miss Housekeeper."

Fuming, Georgiana picked up the bowl and followed him. Teeth chattering, she locked the game larder as they left, then stomped after Nick. Soon they were in the house again and climbing the curved staircase. Georgiana grew uneasy when she realized they were headed for Nick's rooms. She halted on the threshold while he disappeared inside. He came back empty-handed to grin in that knowing, evil way of his.

"Afraid to trust yourself in my bedroom?"

"Here." She shoved the bowl at him and turned to go.

He took the vessel but at the same time thrust his
arm in front of her, swept her inside, and shut the
door.

"Mr. Ross, you're too familiar."

Nick set the bowl aside with a chuckle and rushed
to her side as she opened the door. He slipped in front
of her and placed his back to the portal.

"Move aside, sir."

Without answering he shrugged out of the old
jacket he'd been wearing and dropped it onto the
floor. Georgiana saw it land and turned a wary gaze
on him. His shirt was open at the throat, and she
could see the cords and tendons of his neck, the way
they tightened into prominence. He'd placed the
sputtering candle on a distant table, but his face was in
shadow. She caught the dim gleam of his teeth as he
smiled. He moved again, and this time his shirt
dropped at her feet. She caught a glimpse of a bare
arm sheathed in muscle and smooth skin browned by
the Texas sun.

"Come on, love. Let's put aside our quarrel and
have some fun. You know you like it, long as nobody
knows you're opening your legs for a St. Giles thief."

Her mouth worked, but she couldn't seem to
make her tongue function. He moved toward her, out
of the shadows. His hands were on the buttons at his
waistband. Georgiana blinked as she noticed the flat
expanse of his stomach. Long fingers separated cloth
to reveal silken flesh covering hard muscle.

Georgiana shrieked. Nick leaped, grabbed her,
and covered her mouth.

"Shhh!"

Enraged, and ashamed of how she'd felt when
he'd opened his clothing, Georgiana poked him with

her elbow, then nipped his hand. He yelped and let her go only to brace his weight against the door with one arm. He shook his injured hand.

"Bleeding hell, woman, you almost broke the skin."

"I wish I'd bitten your hand off, you evil-minded wretch. Now, let me out of this room before I—I throw myself out a window."

"A little dramatic, don't you think? How about it, love? Who's to know?"

"I'll count to three, Mr. Ross. One."

"I'll make you scream with pleasure, over and over again, and we can try one of them tricks in Evelyn's engravings."

"Two."

"We already know you don't like the all-fours one." Nick snapped his fingers. "I know. I bet you'd like it if I tied your arms and legs to the bedposts."

"I said 'Two,' Mr. Ross."

"No, no, not you. You'd like it if you tied me up. I'm willing. Then you can get on top."

"Three!"

Georgiana took a deep breath and prepared to scream. Nick chuckled and opened the door with a flourish. He leaned toward her and whispered with such precise enunciation that he made her feel like a simpleton.

"You really are a fussy little prude, aren't you? Be careful, Your Royal Purity, or you'll end a dried-up, barren, mad old spinster. I can see you now, roaming some big house with fifty cats at your heels and drool coming down the corner of your mouth."

"Better than ending up your harlot!"

Nick clucked at her. "Now, George, you can't say

that, not after rolling across the floor with me stuck inside you, moaning all the while."

Her fingers curled into claws, and she almost tried to scratch his leering face. Making fists instead, Georgiana rushed out of the room as he leaned against the door frame, and hardly heard his parting words.

"Lock your door, Your Royal Spinsterness. There's still a murderer about."

Georgiana heard his door close as she hurried down the hall and across the landing. When she reached the top of the stairs, she paused. Glancing back to make sure Nick hadn't followed her, she braced a hand on the banister and let out a sigh that was part wail. The wretch was trying to blame her for their estrangement.

Her mother had always cautioned her about such men, who adopted charming, alluring demeanors to trick innocent girls into allowing intimacy only to turn on them once the conquest had been achieved. Georgiana had always prided herself on being able to see through the ingratiating, glutinous machinations of such men.

But Nick had been too clever for her. She had succumbed, and God was punishing her for her sins. If she had been a plump, pretty little thing rather than a loping giant, she might have gained more experience with men that would have enabled her to withstand Nick Ross. But no one had ever bothered to try to seduce her before.

She would simply have to be brave and endure his presence a while longer, until the murderer was unmasked. There she had the advantage. She knew the family. She knew Ludwig incapable of murder, and Evelyn too full of his own sense of privileged nobility to commit murder. Prudence, however, would kill her own child if he stood in the way of a coronet. And Augusta had already tried to kill several times.

There was no proof of anyone's guilt. How was she going to determine which suspect had committed the crime? Perhaps she could learn something by talking to both women. With discreet questioning one of them might make a mistake and implicate herself. She would begin tomorrow after the earl's funeral. The sooner she solved the mystery, the sooner Nick would leave, and then she would be rid of the pain of seeing him.

"Georgiana?"

She jumped and cried out, then leaned over the banister to see Ludwig at the bottom of the stairs. He was holding an armload of books.

"Ludwig, you frightened me."

"Oh, my heart, I'm sorry. I was on my way to the Egyptian Wing and saw you standing there. What are you doing up so late?"

"Oh, well, I'm so distressed about Threshfield. I couldn't sleep." She glanced over her shoulder in the direction of Nick's room, apprehension making her movements jerky. She expected him to leap out at her at any moment and spew obscene suggestions at her. She descended the stairs. "Um, let me help you with those books. It will give me something to do, since I can't rest."

"You should have the doctor give you something," Ludwig said. He hugged his books to his chest when she tried to take some from him. "I mean, they're not heavy."

In the workroom of the Egyptian Wing they sat down at the table beside the red-granite sarcophagus.

Georgiana took a surreptitious glance inside the stone box, just in case Nick had decided to sneak in ahead of them. It was empty, and she scolded herself silently for her fears.

To cover her nervousness, she picked up the top book from the stack Ludwig had set down on the table. It was a translation of a German work on ancient Egyptian life, covering everything from history to family life and religion. She flipped through the pages and noticed a section on learning—astronomy, mathematics, the magic arts including medicine, and geometry.

She heard a rattle and looked up to find Ludwig balancing dozens of small faience cosmetic jars and bronze votive statuettes on a tray. Setting the book aside, she rushed to help him steady his precious burden. Once the tray was safely on the table, Ludwig swept the books off it and took them to their proper place in the next room.

He returned dusting his coat. "I have been looking for those books for two weeks. Uncle carted them to the library and didn't tell me."

Georgiana sat down beside the cosmetic jars and statuettes and watched Ludwig compare the items with a packing list.

"Ludwig, don't you think Threshfield's death was sudden?"

"I suppose, but, then, Uncle had been ailing for many years."

"True. Do you know if anyone in the house uses belladonna?"

Ludwig was examining a votive statuette of a scribe seated cross-legged with a papyrus stretched across his legs. "What? Belladonna?"

"Nightshade," Georgiana said.

"Nightshade, nightshade." Ludwig picked up a magnifying glass and examined the inscription on the base of the statue.

"Ludwig."

"Yes, my dear. Oh, belladonna. That's some kind of drug, is it not?"

"It comes from the nightshade plant."

"No, I don't think I've ever heard anyone talk—wait. Now that you mention it, Mother used to use it to treat colic, but that was long ago. Why? Are you ill?"

"No, just curious. I saw some growing in the wood. Do you think Prudence would have some?"

"Perhaps. She fancies herself an authority on children's ailments, and those of adults, for that matter. She was always telling Uncle what medicines to take."

"Was she?"

"Oh, my heart, yes. He got awfully testy when she did, so she had to stop."

"Threshfield could be so difficult," Georgiana said. "It's a wonder people didn't threaten to kill him, he was so, well, mean sometimes. Did you ever hear anyone threaten to kill him?"

Ludwig glanced at her over the magnifying glass. "What is all this talk about nightshade and threats, Georgiana?"

"I'm just curious."

"Are you suggesting Uncle's death wasn't natural?"

"Oh, no. No, no. It's just that he died so suddenly."

"I think all death is sudden, in that we don't want

it to happen, especially to those we love. Oh, my heart, yes.''

Georgiana looked at Ludwig poised over his cosmetic bottle, squinting through his magnifying glass, and she smiled. "You're a kind man, Ludwig."

"Hmm? Oh, thank you, my dear. Look at the quality of this faience, such a deep, dark blue."

"I think I'll go to bed," Georgiana said. "You should too. It will be dawn in a few hours."

"I'll be along in a while. I want to find a box for these bottles."

Georgiana left shaking her head. Ludwig would forget what time, probably forget what day or night, it was, and fall asleep at the worktable. She hurried through the Egyptian Wing and entered the curved corridor in darkness. Frost had formed on the windows and on the lawn outside. She rubbed her upper arms, again feeling the chill. A shadow detached itself from those along the wall ahead of her, causing Georgiana to stop suddenly and gasp. It lunged at her, sweeping her against the cold window.

"You're a fool, young George."

"Mr. Ross, I've had enough of your sneaking and spying. Release me."

"You just let old Ludwig know you're suspicious. That was a stupid thing to do. What if he's the killer? Didn't even think of that, did you?"

His arm was pressing against her breasts. Georgiana pried her own arms between his and her chest but couldn't break his hold.

"It's just like you to disparage Ludwig, who is a man of character. He's kind and gentle and mannered and wellborn, and you can't stand that."

Nick's face appeared close to hers so that she

could make out the sharp angle of his jaw. "If he's so bloody wonderful, why don't you marry him?"

"I would," she snapped, "but I don't want to be a countess and have to take on the burden of those kinds of duties as well as my home for children. And besides, I don't lo— he's not nearly old enough."

"What does that matter?" Nick asked. He was so close she could feel his heartbeat, steady and rhythmic. The sensation penetrated her—thud, thud, thud—and aroused her body in spite of her anger.

He went on. "Old Ludwig would do whatever you wanted him to. If you married him, you'd almost be the husband. No worries about being a slave."

"I told you. I won't marry a young man."

She heard a low, evil laugh.

"Of course you won't. Not now."

"What are you talking about?"

She pushed at his arms, but he only pressed her against the wall and put his lips to her ear.

"It's simple, love. You're afraid to marry a young man, 'cause he might do this."

Too late she realized what he was going to do. His lips descended upon hers. His tongue snaked into her mouth and he pulled her against his body. She froze for a moment, feeling his strength and the heat of his skin, the suppleness and texture of his lips; then she pounded his shoulders. Before she could bite his lips, he pulled away and released her. Damnation to him. He wasn't even breathing hard, and she just knew he was grinning at her with that off-center smile.

His voice calm, Nick said, "Or maybe you're

afraid no one else can make you feel the way I just
made you feel."

Georgiana dashed the back of her hand across her
mouth and tried to get out a retort, but Nick was
already gone. He was no more than a shadow gliding
along the corridor, and she was left shaking, her skin
hot, her feelings in a turmoil. Not wanting to meet
him again on her way to her room, she turned and
pressed her hot forehead to a windowpane.

She couldn't endure his persecution much longer.
If he touched her like that, she would go mad with
hating and wanting him at the same time. He knew it,
and he was using her own feelings against her. He was
evil, and she had to escape him. If she hadn't found
Threshfield's killer by tomorrow, she would call off
the wager. Better to dishonor her word than to suffer
such damnable torments at the hands of this man. One
way or another, she was going to get away from Mr.
Nicholas Ross.

18

Nick watched Georgiana surreptitiously from his vantage beside a drawing-room window festooned in black crepe. She was talking to her aunt in the midst of a group of Threshfield family members. True to custom, she had put on a deep mourning costume of the darkest, dullest black bombazine he'd ever seen. He would have thought she'd look like a slender crow in it, but instead the unrelieved blackness highlighted her creamy skin and the primrose color of her cheeks. The jet beads at her throat only enhanced the startling green of her eyes and made them shine like polished malachite.

He shouldn't stare at her. Nick directed his attention to the line of carriages waiting to pull up in front of the portico. The funeral services had been held at the church in the tiny village nearby, and the earl had been deposited in the vault in the family chapel in the park. Being an earl, Threshfield's mourning observances had been elaborate in accordance with Evelyn's and Prudence's estimation of the pomp and ceremony due their new rank.

Nick had thought the Egyptian Wing the most bizarre thing he'd ever seen, until he witnessed the gruesome spectacle of upper-class mourning. Everyone was shrouded in murky, somber black—black silk, black crepe, black plumes, black handkerchiefs, mourning bands and ribbons, and, of course, the favorite bombazine. Bombazine was esteemed because it was so dull, it reflected almost no light.

The whole ritual affected to demonstrate how much Threshfield had been loved. Nick thought it demonstrated how rich Evelyn was that he could afford to waste money on meaningless display. All this fuss wouldn't convince anyone who knew the family that Threshfield would be missed, at least not by the new earl and his wife. They hadn't shed a tear today. But Georgiana had.

He'd almost forgotten her callousness toward him upon witnessing her grief that morning. His sympathetic weakness had passed, however, when, upon arriving back at the house, she had avoided him as if he were a consumptive. He had kept an eye on her, however, because he'd expected her to indulge in more futile attempts to prove her suspects guilty of murder and save herself from him.

Unfortunately, spending so much time in her presence kept him from forgetting his unhappiness. The drawing room further enhanced his mood, shrouded as it was in black crepe. The windows, mantel, pictures, mirrors, and doors were smothered in black.

Never had he expected Lady High-and-mighty to agree to the terms he had set for their wager. Perhaps he'd been more right about her than he thought. She wanted him as much as he wanted her, only she was ashamed of her desire for the likes of him. This humiliating thought kept circling around in his head, exploding whatever peace of mind he managed to garner. Each time it happened, his misery provoked a desire to make Georgiana as wretched as she made him.

In this foul mood he lurked nearby while Georgiana cornered poor Lady Augusta and asked questions about her activities the day of Threshfield's death. As he'd expected, the effort was wasted. Lady Augusta wasn't about to confide in a French spy, and she scurried away as soon as she could.

"Ah, Ross, I've been meaning to talk to you."

Nick turned around to find Evelyn at his elbow looking like a scrawny black eagle in his mourning suit. "My condolences, Hyde."

"It's Threshfield now."

"Right. I say, old chap. Terribly unexpected, the old earl's death."

"Yes, but that's not what I wished to discuss."

"I remember what I was doing that day. Tragedy always fixes these things in one's head, wouldn't you agree? I met the ladies while they were shopping in town. Do you remember what you were doing?"

"No."

"Did you do any shooting, drop by the game larder?"

"No. What I—"

"I bet old Threshfield had you ready to piss in your pants with his story about Lady Georgiana. Bet you thought you'd lose everything to an infant heir."

Evelyn sighted down the length of his substantial

nose and said, "On the contrary. I never believed that ridiculous lie."

As he spoke, Evelyn's gaze drifted to Georgiana. His thin, tightly pressed lips went a bit slack, and he swallowed. Nick watched his throat muscles contract and a flush creep over his face. His gut contracted at the idea of Evelyn's nasty mind contemplating Georgiana.

"Look," Nick said. "Lady Georgiana is talking to Lady Prudence. Fine, upstanding wife you got there. She'll take you far, I'm sure."

"Who?"

"Your wife." Nick nodded in the direction of Prudence's stocky figure. "Remember her?"

Casting a glance of dismay at Prudence, Evelyn deliberately turned his back on her fishbowl crinoline and thick figure. "Don't distract me, Ross. I wanted to ask you how long you'd be staying now that my uncle is gone?"

"Can't wait to get rid of me?"

"I'm sure you won't wish to remain in a house of mourning."

"Doesn't bother me."

"When are you going, Ross?"

"In a few days," Nick snapped. "As soon as Lady Georgiana leaves."

"I've asked her to stay as long as she wishes."

Nick said nothing at first. Then he moved closer to Evelyn and whispered, "You go near her, old cock, and I'll put you in a vault right next to your uncle faster than you can say bleeding lecherous old sod."

"How dare you, sir!"

"You sound like a wounded virgin. Just remember what I said." Nick saluted Evelyn. "When's the luncheon? I'm hungry. Think I'll join your wife and Lady Georgiana. See you, old toff."

Grinning while Evelyn sputtered and gawked at him, Nick sidled over to where Georgiana and Prudence were sitting on a couch near the fireplace. On the way he picked up a cup of tea from a tray. The drawing room was crowded with relatives and friends talking in subdued voices. They clustered together in little milling groups like depressed and not very intelligent doves.

A life-size portrait of the old earl hung over the mantel. It was smothered with black, and Threshfield looked down on the assembly with that familiar expression of malicious amusement. Nick sipped his tea and stealthily edged his way around a clump of mourners until he was standing behind Georgiana with his back to the couch. From his post he could hear her conversation with Prudence.

"I'm sure you're right," Georgiana was saying. "But what about colic?"

"Oh, if it's a bad case, you should use a little belladonna. It works excellently."

"I was wondering," Georgiana said. "Because when I establish the home, there may be quite a few infants."

"Really, Georgiana, all that kind of thing is best left to a housekeeper or a superintendent. You must engage a suitable staff of good character, preferably people of experience."

"I know, but colic is such a problem."

"True," Prudence said. She stirred her tea, clinking her spoon against the porcelain of her cup. "By the way, I was wondering how much longer you intended to stay at Threshfield."

"Not long."

"Of course, propriety dictates that your with-drawal not be precipitous."

"Of course," Georgiana said.

"But, after all, this is a house of mourning."

"Indeed."

"A week, perhaps?" Prudence asked.

"Perhaps."

Nick heard Prudence's cup rattle. "I'll tell the housekeeper, then."

Prudence excused herself and went to meet Eve-lyn, who was announcing luncheon to his guests. Droves of black-clad funeral-goers milled toward the saloon, intent on filling their stomachs at the new earl's expense. Out of the corner of his eye Nick saw Georgiana rise. He set down his teacup and nipped around the couch.

"Did you expect her to take fright and blurt out an admission?" he said.

Georgiana gave a startled cry and whirled around to face him. "Why must you skulk around and spring out at me like that?"

"She wouldn't admit being familiar with bella-donna if she was guilty."

"She would if she was trying to appear innocent."

"Right," Nick said with a roll of his eyes. "And that was clever, trying to question a silly old bird like Lady Augusta."

Georgiana glanced around at the fast-emptying room before replying, "Well, Mr. Know Everything, I found out she takes what she calls her elixir. The doctor prescribed it for her nerves, she said. If we ask the doctor what's in it, I'm sure he'd say belladonna.

No doubt Augusta thinks it's an antidote for French poison."

"Shh." Nick glanced behind Georgiana as Ludwig approached with Lady Augusta on his arm.

"Aren't you two coming in to dine?" Ludwig asked.

"In a moment," Georgiana said. "Lady Augusta, I was just telling Mr. Ross of your marvelous elixir."

"It makes me invincible against poisons, so don't try to kill me that way, Madame Spy. And Ludwig told me he knows all about you and how you sneak around gleaning secrets for Napoleon, and he's going—"

Ludwig patted Augusta's gloved arm. "Now, Auntie, is that the way to talk on the day we buried dear Uncle?"

"Oh, poor, dear Threshfield," Augusta said on a sob. She sniffled into a black lace handkerchief and cast suspicious glances at Georgiana.

Ludwig said, "What you need is some food and a bit of sherry."

"Yes, sherry, a great deal of sherry. For my nerves, of course."

Augusta trotted off in search of a footman to bring her a bottle. Ludwig inserted his round body between Nick and Georgiana and took Georgiana's hands in his. Nick felt a stab of irritation at the familiar way Ludwig touched her.

"I'm sorry about that," Ludwig said as he gazed into Georgiana's eyes. "She's terribly upset about her brother, and she's imagining things more and more."

Nick snorted, but they ignored him. His irritation began to smolder into something greater as the two moved close together.

Georgiana kissed Ludwig on his cheek, and Nick's muttered curse went unnoticed.

"I know it's not your fault," she said to Ludwig. "You look tired. You should rest tonight instead of working so late."

"I will, thank you, dear Georgiana. You've such a kind heart, oh, my, yes." He returned her kiss. "Perhaps tomorrow you might help me with one of the mummies. Its bandages are rotting off, and I've got to do something to preserve them. Did you know that the ancient Egyptian embalmers removed the brain of the deceased through the nose? They had this long tool with a hook on the end."

"Jesus!" Nick cried. He shoved his way between Ludwig and Georgiana.

Georgiana drew herself up to a regal height. "I beg your pardon, Mr. Ross."

"Don't look at me like I'm a hedgehog tracking muck on the carpet. You two make me sick with your kissing and your talk about mummies and brains." He turned on Ludwig. "You just watch who you slobber kisses on, Hyde. And keep your paws to yourself."

Georgiana took offense, but Ludwig only goggled at him, which made Nick even madder to think that Georgiana could harbor affection for this dusty, spineless little clerk.

"Oh, my heart."

Nick thrust his hands into his pockets and gave Georgiana a derisive look. "He sounds like a bloody nun."

"You should apologize to Ludwig," Georgiana said.

"Oh, sod it," Nick snarled as he watched her pat Ludwig's arm.

Georgiana scowled at him and said, "Your language, sir."

"Oh, my heart, yes," Ludwig chimed in. He offered his arm to Georgiana, who slipped hers through his. "It isn't mannerly, using such colored language to a lady."

Nick put his fists on his hips. "You want to teach me manners, toff?"

"That's enough, sir!" Georgiana tugged Ludwig out of Nick's reach. She hissed under her breath at Nick. "You should be ashamed of yourself, picking on a sweet person like Ludwig. You're not fit to—to wash his linens." She flounced away with her charge. "We're going in to luncheon."

"Going to cut his meat for him?" Nick called after them.

Only a few people were left in the drawing room, and all of them stared at him. Nick glared back, then stalked over to a window. He batted at a length of crepe that snagged on his coat, muttering to himself.

"Bleeding white-livered little field mouse. Just the type Georgiana would like to marry. No guts, pudding in her hands."

Wait. Why was he so fizzed? He'd never have worried about the likes of Ludwig Hyde before. But, then, he'd never had to stand by and watch Georgiana kiss him before.

Bloody hell, he was jealous. The thought of Ludwig putting his damp, soft hands on her drove him into a killing rage. When the little toad had kissed her—Nick realized what a feat of self-governance it had taken not to grab Ludwig and toss him into the fireplace.

By God, he was jealous. What was it that Pertwee

had read to him by that old Roman fellow? Ovid was his name. Ah, yes. "Love that is fed by jealousy dies hard."

Nick groaned and pressed a cheek against the cold windowpane. "Strike me blind. Love. Bloody, everlasting hell."

Later that night Nick was lying fully clothed on his bed after assuring himself that Georgiana was locked in her room. She was still shoving furniture in front of her door, so he was confident of her safety. No one else but he could pick locks, or so he assumed. He had sent off the rabbit carcasses and stew to his doctor friend in London. He'd listened to Georgiana's inquiries of her suspects, and he'd made his own concerning Evelyn and Ludwig.

In order to keep himself from dwelling on how much he would like to show Georgiana she still wanted him, he was reviewing what he knew. As usual Ludwig had spent his time among his antiquities the day Threshfield had died. He could have slipped out of the Egyptian Wing to poison a rabbit, and no one would have missed him. Evelyn had gone for a long walk and could have done the same. He could even have paid a hansom cab to run down Georgiana while she shopped. Nick still had his suspicions about that incident, although Georgiana put it down as one of Lady Augusta's mischiefs.

Georgiana's accidents had stopped. Nick thought it was because Threshfield had died before he could change his will or marry her. Georgiana thought it was because Lady Augusta was too grief stricken to make attempts at the moment. Whatever the case, time was running out. Both he and Georgiana would be leaving Threshfield soon, and if they didn't find a murderer before they left, they probably wouldn't find him at all.

He needed to question the servants about Evelyn's and Ludwig's movements on the day and evening of the murder. However, the separation between servants and family and guests was marked in gentle households. If he approached even a footman with such questions, word would quickly reach the butler and housekeeper, who would take the matter up with Prudence. Like Georgiana, he would have to work through his own servant, Pertwee.

Nick was making a mental list of the questions he wanted the valet to ask when he heard a single soft knock at his sitting-room door. It was dark except for the small glow of light from a candle by the bed. He picked up the candle and went to answer the knock.

Opening his door, he found a deserted hall. Was he hearing things? Not likely. As he shut the door, he felt something under his boot. He stooped and picked up an envelope. Within was a note on Threshfield stationery. It was printed rather than written in cursive and bore Georgiana's name at the bottom. She asked him to meet her in the Egyptian Wing at two o'clock that night.

Nick put the note back in its envelope. Her Royal Pureness must think him barely literate to print the blasted thing. And she must have found the murderer! Why else would she want to meet him secretly when she obviously found his company so disturbing?

"Strike me blind," Nick muttered. "If she's found the prig, I'll have to go back to Texas."

He'd failed. No doubt Prudence had killed

Threshfield to assure her place in Society. He felt his heart sink, as though bound by the weight of a hundred sarcophagi. He would have to face Georgiana's triumphant derision. No, Her Grace was too well mannered to jeer. She would present her discovery without flourish and politely request that he take himself across the ocean and never bother her again.

And he would have to go. The note slipped from his fingers to the floor, and he stared blindly at the candle he was still holding. Why couldn't his love have been like Jocelin and Liza's? His was more like that chap Othello and Desdemona's—doomed. Doomed, doomed, doomed. Only Georgiana wasn't nearly so faithful as Desdemona had been.

No, she wanted him gone. But he wouldn't go like a kicked mongrel. He'd go with refinement and grace, and show her he didn't care that she considered their lovemaking a dirty secret best forgotten. Or maybe he should show her what she'd be missing. He had a little time to decide, but one way or another, Georgiana was going to regret what she'd done to him.

Despite his preoccupation with revenge, two o'clock was a long time coming for Nick. While the ormolu clock in his chamber struck a chime at a quarter past one, he was holding a lamp and gliding down the chilly, curved corridor outside the Egyptian Wing. Rather than appear to obey Her Royal Highness's summons, he had set out early. He was going to find a good hiding place. Then he would watch her arrive and let her wait for him a good long time before he suddenly appeared out of nowhere. She would be nervous after the wait in that black morgue of a place, and she would be mad. But he would play the gentleman, pretend surprise that she'd had to wait.

Nick hesitated as he entered the long hall of the Egyptian Wing. Glancing aside at a tall display case, he caught sight of his formal evening clothes, a black and white reflection in the glass. His gaze fell to a row of linen-wrapped bundles. Georgiana had told him what they were, the mummies of a cat, two falcons, a dog and a baboon, all carefully preserved for the afterlife in swaths of bandages darkened with age. Beneath the mummies lay a shelf filled with the amulets of carnelian, malachite, alabaster and lapis lazuli. Egyptian embalmers placed them between the layers of bandages to protect the dead in the journey to the netherworld. Nick figured that the way his luck was running, he could use a few hundred amulets himself.

He moved on, searching the darkness for a suitable place to hide. He wouldn't lurk inside a mummiform coffin. Furious as he was with Georgiana, he didn't want to see her frightened and crying. Besides, most of those standing against the walls were too small for him. And jumping out at her wouldn't produce the polished and reserved impression he desired. Perhaps he should wait in the workroom.

Nick shoved open the door and held his lamp high, noting the table littered with archaeological tomes, small statues and the mummy of a small crocodile. Closing the door, he dragged an armchair from the table and placed it facing the portal with his back to the library door. He set the lamp on the floor and dropped into the chair.

He took out his pocket watch and saw that he still had a good twenty-five minutes to wait. Replacing the watch, he straightened his coat. It was of fine black Saxony and set off his white waistcoat with embroidered border. The diamond studs in his cuffs flashed even in the dull lamp light.

It was so quiet he could hear the ticking of his watch. He got up and plucked a book from the table. Holding it near the lamp, he tried to read, but he was too tense. He set the book on the floor. The place was beginning to irritate him—all the dead bodies, the strange objects made by people who had lived three thousand years ago, the coffins.

Nick's brow furrowed. Something wasn't right. He picked up the lamp and strolled over to the table again. Surveying the stacks of books, he hesitated. Slowly, a frown dragging at his lips, he turned around and held the lamp high. He hadn't noticed before. The space next to the table, it was empty. What had happened to the red granite sarcophagus?

He swept the lamp at arm's length and walked farther into the darkness. No sarcophagus. Then he whirled around as he heard a long, loud creak. The library door opened, sending a flood of light into the room. Nick scowled, set down the lamp and stalked over to the newcomer, who was holding a candelabra.

"Bleeding hell, what are you doing here at this time of night?"

19

Georgiana was early for her meeting with Nick. She threaded her way through the cluttered hall of the Egyptian Wing holding a candle aloft in the dusty darkness. Her spectacles had slipped down the bridge of her nose. Her hands shook as she shoved them back with a finger, and she tried to fight her dread that Nick would insist that he'd discovered Evelyn's guilt when she was certain that Prudence was the murderer. She wanted no more arguments, especially ones in which he taunted and tempted her.

Was it only agitation that made her turn sharply to look behind her, or had she really heard a footfall? Nonsense. There was no one behind her. Coming to the large workroom, she lowered her candle, for a bright glow spread forth from the threshold. The room was deserted. Inside Georgia stopped in amazement to behold an avenue of light formed by two parallel lines of candelabra on stands almost as tall as she was.

The avenue led across the workroom and disap-

peared into the library. She walked between the two
rows, noticing as she went that the red-granite sarcophagus had vanished. Ludwig must have had it
moved, but he wouldn't have left all these candles
alight. This bit of theatrics was Nick's doing.

Georgiana set her jaw and marched down the
golden path into the library. There a shelf with cubi-
cles designed to house papyrus rolls had been moved
from its place against the wall, and the rows of candelabra continued through an opening. Georgiana
stepped through it to find herself on a small landing.
Growing more and more curious and mystified, she
descended a short staircase, her way still lit by tall
candle stands. From below she could hear a light tapping noise.

At the bottom of the stairs lay an open door beyond which she could hear the tapping. Georgiana
walked into a rectangular chamber alight with brilliant
color. She paused in the doorway and blinked hard,
for the room had been plastered and painted in regis-
ters to imitate an ancient Egyptian tomb. Pushing
back her spectacles again, she found the chamber's
only occupant. At the far end of the room Ludwig was
working on one of the dozens of coffins in the collection. The mummy case rested on the red-granite sarcophagus.

Standing on a stepladder with his back to her,
Ludwig was hammering slender nails into wood near
the foot of the coffin. Speechless, Georgiana glanced
around the chamber. Another sarcophagus rested beside the one on which Ludwig worked. Inside it lay a
series of nested coffins. The sarcophagus lid leaned
against a wall.

In various neatly disposed collections lay the accoutrements of the Egyptian afterlife. Magical shabti figurines stood in a group ready to do the labor required of the deceased in the afterlife. Baskets and boxes of food insured the soul's sustenance. Ludwig had also included the furnishings of a well-equipped tomb—low gilded couches with legs in the form of lion paws, cedar and ebony chairs, stands that would hold wine jars, alabaster jewel caskets. Near the coffins sat a shrine that contained canopic jars that held the internal organs of the deceased. There were even personal possessions, mirrors, shaving razors, scimitars, and bows.

Georgiana turned around in a circle, marveling at Ludwig's attention to detail. "Ludwig, how marvelous."

Ludwig cried out and dropped his hammer.

"Georgiana, you're early!"

"Was this supposed to be a surprise? I'm sorry."

Ludwig came down from the stepladder as she approached and smiled at her shyly. "Do you like it?"

"It's amazing." Georgiana looked around the room at the painted scenes that decorated the walls. "You've copied some of the best tomb paintings."

One wall was devoted to a scene of a man watching his servants harvest a field of grain; another depicted the Day of Judgment in the Hall of Osiris, where the dead man's heart was weighed against the feather of truth. All of it was done in brightly painted red, black, blue, yellow, and green.

"It's all so authentic," Georgiana breathed. Then she remembered why she was there and frowned. "Have you seen Mr. Ross? I was supposed to meet him in the workroom."

"Oh, my heart, no. I haven't seen him. Why

would he wish to meet you at such an unseemly time, and alone? It's not done, my dear."

"It's a private matter. I've misjudged the time, I suppose."

Ludwig produced a pocket watch. "Oh, my, it's a quarter past two."

Turning away, Georgiana said, "I'll go back to the workroom. He's probably there by now."

"Wait. He'll find us by the candelabra. Don't you want to see what I've done?" Ludwig trotted over to a table beside the coffin he'd been mending and picked up a roll of papyrus. "I've made an exact copy of the *Book of the Dead*."

Georgiana wandered over to the table. "That's lovely, but I'm quite distracted at the moment, Ludwig. Perhaps tomorrow you could show me."

"This will only take a moment." Ludwig picked up a ceramic flagon and poured wine into a faience goblet. "I've even provided wine as it would have been stored for the deceased. See those jars over there? They all have clay seals bearing the name of Ramses II. . . ."

While Ludwig chattered, Georgiana tried to think of a way to extricate herself without hurting his feelings. Ordinarily she would have been fascinated by Ludwig's replica, but all she could think of was what Nick might do to her when she told him their wager was off. As she worried, her gaze wandered from the wine Ludwig was offering her to the coffin.

The lid to the red-granite sarcophagus had been put in place, and the coffin rested on top of it. The coffin was that of a man and had been fashioned in the New Kingdom anthropoid shape. Painted black and gilded with gold, it bore the features of some Egyptian nobleman who had died thousands of years ago. His arms were crossed over his chest. His hands held magical amulets.

Near the other end of the coffin the wood had split, and Ludwig was attempting to mend it with new wood, which added at least a foot in length. Georgiana frowned and moved nearer the coffin. She was wrong. The wood hadn't split with age; it had been cleanly sawed. Ludwig was adding length to what were essentially the legs of the coffin. Setting her goblet on the floor, she touched the new wood, and Ludwig stopped chattering.

"What have you done to this coffin?" Georgiana asked.

"It was about to break, so I thought that as long as I had to repair it, I would make it fit the new sarcophagus."

"Make it fit?" Georgiana stared at Ludwig. "This isn't like you, to tamper with an important piece. This is a fine example of a New Kingdom—what was that?"

Ludwig walked away from her and around the other sarcophagus. "What?"

Georgiana was glancing around the chamber.

"I heard something."

As she searched the room, the sound came again, this time from the coffin. A short groan issued from it, and she gaped at the painted features of the nobleman, the black eyes, the full mouth and long, straight nose. There was a loud rap against the wood. Then the face seemed to jump at her.

Gasping, Georgiana jumped away as the coffin lid burst up from the base and clattered to the floor. Nick sat up, then lowered his face to his hands. Georgiana crossed her arms over her chest and glared at him.

"What a foul trick, Mr. Ross. If you've damaged that lid, you'll be sorry."

While she chastised him, Nick looked up and glared at her, then winced and touched the back of his head. His hand came away bloody, and Georgiana's tirade faded as she watched him stare at his hand.

"He wouldn't drink any wine either, so I had to hit him."

Ludwig stepped around the second sarcophagus holding a pistol. Her mouth falling open, Georgiana drew nearer to Nick. He swore and got to his knees inside the coffin.

"The fat little weasel lured me down here and hit me from behind."

Georgiana took a step toward Ludwig, who raised the pistol higher. As he got out of the coffin, Nick grabbed her arm and pulled her behind him.

"Ludwig, have you gone mad?" she asked.

Ludwig drew a black-bordered handkerchief from his coat pocket and wiped a tear from his eye, all the while keeping his pistol aimed at them. "No, I haven't gone mad. Oh, my heart, no, but you've both refused to accept Uncle's death. I heard you asking questions. I even saw you searching, prying into the game larder."

"You followed us?" Georgiana asked weakly.

"I was so frightened you would expose me," Ludwig said with a sniffle into his handkerchief. "Until I got the idea of using the tomb. You both will vanish, elope, and no one will ever think to look inside the coffins. No one comes here but me now that Uncle is dead, and you're going to be."

Nick began to edge around the granite sarcophagus as Ludwig spoke, pushing Georgiana with him.

"So you poisoned old Threshfield," he said.

Ludwig cocked the pistol. "Please don't move anymore, Ross."

Nick stopped. "Why did you do him, Hyde old chap?"

"Yes," Georgiana said in bewilderment. "Why?"

A tear rolled down Ludwig's nose and dropped off the end. "I didn't want to, but he said he was going to give my beautiful artifacts to Georgiana, and—and he disparaged her honor!"

Georgiana tried to move from behind Nick, but he yanked her back.

"Bloody hell," Nick said. "You don't care about Georgiana's reputation. You were just worried about your moldy old pots and coffins."

All at once Ludwig stopped snuffling. "That's not true. I would have asked for her hand to save her honor, but you, *you* ruined her."

"What?" Georgiana cried.

The pistol jabbed in Nick's direction. "Everyone thinks I'm too absorbed in my studies to notice anything, but I saw how he looked at you. I've seen you together, in the grotto, here, that day on the lawn when Aunt Augusta tried to shoot you." Ludwig glared at Georgiana. "Uncle told me what was going on, but I didn't believe him until I saw for myself, and then I realized you would give up our glorious studies for him, a common thief."

Shaking her head, Georgiana tried to make sense of Ludwig's ramblings. "You poisoned poor dear Threshfield to keep the collection."

"It's mine!" Ludwig shouted. "I take care of it. I

keep it safe. I study the objects. He had no right to threaten to give it away. When he did, I realized it would never be safe until he was dead." He stuffed the handkerchief into his pocket. "And I once thought we were twin souls in our love of scholarship, but now you've ruined everything. You were going to find out about the belladonna in the rabbit stew, and then I might have been accused of murder. If that happened, I couldn't take care of my collection. I couldn't be separated from my collection. Oh, my heart, no."

As Ludwig spoke, Georgiana felt Nick's hand clasp hers. It was warm and steady, while hers was cold and trembling. Nick had managed to put them in a position at the corner of the sarcophagus. His left leg was partially hidden by the stone container, and she felt it move surreptitiously. She sneaked a glance and saw his boot edging the discarded hammer toward them.

"I don't want to fire a gun in here," Ludwig was saying. "The bullets might damage my tomb paintings, but I don't suppose either of you will drink any wine."

"You put belladonna in it," Georgiana said.

Ludwig nodded. "I thought surely you noticed the passage on nightshade in the book on Egyptian medicine. Since you won't have any wine now, I'll have to shoot both of you. We're too far away to be heard by anyone in the rest of the house, and I'll just have you kneel so that I can aim down." He brightened and smiled at her. "And then I'll be able to replicate the embalming ritual. I have the natron salts ready to dry the bodies, and the tools."

"Holy bleeding hell," Nick said in a hushed voice. "The lunatic is going to wrap us up like them

mummies and stuff us in there." He pointed to the
mummy cases.

"Yes," Georgiana said, her voice shaking. "That's
why he had to lengthen the coffin, to fit you. It's a
clever idea."

Ludwig was beaming now. "I knew you'd appre-
ciate it. Please kneel, both of you."

Nick thrust Georgiana farther behind him.
"Leave her alone. She won't say anything."

"I'm not the fool you think," Ludwig said.
"Once I killed you, she would never rest until she
destroyed me."

Georgiana escaped Nick's grip and slipped around
to his side. "You're right, Ludwig dear, but there's no
need to kill either of us. We won't reveal your secret."

"I'm sorry, dear Georgiana, but I don't believe
you. Please kneel."

While Ludwig continued to ramble on about his
plans, an odd scraping sound had caught Georgiana's
attention. Evidently his own voice had concealed the
noise from Ludwig. She glanced at Nick, whose eyes
were fixed on the source of the scraping. Lady Augusta stood just inside the doorway, clad in an elaborate lace-and-lawn robe and cap. She was tamping
down a charge in her musket with a ramrod. Nick
drew in his breath as Augusta raised the weapon.

Ludwig pointed the pistol straight at Nick's heart.
Georgiana's gaze fixed on the finger curled around the
trigger. She saw it move. Nick cried out and tried to
push her out of the way. At the same time, Georgiana
threw herself between Ludwig and Nick so that Nick
missed when he tried to shove her. The report nearly
deafened her as Georgiana hit the floor. She felt a

sting in her side, but it vanished before Nick's body plummeted on top of her.

His arm came around her and he rolled, bringing her with him so that they ended up behind the sarcophagus. Nick grabbed the hammer and jumped up to peer over the sarcophagus and coffin. Georgiana sprang to her feet beside him in time to see Ludwig whirl around to point the pistol at Augusta. There was a loud crack. Smoke curled from the musket, and Ludwig dropped with a hole in his head. Georgiana's vision filled with the sight of blood and bone. Her knees felt weak, and she heard herself whimper. Nick slipped his arm around her. They exchanged stunned glances, then turned to peer at Augusta.

The old lady hooked her arm around her musket and glared at Ludwig's body. "I told you to kill the spy, not Wellington." She spun around and marched out the door. "Daft young rotter."

Nick slipped his arm around her waist, and they emerged from the protection of the sarcophagus to stand over Ludwig's body. Georgiana glanced at the spattered blood, then looked away. Nick placed his body between her and the dead man. His fingers lifted her chin. She raised her eyes to find him looking at her with a gaze of wondering gentleness. His burnished hair gleamed in the candlelight. His eyes glowed like indigo fire.

"You put yourself in front of a bullet meant for me."

Her gaze wavered. "Dukes' daughters are taught to be brave."

"Do they always risk their lives for common thieves?" His voice was growing even softer, which increased her alarm.

"Constantly," she said.

"I don't believe you."

She cleared her throat. "Poor Ludwig."

"Sod poor Ludwig. He tried to kill us." Nick began to approach her.

Georgiana backed away. "Do you think madness runs in the Threshfield family?"

"I'd make a bet on it."

No matter how much she avoided him, Nick kept coming toward her. Georgiana backed all the way to the wall, where she bumped her head and tried to slide sideways. His arm blocked her. She slid the other way; his other arm came up to bar her escape. He bent down so that his lips were almost touching hers.

"Say it, love," he breathed.

"What?"

"Say why you risked your life for mine."

She was surrounded by him. Her breath was his, her skin tingled with his heat.

"Why?" he whispered. He touched his tongue to her earlobe.

Georgiana gasped and blurted out, "I couldn't let you die! Please, Nick, I want to get out of this horrible place."

"Not until you tell me why."

The blood, the thought that he almost died, drove her to cry out, "I love you! There. Are you satisfied? I love you, now let me go."

She thrust against him with both arms, hard. That was when she noticed the pain. She cried out again and clasped her side. Nick stood back, and they both looked at the blood that soaked the bodice of her gown. Georgiana glanced up to meet his alarmed stare. She smiled weakly.

"Oh, my."

Nick grabbed her as her legs buckled. She felt her body sail into the air. Dizziness forced her to close her eyes. Her head dropped to his shoulder, and she could hear him swearing as he hurried from the tomb chamber. She could still hear his voice, as if at a distance, while she floated in some undefined space filled with pain and nausea.

"Hang on, love. Hang on."

20

Hang on, hang on. Those two words chased each other inside his head as Nick carried Georgiana upstairs to the workroom. She had taken a shot meant for him. Deliberately. She'd risked her life, which meant she valued his before her own.

He'd never been so confused, for no one had ever done such a thing. Always in the past he'd been the one to save people—his mother, his sister, even Jocelin. Now Georgiana had saved him, and he didn't know how to feel about it.

Sweeping books and papers from the table in the workroom, he lowered her carefully and grabbed one of the candelabra for light. He set the stand beside Georgiana, who pressed a hand to her wound. She lay still, biting her lower lip, her eyes closed.

"Hang on, love. Move your hand so I can see."

He eased her hand away from the wound. Swallowing back dread at what he might find, Nick lifted the torn edges of her bodice. The bullet had sliced through her flesh between two ribs, but the injury was shallow. The bleeding had already begun to slow. Relief flooded through him as he took out his handkerchief and gently placed it over the wound.

"Is it terrible?" came Georgiana's shaky inquiry.

"No, love. Just a nick." He bent over her and kissed her lips, causing her to open her eyes. They were brilliant with unshed tears.

She winced. "A nick. How appropriate."

"You don't look too good, love. Rest a moment, and then I'll carry you to your room and get a doctor."

He didn't like the way she'd lost all color in her face. When she began to cry silently, he grew alarmed.

"What's wrong?"

"Poor, poor Ludwig. Poor Threshfield. If only he hadn't made up that tale about giving away the collection, neither of them would have—would have . . ."

"Bleeding hell, that lying old skeleton should have known better, and Ludwig almost killed us!"

"Where is Lady Augusta?"

"Scarpered, love. Now, be quiet."

She had gotten control of her tears, but she grimaced again as she said, "You were right all along."

"About what?"

"The balcony railing, the hansom cab. Neither was an accident."

"Right, love, but we may never know if Ludwig had a hand in either. Me, I still think Evelyn bloody Hyde has got to answer for those little incidents. Which means there's nothing to worry about now that the bastard has his title."

Biting her lip, Georgiana fought back a sob. "Nothing to worry about."

"Here! You keep quiet like I said. You're just up-
setting yourself more with all this talk."

Nick squeezed her hand. Then he found a pitcher
of water, tasted it just in case Ludwig had put something in it as well as in the wine, and brought a glass to
Georgiana. He helped her raise her head and held the
glass to her lips. She took a few sips, then pushed the
glass away and lowered her lashes so that he couldn't
see her eyes.

"Don't worry, Mr. Ross. I'm not going to take
advantage of you. You won't have to sacrifice yourself
simply because I was foolish enough to get shot."

His brows drew together as he set the glass down.
"What do you mean, sacrifice myself?"

"By having to marry me," she whispered.

He said nothing while he absorbed yet another
shock. Georgiana thought he didn't want her. Had
she felt this way all along, and how could she think
such a thing?

"But you thought I wasn't good enough for you,
my being from St. Giles and all."

Georgiana's eyes flew open, revealing astonishment and pain. His arm still cradled her head. She
tried to sit up but fell back, gasping.

"You fool," she said, and she fainted.

A week after Ludwig was killed, Nick rode into the
hills that formed one of the borders of the Threshfield
estate, with Pertwee in attendance. Their destination
was a rotunda, a gleaming white stone pavilion open
to the air and set on a rise overlooking the house,
park, and woods. Slender columns rose to support a
high domed ceiling upon which was set a statue of

winged Mercury. Beneath the dome sat a telescope intended for the enjoyment of the earl's guests.

Nick walked his horse up the slope and cast a morose glance back at his valet. Pertwee had badgered him into coming there, saying he'd spent the whole week slouching about the house, casting even more melancholy upon an already beleaguered family. Nick didn't care where he went.

After he had taken Georgiana to her room and seen her cared for by the Threshfield doctor, Nick had been plunged into the furor of the inquiry into Ludwig's death. He'd answered questions from constables, a justice of the peace, a coroner, and even a queen's counsel and a home secretary. During it all he had been subjected to the arrogant assumption that since he was the one of low birth, he must have been responsible for Ludwig's death.

Georgiana had set them all straight in a gallant, pale-faced appearance in the drawing room before the queen's counsel. Then she'd vanished into her rooms, pleading illness from her wound. She refused to see him or anyone, except Lady Lavinia. Alarmed messages arrived from her father demanding explanations and the return of his daughter.

Lady Augusta was remanded into the permanent care of a staff of nurses whose business was to watch her day and night. Finally the aristocratic queen's counsel sent a lowly constable to tell Nick that Ludwig's death would be ruled an accident—to spare Lady Georgiana and Lady Augusta. No one cared if Nick was spared.

In all the confusion Nick had longed to talk to Georgiana, but she didn't seem to want to talk to him. He asked several times to be allowed to visit her and was refused. He was left to suffer in his confusion. He still couldn't believe she loved him, or that she loved him enough to defy Society and marry him. He was afraid to ask her and receive the answer he knew she must give. In any case, nothing had changed. He couldn't dishonor her and Jocelin.

Dismounting at the summit of the hill, Nick handed his reins to Pertwee and walked slowly to the rotunda. Beneath the dome near the telescope were wrought-iron chairs and a table. Nick sank into a chair and propped his boots on the table, crossed his arms, and sank his chin to his chest.

"Well," he said to Pertwee. "I'm here. Now, where is this Al fellow?"

"Al, sir?" Pertwee asked as he carried a basket to the rotunda.

"You said we were dining with Al somebody."

Pertwee's nose quivered as he set the basket down on the table. "Sir is mistaken. I said we would dine *alfresco*, which means outdoors."

"Well, why didn't you say so, damn it?"

Pertwee sighed. "Perhaps it would take sir's mind off his troubles if we discussed Plato's ideas on tyranny as set forth in The *Republic*."

"It would give me a headache," Nick snapped.

Pertwee drew a pristine-white tablecloth from the basket and shook it. The linen snapped and caught a breeze. Nick glared at it, rose, and went to the telescope. Pertwee had already instructed him in its use, so he closed one eye and focused. He turned the instrument on the house, searching for the balcony and windows of Georgiana's room. He found them but couldn't see inside. Around him the afternoon sun bathed the autumn countryside in gold. He lowered

the telescope a bit to scan the terrace, the lawns, the
lake and fishing pavilion.

He was moving on to the woods beyond the lake
when he glimpsed something black. He turned the
telescope back to the lake, to the Palladian bridge.
Rounded arches dipped into the glassy blue water.
Upon the bridge walked Georgiana, and she was with
someone. His hand jerked, causing him to lose sight of
the couple and their chaperon, Aunt Lavinia. He
swore and refocused, twisting the instrument until it
cleared. When he was finished, Georgiana stood in
the circle of his lens beside a tall, elegantly clad young
man with golden hair.

"Bloody hell, it's Dallas!"

"Sir?" Pertwee asked.

"What's Dallas bloody Meredith doing here?"

"Ah, Mr. Meredith."

Nick whirled around to stare at the valet. "You
know Meredith?"

"Had sir been in a communicative mood these
past few days, I could have informed him of Mr. Meredith's impending arrival."

"Well, tell me now, blast you. What's he doing
here?"

"Sir will be surprised to know that Mr. Meredith
belongs to the family, the Hydes, that is. Mr. Meredith's grandfather, the old earl's younger brother, was
sent to the Colonies in disgrace over a gambling incident long ago. He changed his name and made his
fortune in America. Due to Ludwig Hyde's unfortunate death and Lord Evelyn's lack of other issue, Mr.
Meredith is now the heir to Threshfield."

"Bloody hell. Secretive bastard." Nick turned
back to the telescope. Georgiana and Dallas were still

on the bridge, and Dallas was standing much too close to her. "Too bloody close," Nick muttered. Pushing the telescope aside, he turned back to Pertwee. "Forget the luncheon, Pertwee, I'm going . . ."

His words trailed off as he watched a party of mounted men ride up the hill. Five of them appeared uncomfortable in the saddle and looked as if they belonged in a gin shop on the London docks despite their expensive riding apparel. The sixth was the Duke of Clairemont, Georgiana's father.

Although he'd seen the duke seldom, Nick recognized him by his emerald eyes and erect military bearing, which Jocelin had inherited. He had also bequeathed his height and jewel-bright eyes to Georgiana, but Georgiana's eyes held warmth, interest, and benevolence. The duke surveyed the world and everyone in it with the cold disinterest of one who knew that he ranked above all he observed.

Nick went down the steps of the rotunda to meet His Grace as he dismounted and tossed the reins of his thoroughbred to one of his men. The duke stalked up to Nick, stuck his hands behind his back, and planted his legs apart in a stance so like Jocelin that Nick was taken aback. "I've been looking for you," the duke said without preamble.

"Good afternoon, your grace. I didn't know you had arrived at Threshfield."

"No one does, Ross. I came by my private railcar in response to a letter from the new earl."

"I understand. This business with old Threshfield and Ludwig—"

"I don't care about Threshfield or Ludwig," the duke said, his voice loud. "What do you mean, sir, by interfering with my daughter?"

Nick adopted an impassive expression. "I don't know what you mean. What has Evelyn said?"

"That you've been sniffing around my daughter like a mongrel after a bitch, and that you've even been alone with her."

Nick kept his mouth shut. The duke turned and handed his riding crop to one of his men, jerked off his gloves, and took back the crop. He began to walk around Nick as if inspecting a horse.

"In the past I've tolerated your presence in my house once or twice because I couldn't make Jocelin give you up, but by God, sir, I'll not have you prowling around my daughter and ruining her. I would have thought Lavinia would have sent you packing, but she seems to have lost her senses where you're concerned. But I'll deal with her later. You, sir, will leave England immediately. Go back to Texas, where I'm sure you'll be comfortable among the barbarians."

Nick had been contemplating such a course, but hearing himself dismissed like compost heap provoked an unexpected rage. He might not be good enough for Georgiana, but that was for him to decide, not the bloody duke.

"I'll go when I'm ready, duke old chap, and I'll see who I want, including Georgiana."

The duke flushed and drew nearer. "You will refer to my daughter as her ladyship, you worthless gutter rat. Lord Evelyn said you'd gotten above yourself, that you'd even put your dirty hands on——" The duke broke off, glancing aside at his men, and lowered his voice. "If you think I'll stand by while you try to defile my daughter with your seed, you're a fool."

"Bloody hell," Nick whispered. "You're not worried about Georgiana at all, are you? You're ready to piss in your pants at the thought of your pure family line being soiled by the likes o' me. I forgot what a sodding prick you are, Clairemont. Always thinking of yourself and your position. You and Evelyn are a pair, you are. Go babble at somebody who gives a bleeding ha'penny what you think or say."

As Nick began to turn away, the duke said, "There never was any use trying to reason with the lower classes." Clairemont raised his riding crop and slashed down, delivering a blow to the back of Nick's head.

Nick felt a crushing sting; his knees buckled. Pertwee cried out and rushed from the rotunda only to be stopped by two of the duke's men.

The duke stepped aside, wiping his crop on the ground to rid it of Nick's blood. "Snead, you have your instructions."

Snead, a mountainous man with a broken nose and fists the size of beef joints, lumbered over to Nick and drew a pistol from his belt. Trying to get to his feet, Nick half turned as the man approached. He was still on one knee when Snead reached him. He felt the man's fist smash into his jaw. His skull exploded with pain.

Nick struck out with his fist, landing a blow to Snead's stomach. Snead grunted, grabbed Nick's wrist with one hand, and raised the butt of his pistol above Nick's head. Nick tried to dodge the blow, but the man yanked him off balance. He felt the pistol butt crack into his skull. Agony flowed from the top of his head straight to his heart. He was sure it had stopped beating before he hit the ground and lost consciousness.

The duke was busy putting on his kid gloves and didn't spare a glance at the struggle. Snead straightened up, looming over Nick's body, and looked at his master. The duke walked over to the telescope and peered through it. Snead joined him.

Training the lens on a flock of ducks near the lake, the duke said, "I've been thinking. It will do no good to send Mr. Ross back to Texas. He'll just sail back here. The solution must be more permanent."

"Your Grace wants me to scrag him afore he comes awake?"

"No, you dullard. I don't condone murder, and in any case, a wealthy man like our friend here will be missed."

Snead's bushy brows drew together as he struggled to come up with another solution, creativity being a concept foreign to him. The duke turned the telescope on the distant hills.

"I think Mr. Ross should return to the gutter he came from. Pick an appropriately squalid opium den in Whitechapel and put him in it. Keep him there until he can't go an hour without the stuff, then let him go. Send his man to pack his kit. He is to return to the railroad car after he has informed Threshfield that Ross has decided to leave the country. Make sure he knows his master's life depends upon his cooperation. You can ship Mr. Ross off in a clipper headed for India or China."

"Yes, Your Grace."

The duke left the telescope, plucked a half-filled glass of wine from the table, and sipped from it while his men threw Nick across the saddle of his horse and began to tie him down. Then he mounted his own horse and walked him over to Nick, whose head started to move. The duke pulled his boot from his stirrup and delivered a kick. Nick's head dropped, and his body went limp once again.

Clairemont sighed and tapped his mount with his riding crop. "A most tiresome business."

21

Georgiana's head felt as if it had swelled to twice its size. She wasn't ill. Her wound was healing quite well, and she'd had enough rest. But the day's events had descended upon her with the force of a brigade charge. First the new heir to Threshfield had arrived without warning. Then this stranger had approached her with startling news. Finally, her father had arrived in a rage, and now Nick had disappeared without a word to her.

She sat at her dressing table, lost in misery while Rebecca searched for a heavy jet necklace to go with her off-shoulder evening gown. Yards of *soie cristal* billowed around her, its hue so dark, it appeared purple. When the Duke of Clairemont graced a household, one dressed as if appearing before a monarch. Georgiana wouldn't have remembered, but Rebecca had been with her so long that the requirements of fashion were an unspoken routine to the maid. Which was fortunate, because Georgiana was too upset to think about clothes.

She had been wrong about Nick. All this time she'd been certain he didn't want her when it seemed he'd been convinced he was unworthy of her. The discovery, coming at the same time as her injury, had stunned her. She'd wrestled with her bewilderment for a while and tried to push aside her conviction that in spite of his affection for her, Nick wouldn't want to spend his life with an ungainly giant. Then it had taken more time to summon the courage to face him again, but finally she had decided to confront Nick, to ask him if what he'd said in the workroom had been real rather than a delusion brought on by her pain and distress.

Only late this morning had she emerged from seclusion. Evelyn and Prudence had been formally solicitous, and she had been about to escape their company and search for Nick when Mr. Dallas Meredith arrived. It was then that she learned of Mr. Meredith's connection to the family. Indeed, his friendship with Jocelin had first come about through a discovery of the connection. Although she wasn't much interested in the new Threshfield heir, he had been so persistent in seeking her company that she had found herself on a walk with him and Aunt Livy.

He had moved beside her with a lithe, smooth gait, his sun-gold hair catching the light, and spoke in a slow, cultured drawl. "Lady Georgiana, ma'am, as you know, I've come from America, where my family has been established for some time. However, you don't know that I've spent many months with your brother."

Georgiana stopped on the Palladian bridge to exchange startled glances with Aunt Livy. "You have?"

"Yes, ma'am."

"Mr. Meredith," Aunt Livy said, "this is all very odd. Your family name isn't Hyde, and yet you're the Threshfield heir, and now you say you've been visiting my nephew."

"Well, ma'am, let's just say my grandfather had a bit of trouble in Georgia a while ago, and when he bought all that land in Mississippi, well, he just changed his name."

Aunt Livy raised her brows. "Young man, one addresses the queen as ma'am."

Dallas gave her a lazy smile. "Then I reckon it'll do for two such regal ladies as yourselves. Just a respectful habit, ma'am."

"Your manner is quite enigmatic, Mr. Meredith," Georgiana said. "You were speaking of my brother?"

Dallas slipped his hand inside his coat and brought out an envelope. "He asked me to deliver this."

"Thank you."

When she made no move to open it, he said, "Jocelin told me it was important, and that you should read it immediately."

Eyeing Dallas's impassive face, Georgiana went a little farther across the bridge while Livy remained with their guest. Opening the letter, she began to read.

My dearest Georgie,

I know you're furious with me for trying to prevent your marriage to Threshfield, but we must put aside our quarrel now. Nick has sent me several agitated letters of late, and I've come to the conclusion that I should tell you about him.

She read about Nick's life—about his drunken, brutal father, his mother, who scrubbed floors until the day she died, about how little Tessie had died because she was a pretty young girl. Jocelin even told her about Nick's help with his crusade to rid the world of degenerates who preyed on children. She had known about her brother's part, but she hadn't realized that Nick had guided Jocelin, shown him how to move around in the squalid warrens of Whitechapel and dockside brothels. Without Nick, Jocelin could easily have ended up a corpse floating in the Thames.

I admire Nick Ross above all men, Georgie. He has my greatest affection, and I would like nothing better than to be able to call him brother.

It was then that Georgiana had realized Jocelin was giving his blessing. Somehow he had guessed what had happened between her and Nick. She had raced back to the house to find Nick, regardless of the courtesy she owed to Mr. Meredith, but Pertwee had packed all his master's possessions and left with them. Nick was gone.

Tears stung her eyes as Georgiana remembered how desolate she'd felt upon learning of Nick's abrupt departure. Why, why, why had he left? Had he grown weary of waiting for her to come to him? He had tried to come to her, and she had been too much a coward to see him. It was all her fault, and now she'd lost him. He probably hated her.

Rebecca appeared with the heavy jet necklace and placed it around Georgiana's neck. Georgiana stared through the window at the black, starless night. The vast, dark emptiness reminded her of the emptiness she felt inside.

It was an emptiness born of not hearing Nick's teasing voice call her "young George," of longing to see his lips part in astonishment while she prattled about the beauties of an ancient statue with the body of a man and the head of a baboon, an emptiness fed by the knowledge that he might never again give himself to her as he had done that night in the cabinet.

Why hadn't he waited just a little longer? Did she dare go after him? Her father watched her every move; she couldn't go after him openly. Could she persuade Mr. Meredith to find him? For the first time since learning of Nick's absence, Georgiana brightened.

Rising from the dressing table, she hurried downstairs in search of the American. She met Aunt Livy on her way to the drawing room, where the family gathered before dinner. All the other guests had departed, and the company would be limited to the Threshfields, the Marshals, and Dallas. As she and her aunt reached the ground floor, Georgiana pulled Livy around to the relative seclusion beneath the staircase.

"Aunt Livy, do you think Mr. Meredith could find Nick for me?" Georgiana whispered, wringing her black lace handkerchief in both hands.

"I knew it!"

Georgiana jumped at her aunt's loud tone and glanced over her shoulder and up the stairs. "Shhh. Please, Aunt."

"I knew you'd come to your senses eventually." Aunt Livy snapped open her fan and spoke behind it. "Mr. Ross is twice the gentleman of any of the lot your father had prowling around you and your fortune. It's taken you long enough to realize it. Do you know how hard it's been to keep out of the way so that you two could be together?"

"Aunt Livy!" Georgiana cried in dismay. "Why didn't you say anything if you liked him so much?"

"Would you have listened?"

"Oh."

"Precisely. And I think Mr. Meredith could find anyone he wanted to find. Come on, now. We don't want to leave the Threshfields alone to greet your father. No telling what disgusting lies they'll tell."

In the black-shrouded drawing room they spent a few minutes in strained conversation with Evelyn and Prudence. Looking like a small black football in her huge crinoline and mourning gown, Prudence was beaming in anticipation of playing hostess to the Duke of Clairemont. Hitherto she'd been spending much of her time in her room grieving for Ludwig, but the arrival of so prominent a guest banished all sorrow within her maternal breast. She hardly noticed Dallas's arrival in the drawing room, which gave Georgiana the chance to pull the American aside.

"Mr. Meredith, I have a great favor to ask of you."

"I am at your service, ma'am."

"I must find Mr. Ross at once, and I can't do it myself as long as my father is about. I wonder if you can help me?"

"It would be an honor to come to the aid of such a lovely lady."

Georgiana gave him a pained smile. "You seem to know a great deal about my private affairs, sir, so there's no need for flattery. I'm hardly the dainty, delicate lady."

"I'm not in the habit of spewing false compliments, ma'am. And as for your lack of daintiness . . . " Dallas looked down at her from his greater stature with a quizzical expression.

"I reckon old Nick's glad to have found a lady he doesn't have to pick up to speak to."

"I beg your pardon?"

"Well, ma'am, Nick and I are about the same
height, and neither of us enjoys getting a crick in the
neck trying to talk to ladies of diminutive height."

"Are you teasing me, Mr. Meredith?"

"Maybe just a little, ma'am."

Before she could reply, the butler announced her
father, and the atmosphere chilled as the duke walked
into the room. Clairemont nodded to his host and
hostess with glacial reserve, then greeted his sister.

"I would like a word with you, Lavinia."

"Fine."

"A private word."

"Oh, do get on with it, Clairemont. You look like
a bishop who's just seen the pope on his chamber
pot."

The duke looked as if he were suffering some
great intestinal pain. "Very well, we will discuss your
shortcomings as a chaperon later."

Georgiana sighed and glanced at Dallas.

"Now he's done it," she said.

"Clairemont," Lavinia purred, "I like Mr. Ross,
and I have no intention of letting you ruin Georgiana's chances with him. Be civil or I'll box your ears as
I did when we were children."

"Really, Lavinia, you're hardly the person to
speak about civility. I'm going to see to it that Georgiana is married to a satisfactory young man."

"Oh, no," Georgiana muttered.

The butler forestalled further argument by announcing dinner. At the same time a distant boom
could be heard rolling down the hall and into the
saloon. It was a wonder the statues didn't crack in
their alcoves.

"What was that?" the duke demanded.

"It sounded like the front doors," Evelyn said.

As he finished, Georgiana heard a loud bellow magnified by the marble and alabaster in the hall. The growling shout grew louder.

"Clairrrrrre—mont!"

Georgiana jumped to her feet. "Nick?"

The doors to the drawing room burst open, kicked by Nicholas Ross, who slammed them aside and strode into the room. He stopped when he saw the duke. Everyone stared at him wordlessly, including Georgiana. Nick wore only a dirty, torn shirt, muddy riding pants, and equally soiled boots. He was breathless and sweating, his face streaked with dirt and blood. His hair was damp and dark except for its red-gold sun streaks. He was holding a pistol.

Georgiana was the first to recover from astonishment and rushed to his side. Putting her hand on his arm, she searched his face, alarmed at the rage she beheld.

"Nick?" she whispered.

The hard menace in his expression softened for a moment as he glanced at her. "Hello, love," he said softly.

Then he rounded on the duke, who was facing him with his hands clasped behind his back. Nick's East End accent was harsh.

"You bloody bastard, you tried to kill me," he said with a calm that alarmed Georgiana more than his rage.

The duke lifted one brow. "On the contrary. If I had tried to kill you, you'd be dead."

"Oh, no. You wouldn't dirty your hands with the job, but you shouldn't have picked such stupid coves for it." Nick touched the pistol in his belt. "Snead tried to slit my throat. He's dead."

Georgiana heard those words and began to feel as if she were in a waking nightmare. And she was growing more alarmed the more she saw of Nick's wounds. Touching a wisp of red-gold hair, she turned her gaze from the disturbing sight of his blood. "Father, what is he talking about, and what happened to him?"

"Tell her," Nick snapped.

The duke shrugged. "I had Mr. Ross detained."

"He had me jumped and beaten up, the sodding coward."

Georgiana stared at her father, shaking her head. The duke hadn't taken his eyes off Nick. Before she could ask for more details, Nick gently removed her hand from his arm.

"This time it's going to be you and me, Clairemont." Nick wiped blood from the side of his mouth. "Take off your coat and put up your fists."

"I don't engage in brawls with gutter rats."

"Father!"

"Too bad, old cock," Nick said with a grin. "Because that's what you're going to do, whether you like it or not." Georgiana put a forestalling hand on his arm again and whispered, "Nick, don't."

"Bloody hell, woman, it's too late for manners and dithering."

Evelyn marched over to Nick. "I say, Ross, this is too much."

Ignoring Evelyn, Nick glanced around the room, then went to a wall display beside the fireplace and removed two swords. He threw one at the duke, who caught it.

"No!" Georgiana cried.

Dallas spoke for the first time over the protests of Prudence and Evelyn. "Ross, this isn't the way."

"I'll deal with you after I've finished with Clairemont," Nick said.

Dallas looked surprised. "Me?"

"You needn't be concerned," the duke said to Dallas. "I won't kill him."

Dallas shrugged. "I was worried about you, Your Grace."

"Both of you stop," Georgiana said. "Father, don't you come near him with that sword."

Nick gave Dallas a look, and the blond man caught Georgiana's arm and pulled her back from the two men.

"Let me go, Mr. Meredith."

"Sorry, ma'am I can't do that."

Georgiana yanked her arm with no success. "Men! You're all lunatics."

While Prudence gasped and fluttered her bejeweled hands, Nick and the duke began to circle the room. Evelyn, Aunt Lavinia, and the butler shoved furniture aside. The duke closed in on Nick.

"This will be over shortly," he said. "Then you can summon the authorities to arrest this creature, Threshfield. I'm surprised you haven't already."

As he finished, Clairemont suddenly jabbed at Nick. Georgiana cried out as Nick danced aside and thrust at her father. The duke pulled back barely in time to escape Nick's blade. Startled at Nick's expertise, Georgiana clamped her mouth shut for fear of distracting him. She spared a glance at Dallas, who seemed unworried.

During that brief glance she heard her father swear. There was a high, hissing sound, and Georgiana saw Nick's sword rapidly clash with the duke's before swirling around and around the blade until it caught the guard. The duke's sword flew from his hand and crashed against a wall. At the same time Nick stuck the tip of his blade under Clairemont's chin. Georgiana hardly breathed, and even Prudence grew quiet as the duke lifted his hands in surrender.

Nick looked at his opponent down the length of his blade. "Nobody kicks me in the head and gets away with it."

"I should think you'd be used to it, given your low origins," the duke said.

Georgiana gasped and pulled her arm free of Dallas's grasp. "Father, for shame."

Shaking his head, Nick threw down his sword, took three steps, and punched the duke in the stomach. Clairemont dropped to his knees, wheezing, his face crimson. He clutched his gut and coughed. Nick planted his boot on the duke's shoulder and shoved. The duke landed on his ass, moaning.

"Some people just don't learn without encouragement," Nick said lightly. "Now, you listen to me, Your High-and-mighty Grace. I ain't going to marry Georgiana because I ain't going to dishonor her and Jocelin, not because you don't want me to. And the next time you try anything with me, I'm going to kick your gut into your throat."

"Marry?" Georgiana heard her voice climb the scale. She rushed over to Nick, her whole body shaking from anxiety and outrage. "Am I to understand that you two have been fighting about me?"

"Course we been fighting about you," Nick said.

"I—you—oh!" Georgiana clenched her fists and

counted to ten. It didn't help. "By heaven, how dare you, Nicholas Ross?"

"What?" Nick demanded as she began to stalk back and forth between him and her moaning father.

Drawing herself up to her most erect and regal posture, Georgiana said, "Now I understand. *You* decided not to marry me all by yourself, without asking me how I felt about it. Of all the high-handed effrontery. You decide what is honorable. You decide what is best for me. You decide whom I should marry. You decide whether I am to risk Society's disapproval. And what makes me even more furious is that you have decided that I haven't the character to recognize that honor, bravery, kindness, and loyalty can flourish in St. Giles as well as Grosvenor Square."

"I was only—"

"You were only deciding the course of my whole life for me, Nicholas Ross."

"But—"

"What if I don't care about Society, or Father, or anyone else but—but you—and me. Did you ever in all your prejudiced deliberations think to ask me how I felt?"

"Well, no."

"There!"

Nick spread his arms in dismay. "I thought I knew how you'd feel."

"Don't ever try to hire yourself out as a reader of minds," Georgiana said. Suddenly she felt tears building. Blinking rapidly, she lowered her voice. "If you had bothered to ask me to marry you, Mr. Ross, I would have said yes."

"You would?" Nick asked in a disbelieving tone.

"No, she wouldn't," the duke said from his perch on the floor. "I won't allow it."

"Oh, shut up, Clairemont," Lavinia said.

Georgiana ignored them. Holding back her tears, she whispered, "But you never asked, Mr. Ross. And you still don't believe me. I don't think you'll ever believe me, because in spite of everything, you still think I'm like all the other trivial-minded young ladies in Society. You're a snob, Nick. A bloody snob."

Without warning Georgiana again imagined a lifetime without Nick, alone, desolate, full of the agony of his loss. She gave a small cry filled with misery and rushed from the room. She heard Nick call to her and began to run blindly. She had exposed her deepest feelings to him, and she was afraid. Running across the saloon, she thrust open a door to the terrace and rushed out into the night.

22

Nick rushed to the door Georgiana had just slammed, but the duke scrambled to his feet and yanked his arm.

"You leave my daughter alone."

Nick was about to knock Clairemont aside when Lady Lavinia grabbed his arm.

"Young man, you've made a mess of everything. I'm beginning to think I should have shot you when you first galloped up the drive."

"But I didn't expect to . . ." Nick bit his lip and winced at the pain from the cut on his head.

Lady Lavinia stood back, waving reflectively with a black lace fan. "You abysmal young fool. Don't you know by now that girl loves you more than her life?"

All he could do was stare at the lady and swallow hard.

"Do you, in your most fevered imaginings, think that a duke's daughter remains in a house where a young man accosts her and makes free with her virtue unless she's hopelessly enamored?"

Around him he heard the duke, Evelyn, and Prudence all gasp and chatter at once. His head was swimming, and his eyes felt as if they'd swelled to the size of goose eggs. Without warning the duke shoved his face in front of Nick's.

"If you say a word about your dealings with Georgiana, I'll put a price on your head."

"Sod off," Nick said. He shoved Clairemont aside and rushed from the drawing room.

He was halfway through the saloon before he heard Meredith call him. Dallas caught up with him at the doors to the terrace.

"Clairemont threatened to come after you, but I convinced him he'd only get another fist in his gut. Before you go to Lady Georgiana, I want to talk to you."

"Keep away from her, Meredith. I won't be as nice to you as I was to the duke."

Dallas held up his hands. "Upon my honor, sir, I have no intentions toward Lady Georgiana."

"See that it stays that way."

Withdrawing an envelope from his inner coat pocket, Dallas smiled and handed it to Nick. "Why do you think I'm here, Ross?"

"How should I know? You were bloody secretive about your connection to Threshfield, and you let me come all the way over here when it was your family that was involved."

"But I don't know them, Ross. I'm American. To me they were mere names, and I had no wish to present myself on behalf of Jocelin only to be mistaken for a poor relation in search of charity." Dallas's glance slid away from Nick. "And in any case, I didn't wish to explain myself or my past to anyone. Ludwig Hyde's death made such privacy impossible for me."

"Look, Meredith, I don't care about your damned toff ancestors. Now, if you'll excuse me . . ."

"Not yet," Dallas replied as he offered the envelope he'd been holding. "Jocelin wanted me to give this to you."

Nick gave Dallas a distrustful glance before opening the letter.

I'm taking a chance, old chap, but Liza says I'm right. I think you've formed an attachment to my sister. I also think you find it impossible to admit your love for fear of Georgiana's refusal. I know you, Nick. You'd rather suffer in silence than cause me pain.

Nick felt the blood drain from his head. He'd been right—Jos didn't want him for Georgiana. Clenching his jaw, he read further.

What astonishes me is that you could share with me what we've shared and not know how honored I would be to call you brother. And I would consider it the greatest of gifts if you loved and married my dear Georgie.

There was a bit more, but he could hardly take in what he'd already read. Nick slipped the letter back into the envelope and cleared his throat as he glanced at Dallas. "Well, strike me blind."

"From what I've seen, it's unnecessary. You've been acting as if you've been wearing a blindfold since you arrived."

"Stow it, Meredith."

Turning on his heel, Dallas walked away.

"Meredith," Nick said reluctantly.

"Yes?"

"Thanks."

"It was nothing, sir," Dallas said in his soft drawl that slid gently over every consonant. "I think you might find Lady Georgiana by the lake. I shall endeavor to keep the duke from harrying you." He smiled and went back into the drawing room.

Nick stuffed Jocelin's letter into his waistband and rushed out of the house. He shivered in the night chill, but running to the lake warmed him. Georgiana wasn't there, nor was she in the fishing pavilion or on the Palladian bridge. He didn't think she'd go to the grotto without a horse. He stood on the bridge glaring at the moonlight dancing on the water and tried to think of where she might go. Then he snapped his fingers, burst into a run across the bridge, and plunged into the wood.

His lungs were heaving by the time he reached the edge of the trees that surrounded the clearing. He slowed and walked into the open, approaching the small Greek temple. Two dark figures stood between a pair of columns. They were huddled together but broke apart when he stalked over to them.

"Who have you met this time?" he snapped. He reddened when the maid Rebecca curtsied to him, ogled him for a moment, and disappeared down the gravel path that led to the house.

Georgiana turned her back to him, her head held high. He noticed that Rebecca must have supplied Georgiana's cloak. Feeling like a fool, Nick mounted the steps and addressed that regal figure.

"Sorry, love."

She turned her head slightly, and the moonlight illuminated her high forehead and the roundness of her cheek, making him catch his breath.

"I suppose the darkness has made me brave," she said. "It's certainly made me see things I didn't want to see."

"What do you see?"

"That all your gallant protests about not wanting to disgrace me with your low birth are a ruse to hide the truth."

"I don't know what you're talking about."

She turned so that he couldn't see her face.

"You don't know it, but I'm a great prize to you," she said. "The common thief has stolen the virtue of a duke's daughter. Don't tell me you're not proud of that. But as for marriage, well, you could have anyone, so why settle for a clumsy giant of a woman when you could have a delicate, wellborn girl who is much more womanly? A girl who doesn't have odd tastes and a desire to minister to urchins rather than serve as your decorative trophy."

Nick swore and spun her around. Grabbing her arms, he made her face him. He caught a whiff of lavender as he said, "Now who's being a—what was it you called me?"

"A snob?"

"A snob." Nick drew her close so that he could see her expression. He berated himself when he saw the tears running down her cheeks. "I am proud."

Pain flashed across her face.

"I'm proud to have won your love, young George. And I don't make any sacrifices I don't want to. Loving you is no sacrifice. Bloody hell, woman. We've both been running from each other because of hurts we suffered in the past. It's time we stopped. Now, what's this about a giant?"

"Oh, it's of no consequence." She hung her head.

"Right." He studied her for a moment. Then, with one swift movement, he swept her up into his arms.

"Mr. Ross!"

He grinned at her and spun around in a circle.
"There ain't any giants around here."

"Put me down."

She gasped as they whirled around and around.
When she shrieked to be let down, he stopped and set
her on her feet. She wobbled and almost fell, so he
picked her up again with ease. She goggled at him in
astonishment.

"There," he said. "Do giants get spun around like
a child's top?"

"I . . . Nick."

The word was like a hot Texas wind, warming his
blood. It shot stinging arousal through his veins. His
smile vanished, and one arm dropped her legs. Holding her with the other, he let her slide down the
length of his body until they were standing pressed
close together.

"You said my name, love." He flattened his hand
on her back and pushed her so that her breasts swelled
against his chest. "I warned you about that."

She lifted her gaze to him and said clearly, "I
hadn't forgotten."

Nick barely heard her for the rushing sound of his
blood. Bracing himself with his palms against cold
stone, he pressed her body between it and his own.
He covered her mouth with his and felt the yielding
softness of her breasts and the stiffness between his
legs. He hadn't touched her in so long.

Exploring her malleable lips, he felt her nails dig
into the flesh on his back. Then her hands touched his
hair. She turned her head.

"Your wounds."

"What wounds? Say my name again."

"Nick."

"Oh, yes."

"Nick."

He skimmed his teeth over her bare shoulder and began to draw up her skirts.

"Nick."

"God, don't say it again or you'll drive me to—"

"No," she said, placing a finger against his lips. "Rebecca said Aunt Livy told her to ready the plunge bath tonight."

Nick was kissing her finger and repeated the words without thinking about them. "Plunge bath." His lips stilled. "Plunge bath?"

Without another word he picked her up and walked quickly into the temple. With each step the heat in his body grew, and the ache between his legs turned to pain as he hurried down the steps to the plunge bath. He smelled jasmine but barely noticed the warm gold light that cast watery reflections on the walls.

In his haste and need he ripped expensive black lace. His fingers trembled as they worked at lacing and yanked down petticoats. His vision narrowed to a field of creamy flesh. Only the shock of water sloshing around him distracted him for a moment.

Warm liquid enfolded him even as Georgiana's arms wrapped around him. His flesh surged, made sensitive and buoyant at the same time. Tense with arousal, he lifted Georgiana, and they floated, their bodies shifting against each other with each teasing little current. She suddenly lay back so that her body floated before him, her breasts rising from the water. Her legs locked around his hips, and she arched her back, pressing against him.

Uttering a strangled cry, Nick lunged at her, sub–

merged with her. He watched her hair float around her like black silk under the water. Then he drew her toward him by her wrists and surfaced, holding her body tightly against him, careful to avoid her healing wound. He kicked hard, bringing them to the steps that descended into the water. He planted his knees on a lower step. Georgiana's bottom fit on an upper one, and he surged against her while her legs wrapped tighter around him. She braced herself and lifted her hips. Nick felt water churn around him as he moved against her.

His hands found sensitive, slick places. His mouth followed until he plunged beneath the surface to find her. When he needed a breath, he surfaced to nip at her breasts as they bobbed in front of him. He could have played with them forever, but her hand found him and squeezed, then pulled him. He answered her urging and plunged into searing, tight heat.

He was conscious only of her body encasing his and of water churning around them, faster and faster. Great waves splashed out of the bath, sloshing over the floor. They frothed and foamed as his movements grew more and more violent. When Georgiana gave a watery shriek, he arched his back and jabbed hard, adding his cry to hers. As they reached fulfillment, he fastened his mouth on hers. She wrapped her arms around his neck, and he stood in the water, ramming her hips against his.

Once he regained his senses, he gripped her tightly, eased onto his back, and floated with her on top. They remained there, a joined island of flesh, floating in a dreamy gold haze of contentment.

•   •   •

Georgiana slipped her arms into the bodice of her gown and turned so that Nick could fasten the numerous tiny buttons at the back. Her body still tingled from their lovemaking, and she could see the flush on her arms and chest. Nick finished the last button, came close, and kissed her bare shoulder. Surfacing from her cocoon of serenity, she felt the heat of his lips and descended into a pool of sensual fire. His voice summoned her from its depths.

"You're sure this is what you want, love?"

"I forbid you to ask me that question when you've so ably proved you're certain of what you want."

"It's just that I'm not sure you realize the consequences of marrying me."

Twisting around, she linked her arms around his neck and rose to kiss him. "Oh, my goodness. Do you think I'll have to give up the season, or all those fascinating balls I'm so attached to?" She put her hands on her cheeks in horror. "Oh, dear. Do you think I'll have to give up calls and making inane conversation? How shall I live?"

"Wait till it happens, then you'll see."

"Oh, bother Society. Neither of us has the time for or interest in balls, calls, and shooting things."

"And what about your father?"

"Blow my father!"

Nick threw back his head and laughed. "Bloody hell, in another week you'll be dropping your H's." He grew serious. "We'll have to set your father straight, love."

"Don't worry. Once he realizes how debauched and depraved I am, he'll drag the Archbishop of Canterbury out of bed to marry us. Anything to preserve appearances." She looked into the depths of his eyes, nearly getting lost in the sparkle of blue and indigo. "Are you certain you want to marry into a family full of shallow and pedestrian fools?"

Settling her cloak on her shoulders, Nick murmured, "I want to marry you, and Jocelin and Liza are the only family we need."

Georgiana bent to pick up an envelope.

"What's this?"

Nick plucked it from her fingers. "Jocelin's idea of diplomacy. You'll be happy to know he's in favor of our marriage."

"So he sent one to you too," Georgiana said. "I think Liza had a hand in this."

"It's like her to be direct and send a letter tackling the problem," Nick said.

"And it's like Jocelin to phrase the thing so diplomatically."

Nick rubbed his arms as if he was cold, and Georgiana threw her cloak over his shoulders.

"No," he said. "You'll get cold."

"You've heated me up, Nicholas Ross, and you know it."

He sat down suddenly on the steps leading from the ground floor to the plunge bath. "I'm a mite tired."

Georgiana rushed to him and examined the cuts and bumps on his head. "You shouldn't have fought with my father. Look at your poor head. It must ache and sting fiercely."

"You made me forget."

"We should go back to the house."

"In a moment," Nick said. "I need to know

you're clear about me, young George. You got to see
me straight."

"I do."

"No, you don't. Quit staring at me like a prowling she-cat looking for a tom and listen. I've been in
the devil and all of trouble in my life, young George."

Georgiana stopped him by taking his face between her hands and kissing him gently. "I already
know. Jocelin told me what you haven't."

"And— and you don't mind?"

"Nicholas Ross, I told you I'm not going to answer that silly question anymore. But there is something you can tell me. Will you mind my plans to
found a home for unfortunate children?"

"I used to be one of them." He took her hand
and kissed it. "I got a home you can use."

"You do?"

He turned her hand over and kissed the palm.
"Uh-huh. Jos says it's as big as that palace in Russia
with all the paintings."

"The Hermitage?" Georgiana said faintly.

"That's it. I hardly use the place. Too big, and I'm
not in the country that often."

Suddenly suspicious, Georgiana withdrew her
hand and grabbed Nick's in hers. "Just how many
houses do you have?"

"Oh, seven, maybe eight now. I'd have to ask my
man in London. I been collecting them for a while.
There's a heap o' toffs who got no business sense and
need cash. I got the cash."

"So you can spare this Hermitage," Georgiana
said, still taken aback.

Nick ran the backs of his fingers down her shoulder and nodded absently. "I think I'm too weak to go back to the house right now."

Georgiana touched his cheek.

"You're warm. Are you catching a fever?"

Nick laid his head on her breast. "Yes."

She wrapped her arms around him.

"I knew we shouldn't have gone into the plunge bath. I should have taken you back to the house."

She felt him turn his face and press it to her breasts. A hot tongue delved into the cleft between them. She cried out and lifted his head so that she could see his eyes, which crinkled with amusement.

"You deceitful wretch."

Nick put the back of his hand to his forehead. "I feel faint." His head dropped to her breast again and he nuzzled her.

Georgiana shrieked and shoved him back. Allowing her to move him, he propped his elbows on a step and grinned at her.

"I hear those ancient Egyptians had several wives."

"Only a few noblemen and the king," Georgiana said as she rose and offered her hand to him. He took it and stood beside her, still grinning wickedly. "I'd think twice before I tried it, though."

"Why?" he asked as they went up the stairs.

She gave him a sideways glance. "Because often a few wives would get together and try to do away with the husband so they and their sons could inherit his riches."

"Bloody hell."

Georgiana slipped her arm through Nick's and smiled into the indigo merriment of his eyes. "By the way, do you think your Hermitage is big enough to hold a few of my artifacts?"

"You mean them mummies and naked statues and such? Strike me blind if I want those things lurking in my house!"

"Now, Nick."

"No."

She stopped, flattened her hands on his chest, and stood on tiptoe. Breathing softly into his ear, she said, "Nick," drawing the word out into a long sigh. "Nick, my love. Sweet Nick."

"Well, maybe a few statues."

"Nick, Nick, Nicholas."

He swore and picked her up in his arms. "Whatever you want, damn it, young George. Whatever you want."

She wrapped her arms around him and let him carry her out of the temple. "Thank you, my dearest love."

"I think I'm in trouble, young George, prime, deep trouble."

About the Author

SUZANNE ROBINSON has a doctoral degree in anthropology with a specialty in ancient Middle Eastern archaeology. After spending years doing fieldwork in both the U.S. and the Middle East, Suzanne has now turned her attention to the creation of the fascinating fictional characters in her unforgettable historical romances.

Suzanne lives in San Antonio with her husband and her two English springer spaniels. She divides her time between writing and teaching.

TITLE:	The Engagement
AUTHOR:	Suzanne Robinson
CATEGORY:	Lead-Hist. Romance
PUBLICATION DATE:	June 1996
ON SALE:	May 1996
PRICE:	$5.50 ($7.50)
LENGTH:	304 pages
ISBN:	0-553-56346-7

Reviewers are reminded that changes may be made in this proof copy
before books are printed. If any material from the book is to be quoted in
a review, the quotation should be checked against the final bound book.

Bantam Books, Inc., 1540 Broadway, New York, N.Y. 10036 (212) 354-6500

UNCORRECTED PAGE PROOFS